What Lies Beneath the Graves

(The fifth Spookie Town Murder Mystery)
*(Sequel to **Scraps of Paper**, **All Things Slip Away**,*
Ghosts Beneath Us *and* **Witches Among Us***)*

By Kathryn Meyer Griffith

Why is the town called Spookie? In this murder mystery series it is a tongue-in-cheek, a tip-of-my-hat to my earlier roots as a horror writer and little else. This book is also for my sweet brother Jim Meyer, who passed away on May 27, 2015. He was a great singer/musician/songwriter and was always my best friend. I miss him. If you'd like to listen to some of his songs, here they are: http://tinyurl.com/pytftzc

What Lies Beneath the Graves

by Kathryn Meyer Griffith

Cover art by: Dawné Dominique
Copyright 2018 Kathryn Meyer Griffith

All rights reserved. No part of this book may be reproduced, scanned or distributed in any form, including digital and electronic or mechanical, including photocopying, recording, or by any information storage and retrieval system, without the prior written consent of the author, except for brief quotes for use in reviews.

This book is a work of fiction. Characters, names, places and incidents either are the product of the author's imagination or are used fictitiously, and any resemblance to any actual persons, living or dead, events, or locales is entirely coincidental.

For Jim…I miss you, Brother!

Other books by Kathryn Meyer Griffith:
Evil Stalks the Night
The Heart of the Rose
Blood Forged
Vampire Blood
The Last Vampire (2012 Epics EBook Awards Finalist)
Witches
Witches II: Apocalypse
Witches plus bonus Witches II: Apocalypse
The Calling
Scraps of Paper-1st Spookie Town Murder Mystery
All Things Slip Away-2nd Spookie Town Murder Mystery
Ghosts Beneath Us-3rd Spookie Town Murder Mystery
Witches Among Us-4th Spookie Town Murder Mystery
What Lies Beneath the Graves-5th Spookie Town Murder Mystery
Egyptian Heart
Winter's Journey
The Ice Bridge
Don't Look Back, Agnes
A Time of Demons and Angels
The Woman in Crimson
Four Spooky Short Stories
Human No Longer
Dinosaur Lake (2014 Epic EBook Awards Finalist)
Dinosaur Lake II: Dinosaurs Arising
Dinosaur Lake III: Infestation
Dinosaur Lake IV: Dinosaur Wars
Dinosaur Lake V: Survivors
Memories of My Childhood
Christmas Magic 1959 short story
*All Kathryn Meyer Griffith's books are here:
http://tinyurl.com/ld4jlow
*All her Audible.com audio books here:
http://tinyurl.com/oz7c4or

Chapter 1

"Hey, slow down Myrtle!" Abigail shouted as the old woman scurried around another prickly shrub, abruptly changed direction, moved through the spaces between the trees and splashed through a trickling creek. The ground was soggy and muddy from the last rain and Abigail had to be careful where she stomped her feet. It wouldn't do to sink her new shoes into the muck or to fall on her butt in a puddle of mud. She hadn't planned on this wild hike through the wilderness and hadn't dressed appropriately. That Myrtle. The old woman had known where they were going, what the terrain would be, and she'd worn rubber boots. Not so Abigail. Abigail was dressed for town and had her good clothes on. "Where are you going, Myrtle?"

"I think I know where my grandniece is. She goes to a special place a lot to think or when one of her intuitions, dreams or trances, or whatever she calls them, have upset her. Just follow me. I know the way and it isn't far." Myrtle dodged a low hanging branch and it almost slapped Abigail in the face. Luckily she ducked just in time, barely. A tiny branch fluttered across and scratched her face and when she reached up her fingers came back with a streak of blood.

"Myrtle, slow down!"

"You know," Myrtle suddenly declared as if the thought had only come to her, "I'm really thinking about going on a world cruise this summer. Leave in July and get back whenever. Maybe I'll be gone for months. Sort of like a birthday present from myself to myself."

For Pete's sake, Abigail thought, but didn't say out loud. The old woman had to be closing in or even past ninety years old. Did ninety year olds really traipse around the globe like vagabond teenagers? Didn't they have to stay close to their doctors and stuff? "You're kidding, aren't you? Remember what happened the last time you went on a cruise…a friend of yours ended up dead."

"Yeah, I remember. But that was a real fluke. It wasn't the cruise that did poor old Tina in, but a land grabbing couple of murderers. I don't expect that to happen again, not in my lifetime. As far as I know no one's out to murder me or any of my friends–right now anyway," she mumbled the last three words though Abigail heard them.

Abigail figured she'd play along. Myrtle did like to daydream about the great adventures she was going to go on. It didn't mean she would actually do them; though she did like to travel and traveled more than any old person Abigail had ever known. "Where are you thinking of going on this cruise?"

"Oh, I'm not sure. I'm still doing research. One of those senior cruises so I don't feel so out of place. Someplace warm, I think. Tropical islands with beautiful blue seas around and friendly natives. Lots of fruity drinks with those tiny umbrellas in them. Oh, and the cruise ship will have to have tons of good food and goodies on it, too. That's a given." The old lady grinned over her shoulder at her. "You know me, I like the water and the sun. The dessert buffet."

"That you do. Let me know when you decide on your itinerary and exactly where you're going. So I can put up a map on my wall and stick it full of pins to follow your bread crumbs."

"Ha, ha. I will. Maybe I could even talk you into going with me, huh? Glinda, too. A women's cruise vacation. I'll pay for it."

Myrtle was serious so Abigail didn't mock her. "I don't think Frank would think me going on a cruise for a couple of months or more was a good idea. Though Laura's away at college, we still have Nick at home. And Frank would miss me. I'd miss him."

"Ah, Frank can come with us. Nick, too. I'll pay for all of you. Nick will be out of school by June and we could go then and be back in time for him to catch the fall semester. I know it'll be a hunk of money, but hey, I can't take it with me so I'm going to spend it. Let me spend it on you guys."

No way. Abigail didn't like big boats on big oceans. They could sink and then they'd drown or sharks would eat all of them. *No, no, no.* But flabbergasted at the sheer generosity of the offer, Abigail could only say, "Uh, let me think about it."

"You do that."

Abigail kept muttering beneath her breath but continued trailing Myrtle through the wet woods. At least the rain had stopped, the fog had lifted and the sun had come out to warm the world around them. Early spring could be so fickle in Spookie, and this morning it was chilly, so Abigail was glad she'd worn a jacket. Myrtle, on the other hand, was wearing her usual colorful collection of layered dresses and a furry coat which would have been more suitable for the deep freeze of the Arctic. It was like following a hobbling and strange looking bear. The comical image made Abigail smile.

They'd been on their way to visit Glinda, their local psychic and Myrtle's grandniece, at Glinda's house, but no one had been home when they rang the bell. Of course Myrtle had known where the spare key was kept, beneath the ceramic frog in the rock garden surrounding the porch, the same place her late sister Evelyn had always kept it, and she had merely let them in. Before Abigail could protest intruding on Glinda's privacy, Myrtle had blurted out, "Oh, I do this all the time. Glinda doesn't mind. Besides, most days she already knows I'm coming and isn't surprised. My home is your home, Aunt Myrtle, she always tells me. Seeing as it did once belong to your sister. Visit anytime you want. So I do."

But Glinda hadn't been in the house, there was only the menagerie of animals, mostly cats, she'd been collecting. Evelyn's ghost must be very happy. The felines darted away to hide like frightened children or meowed at them from dark corners.

"That girl," Myrtle complained, finding and picking up a blue cell phone from the kitchen table. "It'd be easier to track her down if she'd just remember to take her cell phone along with her. She's always leaving it somewhere. Once I found it in the freezer. No joke." The old woman took the phone and dumped it into her jacket's pocket.

What Lies Beneath the Graves

"When we find her I'll give it to her."

"Then we're going to kept looking for her?"

"Of course," Myrtle replied, "I've had this feeling all morning I had to speak to her. It's important."

"Oh, okay. Lead on."

Then Glinda's main cat, the gray one called Amadeus, was at the house's entrance in front of them. It gave them one of its weird looks and dashed out the open door. "We'll follow that critter. I'm sure he'll lead us right to Glinda."

"I thought you said you knew where your niece was?"

"Well, I have a good idea, but I'm sure the cat will find her first and take us right to her. It has that power. Let's go."

They went out the door, closing it behind them, and looked for the cat. It was nowhere to be seen.

"Darn. He did that disappearing act on purpose to taunt me. That cat hates me," Myrtle had grumbled as they'd walked behind the house. "Though I am so nice to him, bring him treats and all. He's a peculiar cat."

"You still believe he's a magic cat?" Abigail had queried, hiding her amusement. She glanced over her shoulder at Evelyn's old house as they left it behind. It looked good, Myrtle had confided to her a while back, better than it had in decades. Glinda had had it painted a cheery yellow and had new shutters, a pretty light jade color, put around the windows. Wooden boxes full of bright flowers sat beneath the windows. She'd cleared out and cleaned up the piles of clutter in the yard which had been scattered around and had planted wild flowers everywhere. There was an antique glider swing for three, topped off with soft cushions, under the oak tree.

The yard's grass was always kept cut and the bushes shaped and trimmed. It was a lovely homestead now and its unique beauty rivaled the best houses in Spookie. Abigail had helped Glinda decorate the inside and, even she had to admit, it was now a beautiful home. Glinda loved it as much as Evelyn once had and it showed. Abigail was fairly sure Myrtle had contributed monetary funds to accomplish the makeover because, according to Myrtle, she spent as much time at Glinda's place as she did her at her own, and she had wanted to help her young niece because, she'd asserted, being a psychic wasn't all that profitable. Then again she and Glinda had formed a tight bond which was touching to behold. The old recluse was becoming more social with every year and that was what was most amazing to Abigail. Myrtle having a young relative to care for had changed the old woman. Abigail reckoned the next step was Myrtle eventually moving in with the girl, which wouldn't be a bad thing. Myrtle's eyesight and hearing were both failing, though Myrtle would never admit it. Ninety-something could be a brutal age for anyone. There were times, though, like now, Abigail couldn't believe how spry her old friend still was. For the time being anyway.

A swallow flew above them not inches above their heads, dipping and sailing like a tiny ship on the air. Abigail shaded her eyes with her hand and watched the bird speed away into the azure sky. Three others joined it and called to each other like old friends.

Glinda had been living in Evelyn's house for over two years and the psychic had settled easily into it and the rhythm of the town and its quirky people, fitting right in. She had many friends and could often be found at Claudia's Tattered Corners book store or Stella's Café conversing or visiting with any number of the townspeople over breakfast or lunch. Sometimes she gave readings at both places. Stella and Claudia welcomed them. It brought in more business. People were curious about Glinda, her visons, her crystals and tarot cards, and loved to crowd around to watch and listen when she was reading someone's fortune. Glinda had become somewhat famous in the area because so many of her predictions came true. These days she didn't have problems getting bookings, yet she refused to raise her prices. Often she would give free readings if the person needed it but couldn't afford it. "I know what it's like to live paycheck to paycheck. I never forget that. Some people need my help and I will not turn them away because of money. I don't share my gift merely for the money. I share it to help people."

The strange gray cat suddenly reappeared ahead of them, tail and whiskers twitching as it paused, stared back at them as if to say *follow me* and scampered off into the woods.

"Crazy cat." Myrtle chortled. "Okay, okay, slow down, you contrary fur critter, we're coming."

Abigail laughed then as the woods closed in

around them. They'd been following the cat ever since, though it kept slinking in and out of their sight and they'd had to keep their eyes sharply peeled to not lose it.

"Uh, where precisely are we going?" Abigail repeated.

"We're here." Myrtle had arrived at an overgrown and apparently long forgotten graveyard. There were many such forgotten family cemeteries around Spookie. They were burial places hidden and lost in the town's forests, dotted with crumbing tombstones with faded inscriptions and paths dense with weeds. Withered trees protectively hung their branches over the spot and a knee-high dilapidated fence encircled it. A small patch of sacred ground, there weren't more than three dozen graves residing there. Abigail had never been to this particular cemetery, though, but sensed immediately the eerie ambience pervading it. She could almost feel the departed lurking behind the tombstones or floating below the ground's dirt. Gentle shivers shimmied along her skin. Good thing the sun was shining and bright. The boneyard would have been too creepy if the day would have been overcast.

Evidently the cemetery wasn't their destination. They skirted around the graveyard and when Abigail looked up a large concrete gazebo loomed before her. She'd never seen one like it. It was quite large and squatted on a hill overlooking the graveyard on one side and a steep drop to the creek on the other. As the cemetery it appeared to have been there a long time, was surrounded in overgrown shrubberies and weeds, but it was a solid edifice, octagonal, and perhaps twenty feet across and fifteen feet or so in height. There were five stone steps leading up and into it. Hard wooden benches encircled the gazebo's inner circumference.

Strange, she thought, to have such an uncommon structure in the middle of the woods and next to an abandoned graveyard. Who would put a gazebo way out here? Well, someone did. Probably the original owner of the property.

Then she noticed who was sitting on the benches inside the gazebo. Glinda and Frank.

"Hey!" Myrtle chuckled, rubbing her hands together gleefully. "Hot dog, the gang's all here."

"Hi Glinda," Abigail greeted the young woman, climbed the steps and gave her husband, Frank, a hello hug. "What's up?"

"I've had an interesting vision…a visit, actually, from someone who needs my–our–help."

"Oh," Myrtle exclaimed. "Yippee, is it another adventure, another grand mystery, for us to solve?"

"We'll find out." Glinda's hands gestured them to sit with her. "That's why you are all here. I have questions to ask and things to learn. The person who contacted me has a favor to ask. And I'm going to need your help to grant that favor."

Oh boy. Abigail caught the eager grin on Myrtle's face. *Not again.* It'd been two lovely peaceful years without any complications, dangers or murders in Spookie and she didn't want it to change. She liked their simple life without criminals or murders to muck it up. Then she noticed Glinda's odd expression, the concern in her eyes, and knew there was already no turning back. The die had been cast. *Here we go again.*

"What's the favor?" Myrtle pressed.

"I'll tell you soon enough," Glinda clarified. "Once everyone takes a seat."

"Ha, if I would have known we'd all be here," Myrtle piped up, "I would have brought a picnic lunch. Ooh, fried chicken and potato salad does sound tasty about now."

After throwing Myrtle an amused grin, Abigail glanced at her husband. "Frank, what are you doing here? I thought you were working today with the police department?"

"I was. Then Glinda called me and asked me to come over. Said she had something to tell me and a request. I needed to get out of the stuffy office, not anything important going on today anyway, the office was dead, so I agreed. It was a nice day, she wanted to take a walk and show me something and here we are." He smiled and spread his hands to include their surroundings. "She said you two would turn up sooner or later. And here you are."

The year before her husband had accepted a consultant's job with the sheriff's department as a part-time detective. It had surprised Abigail because he'd been retired from the Chicago Homicide Department for as long as she'd known him and seemed happy with his new mystery writing career and their simple life at home with the kids. He had become quite the local celebrity with his best-selling mystery novels. At the time he'd taken the consulting job, though, he'd confessed he had become restless just writing about crimes and no longer actively being able to solve them in the real world. The mysteries they'd cracked with Myrtle the last couple years had reawakened his sleuthing instincts. So he had taken the offered job with Sheriff Mearl and seemed content with it. It got him out of the house more, he said, and kept his brain sharp for writing his mysteries.

"Yeah, about where we are," Abigail sat down beside her husband, her eyes taking in what was around them, "what is this place? And why is there this lovely gazebo way out here in the middle of nowhere…and so close to a run-down weed-filled cemetery?"

Myrtle, who'd settled down on one of the gazebo's steps instead of sitting on one of the benches, piped up, "This gazebo has been here forever. Since before my sister and I ever came to town. When she got married and bought this house, we discovered it one day while we were out traipsing around in these woods. We used to come out here and have picnics with our husbands and our children when we were younger. I was told that years ago, in the late nineteen hundreds or so, there were even town picnics and events out here for a time. Bands would play in the gazebo and the townspeople would dance and eat picnic lunches on blankets in the grass. But it's been forsaken and forgotten now for ages. I showed this place to Glinda soon after she took possession of the house. I and my sister always enjoyed coming out here to escape the world and her house full of yakking, yapping critters." Myrtle chuckled. "At least it was quiet."

"I love it out here," Glinda said. She grinned at

Abigail. She was wearing one of her long flowing skirts and a ruby silk blouse under a heavy purple sweater. Glittery silver tennis shoes. No jewelry except some dangling silver earrings. Her green eyes flashed. "I come out here every chance I get. It relaxes me when my visions drive me a little nuts."

"I know," Myrtle remarked. "Like I told Abby, if I can't find her at the house this is the first place I look." She took Glinda's cell phone from her pocket and handed it to the young woman. Glinda nodded her thanks.

"So, Niece," Myrtle wanted to know. "What about this vision you've had?"

The young woman tilted her head and offered them an enigmatic curve of her lips. "It was a strange one as many of them are, with missing pieces. I'm not sure exactly what the visitor in my vision wanted, not yet anyway. But I can tell you this. It was the ghost of a young man with red hair and a beard. Good looking fellow with a winning smile. Handsome, even though he had a scar on the left side of his face. The way he was dressed, clothes perhaps from the early twentieth century, his head gear, gave me the impression he was a sailor of some sort. In the vision he was on the deck of a boat or ship. I couldn't tell which one. The seas were calm around him and I could hear the shouts of other sailors on the ship with him."

"What did he want?" Myrtle again. Her eyes were firmly fastened on Glinda's face.

Glinda tilted her head and replied in a soft voice, "He told me he needed my help, our help–he actually mentioned all of you–to right a terrible wrong he'd done in his life to his young wife and daughter which is keeping him from moving on."

"He asked for us by name?" Now Abigail was also intrigued.

"Well not by name, more by his thoughts," Glinda explained with a casual wave of her hand as she leaned back against the gazebo's railing. The sunlight which caught at some of the strands of her silver hair made them sparkle. "He gave me glimpses of Myrtle, Frank and you and made me understand whom he was speaking of."

"What else did he give you *glimpses* of?" Frank caught Abigail's eye. She smiled back at him. The mystery had begun.

"Not much more than that. For now. He said he'd see me again. So I thought because you, Frank, grew up here and Myrtle," she met Myrtle's gaze, "have lived here so long, one of you might make a connection of some sort for me."

"Hmm," Abigail interjected, summing up the clues, "a sailor from another century, a possible wrong done his family, a wife and a daughter, which he now wants to right. That's not much to go on."

"I know I haven't heard the last from our sailor." Glinda exchanged a look with Frank as she said it. "Ah, you've remembered something, haven't you, Frank?"

She said that because Frank's expression was one of deep contemplation then sudden enlightenment. Abigail had seen that look before many times. He'd made a connection or had recalled something. "Maybe. Glinda, you said you think he was a sailor from the last century…perhaps around seventy, eighty years ago? There was a young wife and daughter wronged in some way and he wants you, us, to help make amends to them?"

"That's approximately what I gleaned from the vision. As you know the images are sometimes fragmented and often difficult to decipher. I need more to really know what he wants."

"So you didn't get any names from him? Didn't get his name?"

"No. But I'll be sure to ask next time I see him, if he does revisit me." Glinda shook her head. "You can't depend on those ghosts for anything concrete, you know. They like to tease and taunt, and sometimes they only let you see scraps or pieces of things. Often they're fickle, vindictive or annoying. They don't live by the same rules as live people do."

Myrtle chuckled and elbowed her niece affectionately. "So true, so true. They are capricious entities. Me, myself, I only believe half of whatever a spirit shows or tells me. You never know what their ulterior motives are."

Frank didn't react to their remarks, but thoughtfully continued on with, "I think I might know who your sailor ghost could be. Truth is, this place, the graveyard, the gazebo, and the original owner, or the builder, of Glinda's house, have quite a local history, almost a legend, to them. All my life I grew up hearing bizarre stories of the man who built and lived in Evelyn's house, now your house. He was quite a character, and he *was* a sailor, oh, about seventy, eighty years ago in the nineteen thirties or forties. Supposedly, before he settled here, he traveled the world seeking riches and plunder. He was a genuine treasure hunter, an explorer. He abandoned his family to seek a very special treasure on some island in the Caribbean and when he returned many years later his wife and daughter were lost to him. Or so the legend says."

"Just like Jack Sparrow in those pirate movies." Myrtle was bobbing her head as she peered up at them from her step. Pursing her lips, she scratched her head. "He was a treasure hunter who sailed the seas and looked for gold. That Johnny Depp, what a cutie."

"And if I remember correctly," Frank added, ignoring Myrtle's comments, "later in his life it was said he tried to find his family. He hired private detectives to search, but his family was never found."

"Did he find the treasure?" Abigail asked.

"Some say he must have because," Frank was studying the landscape, the graveyard, "he eventually returned to Spookie, throwing cash all over the place, bought a large parcel of land, this land, and built what one day would be Evelyn's house. But he kept to himself. At the moment I don't recollect his name, but perhaps it'll come to me in time. He was an eccentric recluse and was rarely seen in town. He had no real friends, just servants and workers, and didn't interact with anyone once his house had been built." Frank paused as if he were dredging up elusive memories from long ago. "I don't recall much more than that, for now."

In the distance a flock of ebony birds flew in circles and arcs, moving in an intricate dance, and swept away beyond the trees. Abigail loved watching the sky acrobats and had to drag her eyes away.

"Well, we'll compile what you two do ultimately remember, what we can find out from the old newspaper articles if there are any, and I'll let you know if the sailor appears to me again," Glinda stated. "Perhaps he'll give me more clues to what he wants from us.

"Well, I hate leaving good company, but it's getting late and I have a client coming at three for a reading. Got to keep making money if I want groceries in the pantry." She stood up.

Abigail rose from the bench and strolled down the steps past Myrtle. "Yep, we need to be going, too. I have some sketches to finish before tomorrow for my next job."

Myrtle was right behind her. "Oh, then you did get that mural commission from that Mexican restaurant?"

"I did," Abigail concurred. And it would be a real challenge; one she couldn't wait to tackle. The restaurant, South of the Border, had recently opened on Main Street and served authentic Mexican dishes in a high class ambience. She'd eaten there twice already and loved how the place was decorated with vivid colors and live plants and flowers. The second time she'd been there the owner, Miguel Angel, had approached her and asked if she'd be interested in painting an authentic Mexican town on three of the walls.

What Lies Beneath the Graves

"I want my customers," he'd explained when he'd pitched the job to her, "to feel as if they are dining in a genuine Mexican village. The people and the buildings must look real. I want my patrons to feel the hot summer sun and smell the brightly colored flowers everywhere, too. Mrs. Lester, I've seen your work around Spookie and I love everything you've done. That wall mural on the side of the building as you come into town is amazing. What do you think? Would you be interested in painting my mural? If you are we can discuss fair compensation later after you've come up with the preliminary sketches. How soon can you have them? I would really love to get started on this."

Of course she had accepted the commission. She'd finished her last job, a painting of someone's house complete with the family and the dog in front of it, the week before and had been wondering when she'd be offered another job. Prayer answered. Before she'd left the restaurant she already had ideas swirling around in her head. As always she was excited at the beginning of a new artistic undertaking. It was one of the things she lived for.

That meeting had been the day before and she'd planned on beginning the sketches that afternoon. She was eager to get home and begin.

The four of them returned to Glinda's house and went their separate ways. Myrtle to her house claiming she had things to do, heaven knew what, and she and Frank went to their home.

Once inside, Abigail inquired, "Frank, are you going back to the office now or are you going to work on the new book?" He hadn't told her much about the new novel. He rarely did in the beginning and she never nagged him. He'd tell her about it when he was ready.

"No, I thought I'd go by the newspaper and do some digging on our sailor ghost. Since our visit with Glinda, I'm intrigued. I just called the newspaper and Samantha is there now getting the new issue ready for press. I mentioned what I wanted, told her about Glinda's ghostly visitation, and she said she'd look in the archives for me before I got there and pull out anything she finds about the situation. She said she'd heard the stories about the sailor who'd built Evelyn's house and his hidden treasure all her life. Seemed real interested in the whole thing. You want to come with me?"

"Nah. I'm going to knock out those sketches for Miguel Angel. He's expecting them tomorrow. You go ahead. You can fill me in on everything you learn when you get back.

"You know, Frank, I can't believe we're on another one of Myrtle's crazy mysteries again. How did this happen?"

"Well, to be fair, it wasn't Myrtle's doing, honey. It isn't one of Myrtle's mysteries at all if you think about it. It is Glinda's. She's the one who was contacted by the sailor's ghost. She's the one who's asked us for help."

Abigail shook her head and released a stoic sigh. "I guess you're right. But she's Myrtle's niece and now we have two of them who see ghosts and drag us into dangerous secrets we are supposed to help solve. You know as well as I that somehow it'll all lead us to a big fat mess of one sort or another. It always does."

Frank hugged her as he chuckled. "You're right about that. But I don't mind. Life was getting too boring anyway."

"Yeah, for you maybe. I like it boring and safe with Laura in college, only coming home on weekends, and Nick following his musical siren by being in a band and practicing almost every night. And your son, Kyle, a busy medical resident hours away. We have the house to ourselves more and it's quiet. Most of the time anyway. Unless Myrtle or Glinda drop in and bring their normal brand of chaos, as they frequently do."

Life was good and Abigail didn't want anything to change it. Nick at sixteen was lost in his music. He could play a melody on his guitar simply by hearing it once and he was already writing his own songs. The boy was a musical genius and as talented in it as his sister was in art. Abigail was so proud of both of them, the adults they were becoming, and blessed the day so many years ago she'd met them in the library, two hungry urchins with big eyes, and the day she decided to take them under her wing and raise them. Now they were her and Frank's children as much as Kyle and as if they'd been born to them. Laura and Nick had made her and Frank's life so much fuller and better. And Kyle was now in his third year of medical residency at a large Chicago hospital and doing exceedingly well. He was on his way to being a good doctor. He wanted to complete a full seven years before he would hang out his physician's shingle…hopefully joining Doctor Andy's practice in Spookie. Frank was thrilled his son wanted to be a small town doctor and he had chosen Spookie to be that small town. The timing couldn't have been more perfect. Doc Andy would be retiring about the time Kyle would be ready to take over. They rarely saw Kyle these days because his schedule was so demandingly hectic at the hospital. Whenever Frank could swung it, though, he'd drive up to Chicago and drop in at the hospital or Kyle's apartment to visit. He missed his son.

"Don't worry. How can a dead sailor's spirit who only wants atonement for his earthly sins, to find his child, and a hidden treasure which may or may not have ever existed lead to any real problems for us? It was all so long ago. Probably nothing will come of any of this. Glinda has trances and dead people visiting her all the time and often they never revisit. That'll end it. But the whole buried treasure scenario fascinates me–everyone loves tales of buried treasure–and I'm thinking I might use it somehow in my new book. The legend, I mean."

"You might, huh?"

He nodded. "So I want to learn more about it."

"I guess I'll see you later then," she said as he headed for the door. "For supper?"

"Since you're going to be busy on those sketches, you want me to bring back something for us?" Frank offered. "How about a pizza from Marietta's?"

"That sounds tasty. Get some of their cheesy bread and salads, too, enough for Nick. He'll be at band practice until eight but we'll save him some." It was the middle of the week so Laura was at art school hours away. The house sometimes felt empty without the children in it, but Abigail looked forward to the evening of solitary drawing. Just her and Snowball. The cat was getting older, no longer a kitten, and in the evening when she was working the cat liked to sleep on the chair beside her.

"I will pick up a pizza and sides." Frank gave her a kiss before he walked out.

Abigail stood at the door for a moment and then gathered her art supplies so she could get started drawing. She had the strangest feeling someone would soon come knocking at her door and disrupt her solitude. Time to get to work before that happened.

Chapter 2

Frank practically bumped into Claudia as he got out of the truck and headed towards The Weekly Journal's building. The sun was in his eyes but he knew who the woman was the minute she spoke.

"Hi Frank. What brings you to town in the middle of the day? Abigail said you were working at the sheriff's department today on your consulting job?"

"Good morning Claudia." He met her eyes as she paused on the sidewalk outside the newspaper's window; clutching a white box he recognized immediately as one from The Delicious Circle bakery. "I took off early. Glinda had to tell me about one of her latest visions so I went to her place. The gang was there, Myrtle and my wife. I've just come into town to check something out at the newspaper. Samantha is expecting me.

"How are you and your husband doing?"

"Oh," she spoke with an amused inflection in her voice, "we're fine. Since Ryan finished the Willowby's kitchen remodeling he's restless. Again. He's back to going on and on about taking that dream trip to Africa to hunt big game before he dies. You know how he is?"

Frank grinned. He knew. Claudia's husband had been talking about a safari to Africa since he'd known him. Thirty years, at least. He wanted to bag a wildebeest or a Greater Kudu or some such beast. Everyone had their dream vacations. Frank wanted to go to Ireland and wander around in the small quaint villages. Abby had always dreamed of visiting England. One day perhaps they'd even go.

"And at the homestead we've been overrun lately with these sneaky raccoons. An entire family of them. They get into our trash cans every week and make a mess of things in the street. One, a baby, even snuck into the house through the dog door the other day and, boy, did Ryan have a wild time getting it out again. It got in the cookie jar and ate half the cookies before we realized it was in the house. It jumped in his face when he first tried to catch it. Small as it was, it sure could run and hide like a little demon. We finally cornered it, tossed it into a bag, and set it free outside where its mother was anxiously waiting for it. She tried to bite him. You should have seen my brave husband fighting that tiny critter. Ha! It nearly got the best of him, let me tell you. And he wants to go to Africa and hunt big game? Yeah, sure. That man!" She was shaking her head.

Frank couldn't help but smile. "Raccoons can be pesky all right." He said nothing about Ryan's forever trip to the Dark Continent. No need to. "How come you're not in your shop selling books?" His eyes were on the bakery box. He'd had an early breakfast but it was past two now and his stomach was growling. He thought he could actually smell the pastries Claudia had bought.

Claudia laughed and raised the box. "I suddenly had the irresistible desire for some of Kate's famous glazed donuts so after lunch I stopped by there and purchased a dozen. Now I'm going back to the bookstore to have some with coffee. Can I interest you in joining me?"

The offer was tempting, but when Frank glanced up he saw Samantha in the window gesturing at him.

"Any other time I'd happily accept, Claudia. You know I love Kate's donuts. But Samantha is waiting for me and you know you can't keep a pregnant lady waiting."

"I'll say." Claudia shifted the box in her arms. "She's so close to the delivery day, we wouldn't want to upset her in any way, now would we? Here," Claudia opened the box and grabbing a napkin from inside wrapped it around two donuts and handed them to Frank, "one for you and one for our pregnant newspaper lady. She's always hungry these days, especially for sweets."

"That's kind of you." Frank took the donuts from her. "Thank you. This'll tide me over until supper and I'm sure Samantha will gobble hers down."

"You're welcome. But the gift comes with a price. When you get the time you must stop by the bookstore and tell me all about Glinda's new clairvoyant insight and what's going on. If Myrtle and Abigail are involved I suspect it's another mystery you all are on."

What Lies Beneath the Graves

"Maybe or maybe not. Glinda has lots of visions. She can't help every spirit who appears to her. This new endeavor might never go any farther."

"Hmm. Well, see you later then." After a quick wave at the woman in the window, Claudia swung around and her heels tap-tapped away from him in the direction of her bookstore. As usual she was dressed in a classy outfit, black slacks and a rose silk blouse. Heels. Watching her stroll away reminded him he'd forgotten to ask about her kids. The five of them were grown and long gone from home but he'd gone to school with a couple of them and liked knowing what they were up to. Well, he'd ask next time he saw her.

He opened the Journal's door and walked over to Samantha's desk. The woman was sitting in her chair, hand on her swollen belly and a distracted look on her puffy face. She'd married her fiancé Kent the year before and was now pregnant with their first child. Kent was more than excited over the prospect of being a father but Samantha, being a working woman and lately eying the political office of town mayor, was more concerned about how she was going to handle it all.

"It won't be long now. The baby's arrival?" Frank sat down across from her in one of the chairs. "The end of May, right?"

"Not soon enough for me." Samantha groaned, rubbing her stomach. "I want this baby born…yesterday. I'm so tired of being so…fat."

"You're not fat, you're just going to have a baby."

"So everyone says. But, lately, I'm not sure if

it's a baby or a kangaroo. The way it kicks me all the time. My stomach inside must be black and blue."

"It will be over soon. In the meantime this will cheer you up. A little present from Claudia." Frank presented her with the donut and was relieved to see her smile. She'd been way too down there for a moment.

"Yum." She accepted the donut and the two of them ate their pastries. "Oh, so good. I was just thinking I was hungry and needed a sugary snack. A pick me up to keep going."

The publisher finished the treat and wiped her hands. "I've been searching the archives and pulling out the old microfiche in the storage rooms since you called me. We have an ancient microfilm machine up in storage, too, and before you leave you can dig it out for me. There's no way I can crawl around up there and bring it down here. It's way in the back and as I recall it is heavy."

"I'll get it down before I leave," Frank said.

"Okay."

"So I guess you haven't uncovered any pertinent information yet about our mysterious sailor ghost?"

"No, not yet," Samantha replied, leaning back in her chair as she rubbed her neck. "But there's so many boxes of microfiche and some of them, I've found, have their years mislabeled. Apparently some of our earlier reporters couldn't count very well. Since you don't know the exact years involved anyway it complicates things even more. So far I haven't found anything concrete on your sailor and

What Lies Beneath the Graves

his treasure, or at least not in more recent years, other than the possibility we might find something in the microfiche files or from people I've asked but I'll keep on asking."

Frank was disappointed but tried not to show it.

"But," Samantha's lips smiled, "after you called and I thought about it I did recall some things I heard when I was a child about the legend of the sailor and his hidden treasure."

"Oh, really? What is that?"

"I imagine you remember my family when we were kids? I was years behind you in school but your parents lived close to mine and everyone on my street knew each other. We were dirt poor. My father, who went from one crazy job to another trying to support us, used to make jokes about sneaking onto Evelyn's land and searching for, as he called it, Bartholomew's Booty. My father was sure the treasure was buried somewhere on the sailor's land, most likely in the yard or the graveyard behind the house. That's what everyone believed. There were even nights my dad disappeared for hours and my mother would jokingly say he was out looking for Bartholomew's treasure. He'd come home the next morning covered in grime and sweat, angry he still hadn't found it.

"Oh, and one time I asked my mother what kind of treasure my father thought he was looking for and she said it was a chest of jewelry and coins, thought to be worth a fortune. I wanted to know how she knew that and she said it was reported in the town's records during her childhood that

Bartholomew paid for the land and the building of his house with some of his gold and a lot of townsfolks believed he didn't spend all he had in his lifetime. He hid the remainder somewhere on his land. Thus the legend took form and grew."

"So," Frank summed up, "the sailor's name was Bartholomew and his treasure was gold coins and jewelry. That's something we didn't know before. I can't wait until you start going through those microfiche." He thought about it and added, "You know I could help you look through them?"

"Thanks. I gladly accept the help. Heaven knows I need it. I have a newspaper to get out and," she patted her stomach again, "this baby of mine could arrive early and Kent and I still have a crib to put together as well as finishing the baby's room. We can't decide on what color to make it." She shook her head but smiled while doing it.

"Good. I can start right now. I could dig out the boxes and the machine." He stood up.

"Excellent," she said. "Oh, and here's another idea to help your paper search…you could check the town's past real estate records for who originally built Evelyn's house and find out the man's full name. Make sure it is the same Bartholomew. And if it is, get an approximate timeline of his life."

"That's another good idea. In fact, I'd already thought of it and I might go ahead and do that first. Then start going through the boxes of microfiche. It could decrease the years I have to look through if I know when the man lived and when he built the house."

What Lies Beneath the Graves

"All things which would be helpful. You know, I'm pleased you're looking into this old mystery. I've always been fascinated with the legend of the sailor and his buried treasure."

"All righty," Frank concluded. "I'm going to city hall to look up some real estate records."

"And I'm going to whip up one last article for our weekly newspaper before I hit publish." She was smiling mischievously. "In the article I'll be asking if anyone remembers anything about this mysterious sailor and his lost treasure. Some of the older townies might recollect something. You know I enjoy helping a fellow writer get the research he needs for his books."

"Now that's another good idea, using the newspaper to ask if anyone remembers anything about the man and his gold. Thanks. It'll be interesting to see what shakes loose. I'll be back later to check out those microfiche." Frank lifted up from the chair and with a courteous goodbye wave of his hand headed for the door.

"Oh," Samantha tossed in as he was at the exit, "I just had another idea. You could stop by the bookstore on your way to the courthouse and see if Claudia has any books on the sailor's legend. Maybe a local inhabitant of the time or soon after wrote something about the treasure. Or there might be a collection of urban town folklore which might mention it."

"I'll do that." Frank was out the door and striding down the sidewalk. First stop Tattered Corners.

"Oh, coming after more donuts, huh?" Claudia

teased when she looked up and saw him. "They're on the table over there. Help yourself." She had a stack of books in her arms and was sliding them into spaces on the shelves.

"Not here for the donuts, but to see if you might have a book about something I've become interested in," he paused for a moment, "which might help me in writing my new novel."

Claudia faced him. "And what book would that be?"

Frank explained about Bartholomew and his undiscovered buried treasure, using a half truth. No need to start the treasure fever bubbling up and over again. Claudia was as bad as Myrtle when it came to spreading gossip. "I thought I might use it as part of a plot device in my new book. Fiction based on real life happenings or truths often make the best fiction. Samantha thought you might have a book here on it since he lived here in town once."

He got more than he expected when she answered. "Oh, that old wives' tale about Bartholomew Masterson's long lost treasure being buried somewhere on his land; probably in an old cemetery somewhere near his house beneath a grave or something?"

Bingo. "So his name was Bartholomew Masterson? Really?"

"Really." Claudia grinned and put the books down on a nearby cart. "No one these days would probably remember where he lived around here, but there were whisperings about him, a recluse who seemed to have secrets, and some mysterious treasure. So he caught someone's fancy enough to have something written about him."

Really?" Frank couldn't believe his luck. A book would make his research a lot easier.

"Oh, it's not a best-seller published by a big publisher. I think it was self-published in the day long before that became fashionable; with a vanity press. It's not even a book only about him." She was on the move now, her fingers brushing along a column of book spines at the bottom of a shelf. "If I recall correctly, it was a homegrown collection of curious town stories written by an older woman who'd lived here all her life and wanted future generations to never forget them. I remember reading it as a young girl and when I opened this bookstore thirty years ago someone anonymously donated a box of them, since it was about Spookie. Most of them have sold over the years to people who live here and care about our town. I thought we had a copy or two left, or I thought we did." Claudia had walked over to another aisle and had continued looking.

"Who was the woman who self-published the book? Do you remember?"

"Not off hand, I can't recall it. She was before my time. But I'll recognize the book when I see it. Someone told me the author was a member of the town's early historical society. You know those members were and are still trying to preserve town stories and legends."

Frank waited, watching as Claudia rifled through more books.

"Yes, here it is," the bookseller announced. "I knew it was here somewhere." She yanked out a worn looking but thin book and gave it to him.

"Can I just borrow it for a while?" he asked as he cradled it in his hand. "I'll return it when I get done reading it. Won't take long, it is a short book."

"It is. Take your time. If it's been on that shelf all these years I don't think anyone is standing in line to buy it. And if it can help you with your new book, then welcome to it for as long as you need it. I love helping authors."

Frank was examining the book. "Hmm, says here the *Odd and Unusual Stories of Spookie* was published by a Lily Merriweather. I've never heard of her." Frank opened the book and took note of the publication date. 1943. He skimmed through the short table of contents. Bartholomew Masterson's Buried Treasure. Page 49. Good. "Thank you, Claudia. I guess I better get going. I still have things to do and places to go."

"Okay, Frank. I hope that little book gives you what you're looking for."

"It might."

Frank left the bookstore and was almost at the truck when he decided to take a quick detour. The taste of Kate's donut was still in his mouth and suddenly he had to have another one and a cup of coffee. He glanced over at The Delicious Circle. It'd only take a minute or two and then he'd be off to city hall.

Walking into the donut shop he spied his friend Kate behind the glass counter putting in another tray of freshly made donuts.

"Hi Frank," she greeted him, straightening up. "How are things going?" Her green eyes met his.

What Lies Beneath the Graves

She'd cut her dark hair shorter than normal, but it and she looked good, happy. Abby had mentioned to him the other day Kate now had a boyfriend named Norman who worked at the local flour mill and they were getting serious.

"Things are fine, Kate. I just thought I'd run in here and get some of your delicious donuts to take home."

"Ah, trying to get points with Abigail, huh?"

"Not really. I have plenty of points with my lovely wife. I'm the perfect husband. Just ask her. Truth is, I wanted some for myself, though she and Nick will appreciate me bringing pastries home. They always do. So please give me six glazed, three chocolate covered custard filled and three of those crème horns." Crème horns were Abigail's favorite. Nick, as most teenagers, liked donuts of any kind. "Oh, and can I also have a cup of coffee to go?" Frank settled down on one of the counter's bar stools and propped his elbows on the counter.

"Sure thing."

"How's your new boyfriend, Norman right, doing?"

Kate laughed. "Oh, so everyone knows about Norman, huh?"

"Small town." He shrugged his shoulders.

"Yeah, small town, big eyes and ears everywhere. Oh, Norman is fine. We've been dating over a month now and I really, really like him. He's a good, solid man and those are hard to find these days and especially in my advanced age group." She smiled. "He works hard, he's kind and he helps care for his ill mother. I'm lucky to know him." She put the paper to-go-cup of coffee in front of him and the box of donuts beside it.

Laying the tome he'd been holding on the counter, Frank paid her.

Kate reached out and tapped the book. "Ah, the *Odd and Unusual Stories of Spookie*. I haven't seen that strange little book since I was a kid. I thought they'd long ago disappeared. You know the author was my great-grandmother?"

"You're kidding?" Frank was taken aback. What a small world it was.

"Nope. My mother used to talk about her nutty, eccentric grandmother Lily all the time. The woman was obsessed with Spookie, its people and history, and the strange stories about it. Lily maintained Spookie was built on haunted Indian land and that's why so many weird things happened to it and its people. She believed the fog hid the dead Indian spirits and they were always watching us, the living."

Frank thought, wait until I tell Myrtle that story. "Well, I haven't heard that particular detail before, but it might explain some things. This town does have its share of weird occurrences–and a lot of eerie fog. And Myrtle is always claiming to see the *ghosts in the woods* as she puts it. Perhaps they are Indian spirits." Frank took a sip of his coffee which Kate had prepared exactly the way he liked it with a teaspoon of sugar and a splash of milk. "What else did your mother say about her grandmother Lily?"

"Only that she was a woman ahead of her time. Odd, yes, but with a truly compassionate and generous heart. She loved our town. Read that book you have there and you'll know a lot more about her." As she answered him Kate's gaze had traveled to something outside the windows. Frank's gaze followed hers.

Someone was coming into the shop. A man. Frank knew most everyone in town, but not the man who came in and shuffled up to the counter, limping with the help of a cane. He looked like a bum dressed as he was in frayed clothing which hung on his skeletal frame. His long wrinkled pants with holes in them were too big and his worn suit coat was dusty. His face was gaunt and he sported a white beard beneath thin lips, a beaked nose and bushy ivory eyebrows. His eyes, though, when they rose to look at Frank, were a mesmerizing blue, but they were tinged with sorrow and regret. Hanging from his slumped shoulder there was a leather bag which looked as used as the man himself. The bag, lumpy and fat, looked full. "Howdy do, my name is Silas," the man said and tipped the black fedora, also dusty and wearing its years, in Frank's direction.

"Hello," Frank replied. "Mine is Frank. Nice to meet you."

"Kate," Kate supplied.

The elderly man zeroed in on her. "Well, Kate, I'd like a cup of that coffee like the young man here has. It smells really good." His voice was soft, cultured and as his eyes were also strangely hypnotic and intelligent Frank had the impression he was an educated man. "If you'd be so kind." He plunked down on the stool beside Frank and began to rummage around in his pocket. He brought out a small pile of dirty coins. Mostly pennies and nickels. Frank spotted a dime or two. "As much coffee as this can buy, my sweet lady."

Frank had to admit Kate was civil, even kind when she requested, "Is that all? Just coffee? Nothing else?"

The old man's eyes were caressing the trays of fancy pastries under the glass. "That will be all."

Frank couldn't help himself. "Kate, give the man a couple of any donuts he wants and I'll cover it."

"No, no I can't accept that," the man in the fedora protested to Frank, but half-heartedly. His eyes were devouring the cherry Danish. His tongue licked his dry lips. "But thank you anyway, young man. It was a kind thought."

"I insist," Frank stated firmly. "Kate, give him what he wants."

The elder remained silent, but his eyes lowered as if he were either ashamed or grateful.

Kate's smile was immediate. "What do you fancy?" she queried the old man.

An arthritic finger pointed to a cherry Danish and a glazed donut. When the old man smiled it changed his face and made him look a decade younger. It was easy to see he was hungry.

Kate took the chosen pastries out and along with a napkin, she placed them before the customer. She poured a large cup of coffee, placed the sugar container and a milk pitcher in front of the old man and then swiped up the pile of coins, depositing them into a cracked cup on a ledge behind her.

What Lies Beneath the Graves

"Coffee refills are free," she told him.

"You are both too kind. Thank you. I guess I'm a little low on funds at the moment. Next time I see you, Frank, I will pay you back." A casual lift of frail shoulders.

"You don't have to," Frank said. "We've all been there. Take it easy, Silas."

"I will…Frank."

Frank laid a ten dollar bill on the counter. As the old man gobbled down the first donut Frank leaned over and whispered near Kate's ear. "Send a few more donuts and another coffee along in a bag with him when he leaves. On me."

Kate tilted her head enough for him to know she understood and murmured, "Was going to do that anyway."

Frank snatched up his box of donuts and his cup and went out the door. He had business at the city hall and then a return visit to the newspaper. And he couldn't be late for supper with Abby and Nick. At least now he had clues to follow up and direct him on his search. The legend of Bartholomew's lost treasure had gotten under his skin and he knew he wouldn't rest until he'd learned more. It wasn't just the old mystery Glinda had presented to him which intrigued him, it was the whole treasure thing. He already had plots and possibilities swirling around in his head for his new mystery book to incorporate it. He'd been searching for a plot device for his new book for a long time and he knew buried treasure was it. Not to mention, since he'd been a child he'd loved the tales of pirates and buried treasure, Black Beard and

Captain Hook. He'd once dreamed of going out to sea himself to look for sunken ships and what treasure they might have carried. Instead he'd grown up and had become a cop.

In the city hall's records department, to his surprise but not shock, he confirmed it was Bartholomew Masterson who'd built Evelyn's house in the year nineteen thirty-eight; earlier than he'd thought. So when he returned to the Journal he knew he needed to look in the microfiche boxes for the late nineteen thirties and early nineteen forties to perhaps discover any articles about the reclusive Masterson and his legendary treasure.

But after two hours of digging through dusty microfiche boxes stacked willy-nilly with no regard to dates he realized it would be more of a job than he'd expected. "I'm cutting out for the day, Samantha," he updated her as he came out of the storage room. His hands were filthy and he was covered in dust. He'd need a shower before supper. "If it's okay with you I'll come back tomorrow and keep rummaging."

"Good timing. I was just coming to look for you. Sure, come back anytime. No luck, huh?" Samantha looked as if she were getting ready to leave as well. She had her jacket on and her purse in her hands.

"No luck. There's too many boxes. And your microfiche machine doesn't want to cooperate. It keeps dying on me."

"It's really old, what do you expect? I'm surprised it still works at all. I open the doors tomorrow at nine."

What Lies Beneath the Graves

"I'll resume the search tomorrow morning…sometime." He retrieved his cell phone from his pocket and tapped in a number. "Right now I need to order a pizza and cheesy bread from Marietta's, pick it up, and get home. Abby gets cranky if supper is too late."

"That she does."

He put in his order and hung up.

"You and Kent need to come out for a visit soon. We haven't seen you in a while."

"I know. Possibly this weekend we'll drop by."

"Give up a call first to be sure we're home."

"I will. Take it easy Frank."

"I will."

Samantha led him out the door and the two went different ways.

Chapter 3

"Myrtle, have you seen your niece since yesterday? Has she seen anything else which might help us find out more about her ghost sailor?" Abigail was putting her sketch book and colored drawing pens away, tucking them into the bottom drawer of the antique sideboard in her kitchen where she kept her art supplies.

"I haven't been there or talked to her yet today. I'm going over for supper, though. We always share suppers on Thursday nights. It's our thing. We visit, play a card game or watch a movie together and I frequently spend the night in her guest room. I think she's making lasagna tonight. She makes a mean lasagna. She puts a ton of cheese in it. And you know I love cheese." Myrtle was sitting at the table watching Abigail. "I haven't even told her Frank suspects the ghost is the original builder of her house. I'll tell her tonight."

It was two-thirty in the afternoon and outside it was raining, not a heavy rain, merely a light sprinkling so prevalent in early spring.

"Frank hopes the ghost will revisit her again and will reveal more. He's really into this buried treasure story now. He wants to use it for his new book."

"Surprise, surprise. That man takes everything that happens to us," Myrtle complained good-naturedly, "and puts it in his books. That's why they all sell so well. We lead interesting lives, we do." Now the old woman smiled devilishly.

Abigail was standing at the kitchen window above the sink, gazing out into the rainy woods. She'd brought the dogs in when the rain had begun and they were in the other room somewhere doing whatever it was dogs did. It was quiet so the dogs must be behaving themselves or napping. It made sense, they were old. Their days of exuberant mischief were mostly over.

As usual, Snowball was curled up sleeping in her cat bed by the oven. The creature loved to sleep somewhere warm on rainy days. She'd wake up when Abigail started making supper. Abigail glanced over at the cat. The critter was four furry paws up and tummy showing. It'd make a cute picture but Abigail restrained herself. There were already enough cute pictures of snowball on her Facebook page. She didn't want the world to think she was cat crazy, even if she was.

"Yeah, we lead such interesting lives," Abigail joked sarcastically.

Myrtle threw her a haughty glance. "We do at times. Murder mysteries seem to attach themselves to us like we were magnets. Killers, too. Ghosts. People come to us for help. No small things. I'd call that interesting."

"If you say so."

Myrtle changed the subject. "How did Miguel

like your sketches?" She plunged on. "You met with him earlier today, right?"

"I did." Abigail joined Myrtle at the table. "And he loved my drawings, my concept for his restaurant. He okayed them and everything I suggested on the spot."

"Can I see them?"

"Sorry, he kept them to show to his family and his workers. I should have made copies on my copier but was in such a hurry this morning before I left adding last minute touches to them, I didn't. But…I did snap a few photos on my iPhone before I left them with Miguel." Abigail reached back, picked her phone up from the counter and showed the pictures to Myrtle.

"They look nice. Great like everything you do. Lots of bright cheerful colors and smiling people. What, no sombreros? Donkeys loaded with pots? No Mariachi bands?"

"No, none of those. I want this to represent and reflect Mexico today. Modern. Even if it's a quaint village representation."

"Humph, they still have Mariachi bands in Mexico today. I like Mariachi bands," Myrtle grumbled in her little old lady pouty voice. "And little donkeys carrying pots."

"You also like delicious food and South of the Border has marvelous food."

"We'll have to go there one day for lunch."

"We will. I'll be there a lot because I'm starting the mural right away. Miguel offered me an excellent payment for doing it and I accepted." Abigail was happy with the commission and the coming work. She was always happier when she was painting something somewhere.

"Well, make sure you leave some time for our new buried treasure ghost mystery. I'm sure there will be more developments here real soon. Glinda doesn't mess around. She'll have more clues for us and we'll be on our way, I bet."

Abigail inwardly sighed but kept a pacifying smile on her face. She knew Myrtle lived for their little adventures and Frank wove them into his murder mysteries–but Abigail not so much. She was tired of running from criminals or her and her friends hiding from murderers. She'd had more than enough of that to last a lifetime. She was not living in a crime drama, though Myrtle would probably like that. Then an idea occurred to her. "You know that world cruise you keep saying you're going on? You ought to book one of those mystery trips where they preform nightly mysteries for the passengers to solve. You'd like that."

Myrtle's eyes lit up. "Now that's a darn good idea. I'll have to look into that. I'd be good at it. Probably solve all the mysteries right off. But just to let you know, I've postponed going on that world cruise for a while." She was getting up from the chair. Dressed in one of her long dresses, she'd layered under two sweaters and a thin rain coat; on her head was one of her woolen sock caps. She grabbed an umbrella which had been hanging on the back of her chair. It looked like one of Claudia's giveaways.

"Oh, yes?" Abigail didn't like the sound of that but on the other hand she wasn't sure she wanted to encourage the world cruise thing, either. Myrtle had a habit of getting into trouble wherever she was, but at least if she was in Spookie, she, Frank and Glinda could keep an eye on her. If she were thousands of miles away on a cruise ship that wouldn't be as easy.

"Yep. That Caribbean island with warm sand and sun or one of those mystery cruises will just have to wait. I have a mystery to solve, a wrong to right, an adventure to seek closer to home. I have the premonition it's going to end up being a really big thriller, too. And murder will be involved."

Oh boy.

Myrtle appeared to recall something. "Where did you say Frank was?"

It would be fuel to the fire, but Abigail chose to tell the truth. "He's at the newspaper attempting to learn more in the archives about the man who built Glinda's house, feeling that the ghost who appeared to her is connected to her house or her land somehow. He's also looking for any articles which might ever have been written about the builder or touched on him. Frank called me a while ago and told me he thinks he's discovered the builder's name. It's Bartholomew Masterson."

"Bartholomew Masterson is the fellow who built the house Glinda now lives in and Frank believes he might be Glinda's ghost?"

"Possibly. He's still digging around in the archives and asking around."

"Hmm, the name somehow sounds familiar." Myrtle cocked her head as if she were listening to something far away. "As if I've heard it before."

What Lies Beneath the Graves

"Maybe Evelyn mentioned him over the years as having been the original owner of her house?"

"She could have. But my old brain doesn't remember it if she did or not. Evelyn said a lot of things all the time, she talked way too much, and mostly I never listened. Bad me. Now that she's gone, I wished I would have. Most of the stuff she said was silly, about her menagerie. Dog, dog, dog. Cat, cat, cat. This critter this or that critter that. Blah, blah, blah. But the name really does strike a chord somehow. I'll have to ponder on it.

"Well," Myrtle announced. "I got to be going."

Abigail smiled. "You're off to pester Frank at the newspaper, aren't you?"

Myrtle smiled back. "You know me so well, Abby. I'm off to help him look. This is my adventure, too, you know. It was my niece the ghost appeared to."

Then the old woman was gone, leaving Abigail to shake her head as she so often did when it came to Myrtle. Though she had to give the old woman credit. To be in one's nineties and still be so involved in the world was a rare thing.

*****

Glinda was sleeping, she knew she was sleeping…she was in her bed, two of her cats, Amadeus and Ebony, curled up beside her. She awoke for a moment and then slipped back into her slumber. Aaah, so nice to be safe and warm, her bed was so soft. Outside the night was singing, full of crickets, frogs and mournful small creatures scurrying from bush to tree in the dark. An unfamiliar sound made her open her eyes and look where Amadeus wanted her to look. Framed in her window she glimpsed the full moon, its light filling her room and softening the world outside. Another strange noise from outside somewhere. It sounded like…the ocean and a…ship's bell or something like it. Weird.

Amadeus hunkered above her and meowed. One of his large paws touched her chest, his gaze going to the window. What did he want? He jumped to the floor and padded to the door, looking backwards at her. He wanted her to follow him.

She rose from the bed, put on a robe and the mule shoes she used for going outside, and left the house. The moonlight illuminated everything almost as clear as if it were day. Her yard and the surrounding woods stretched out before her in the night. The rain had ceased but had been replaced with a thickening mist covering the ground and creeping up the trees. She'd learned to love the fog in Spookie in all its incarnations. Sometimes it was as fine as spider webs, clinging to the grass, trees and shrubs and sometimes it was a fluffy gray blanket hiding everything in its path. Tonight it was swiftly becoming the blanket, but so far restricting itself to the ground. For now. The thought crossed her mind she shouldn't stay out too long or the fog would hide the forest world completely and she'd be trapped, lost, and unable to find her way home.

She'd lost sight of her feline guide, had stopped, and called out into the dark. "Amadeus, where did you go?" He meowed and must have waited for her because there he was at her feet.

"Why are you dragging me out here, you silly

puss? It's chilly and wet. Amadeus!" She was shivering. She should have grabbed a coat but she'd been in such a hurry to tail the cat, she hadn't thought of it.

Amadeus had bounded ahead through the brush and, with an exhaled breath, she continued to run after him. He seemed insistent she follow, so she would.

She saw the graveyard first. It was eerie beneath the full moon above and with the surrounding woods in deep shadows. It was a good thing graves and tombstones didn't bother her. She talked to the dead often enough that their final resting places didn't unnerve her or too much anyway. Night birds were chirping in the branches around her. It was still a spooky place.

Amadeus was perched on one of the rails of the gazebo. His tiny silhouette stark against the night's background. A small cluster of early fireflies were flickering around the animal.

Glinda went up the steps and once inside the structure sat down on one of the benches. The wind was whipping through the openings and she could smell the musky wet earth, mud and tree bark. Nature. She loved that smell. Amadeus jumped into her lap. The fireflies flew away into the woods.

Again she could hear an ocean's waves and what she believed was a ship's bell. Ringing. Ringing. She closed her eyes and that is when the trance overcame her.

Now the ringing bell was louder, nearer, and the sound filled the air around her. She was no longer in the gazebo. It was as if she were seeing from another's eyes. She was on the ocean–which would account for the splashing of the waves she was hearing–and there was water everywhere. She felt the ground shift beneath her, a sort of rocking motion, looked down, and realized she was on a deck of some kind. She wasn't really knowledgeable about ships and things that sailed the seas so she had no idea exactly what sort of vessel it was. Her eyes scanned to her left and the right, up into the clear blue sky and down. Yes, she was on a ship and by the looks of it, an older, smaller ship; not one of those huge shiny metal and plastic cruise ships, either. The wooden decks were scuffed and nicked with years of boots treading across them. The paint around her on the walls and enclosures were flaking. There were three masts rising above her into the sky, canvas whipping in the breeze, so the ship was a sailing vessel of some kind. On one of the circle-shaped life preservers there was a name: Black Ghost. So the ship was called the Black Ghost.

She could hear men talking and whispering around her, yet when she looked there were only shadowy figures moving about the deck. Working men from another time. It was hard to see them in too much detail, but they appeared to be dressed as perhaps sailors would have been in the early twentieth century. They weren't in uniforms, so they weren't soldiers or military and they didn't look to be pirates, merely seemed to be normal men of the time laboring on a ship. But was it a fishing ship or an exploration vessel?

Then some of the conversations became

audible, as if someone had shifted the dial on a radio and finally found the true channel. The voices came through clear.

"That treasure is there, I tell you," one shadow was saying to another. "The ship, the Sea Lord, went down on the sharp reefs around this island during a terrible storm and with it the shipment of gold supposedly for the war effort in England. It never got there, of course. Soon after it left America's shores the ship was smashed to smithereens on the rocks, all men on board vanished, died, most likely. I have been hearing about it for years. The wreck is down there in shallow water among the fish, rocks and sand. Easy to salvage with divers. Chests and bags of jewelry and old Spanish coins stolen, though no one knows from who. But those who speak of it say the treasure is cursed. That's why the ship sank and the gold was lost and not for the first time. So anyone who touches any of it is fated to die. That's what they say."

"Who cursed it?"

"No one knows. Could be the pirates who are rumored to have first collected it years past or the original owners whoever they were. This is an old treasure. Long lost and recently found."

Another shadow floated up to her, or to whomever she was supposed to be in the vision. "Bart, the captain is calling us all together for a meeting. Now."

She heard her lips mouth the response, "We must be close to where the Sea Lord went down, Owen, my brother." A pause. "We've found it. After all these months searching for that treasure the captain must believe we might have found it."

Brother?

"We might have. The others believe so as well. Just think, Bart, if we actually do find it we will all be wealthy men. Filthy rich like kings. All twenty of us. Why, you can return to your beloved Darcy and give her anything she wants. Anything. She'll forgive you then, I'd wager, for leaving her, the babe, and being gone for so long."

"I can only pray it will be so, Brother. It has been so very long since I saw or spoke to her. Has she stayed faithful to me? I don't know if she has. She swore she would. I must get back to them soon. I promised. Let's go...." And the shadows and the voices dwindled away. For a moment more Glinda could see the ocean around her, hear the waves and inhale the tanginess of the salty sea, then everything receded into blackness.

She opened her eyes to sunlight and was surprised to find herself in her bed, Amadeus snuggled beside her along with two other of the cats, Gizmo and Big Paws. She'd never left her own bed, her room or her house; had not wandered into the night woods and sat in the gazebo. It had all been a dream. A dream, like the ship and the talking shadows.

But who were Bart and Owen and why were they haunting her? And that treasure…had they ever found it? She didn't know either thing but she had the feeling she'd learn soon enough.

Chapter 4

Frank was taking a break from rummaging through the microfiche boxes, his feet up on Samantha's desk, sipping on a cup of cold coffee he'd brought with him earlier, and had opened the book *Odd and Unusual Stories of Spookie* to read. He hadn't had time before then. The previous night after their family pizza supper he'd spent playing Monopoly with Abby and Nick, who'd been home unusually early from practicing with his band, The Young Ones. Then, the following morning, Frank had gotten up early and driven into town to the newspaper to continue his research on Masterson.

Samantha had been in and out of the office already, some story she was on, and the other two junior reporters in the office, Jasmine and Toby, were clicking away in the far corner on their laptops. They were new reporters, fresh-faced, technology savvy, idealistic and they worked for minimum wage, which was about all Samantha could afford. The newspaper world wasn't what it had once been. The Internet, all things online, had taken over print. Frank often wondered how Samantha kept the Journal afloat. Good stories, home town stories about the people Spookie cared about, was what she'd always say; stories they wanted to read.

Frank's fingers flipped the book's pages to number forty-nine and he began reading. The chapter wasn't very long, barely two pages. As chronicled in the book Bartholomew Masterson had been a retired sailor and treasure hunter who came to Spookie in nineteen-thirty nine and built the house at number ten Blossom Road. That location was once Evelyn's house and now Glinda's home. The book spoke about the wealthy man and how reclusive he was, even as the house was being constructed, and the rumors he'd found a treasure of gold from a ship wreck earlier in his life and had brought it back with him from the sea. No one had ever seen the treasure itself. The man would never acknowledge he had it and never talked about it. He lived, alone and friendless, in his house until he died and only after his death were papers found hidden in his attic which referred to a long vanished, and unnamed, wife and a possible child. Also among the documents he left behind was a simple diary which stated how, in his old age, he had come to greatly regret not ever being able to find his lost wife and progeny and how he'd spent many years and limitless money searching for them; going so far as to hire a string of private investigators to look across the country. According to the book, he never found them.

And here, too, was where one of the places the legend of Masterson's secret treasure had been given birth, because the diary and other discovered records also hinted at the possibility that Masterson might have buried the remainder of his gold somewhere in the ground on his land. Somehow the information from the diary leaked out and the treasure hunt had begun. But his property covered twenty acres, included deep woods, valleys, a creek, and a sprawling graveyard many of the early townspeople had been interred in. If Masterson had buried the remnants of his gold before his death it could still be in the earth somewhere. *Odd and Unusual Stories of Spookie* didn't say how much of the gold he'd left at the end of his life but it did say many people believed he'd buried it somewhere beneath a grave in the graveyard. Clues they'd somehow gleaned from some of the things he'd said while he'd still been alive and later in his writings. And after his burial, when the house had been empty, it had been ransacked, his grave had been vandalized and dug up, along with many others in his cemetery by townsfolk searching for what was left of the gold. Apparently no one had ever found it or if they had they'd kept their mouth shut and ran off to liquidate and spend it all.

And so the legend of the lost treasure grew, yet when never found, over the following long years it slowly faded again in peoples' memories.

So, Frank closed the book after coming to the end of the two pages and reading all there was to read, could this be who the sailor ghost really was? Masterson? And, if they were one and the same, was the ghost's reason for appearing to Glinda so they'd resume searching for the rest of the gold? Why? For the ghost's long lost wife? No, she'd be dead by now. Or…for his child, whomever and wherever she was?

For the child then?

Frank put the book down. Time to return to the dusty boxes and the sheets of ancient microfiche film. He'd have to ask Samantha why she didn't just take the old film and have it transferred to digital files. Maybe because it would cost her in manpower to transfer all the microfiche to digital? Probably. But getting rid of the dusty boxes and putting the old records and newspapers on the computer would free up space in the back rooms. Samantha had done so much to the newspaper's offices, beautifying and updating them, perhaps she hadn't got around yet to modernizing the old information in the storerooms. Frank looked at the beautiful mural Abby had painted on the wall two years before. The room really did look welcoming. It was an appealing place to work in and the mural made a person realize the long respected history of town newspapers and how important they'd always been to the villages they served. He hoped the newspaper would continue to exist for many more years. He enjoyed opening it every week, hearing the crackle of the paper between his fingers as he turned the pages, and reading up on what was going on in his little town.

"Good book?" Toby had come up beside him. The young man, the satchel which held his laptop hanging at his side, was on his way out.

It was at that moment Frank had the random thought he should keep the information concerning the remainder of the buried gold to himself. For now. He didn't want the town going crazy again and embarking on another Spookie gold rush, digging up Glinda's house and land searching for a buried treasure which may or may not exist any longer.

"Not really. Pretty dull. I'm gathering research for my new book, that's all."

The young reporter was studying the book cover. "*Odd and Unusual Stories of Spookie*, huh? It doesn't sound dull to me. Spookie is and always has been an interesting place, or so I've been told."

"Yes, it has been, it is, an interesting town." Frank knew Toby was new to the village, had only been living there a handful of years, but he was a curious individual and a…reporter. Everything he saw, learned and overheard was fair game for publication to him. Frank didn't want the treasure story posted all over the Internet tomorrow so he was careful with what he said and how he said it.

"What's this novel going to be about? You know, I've read all your books. I really like them. They're great murder mysteries. I'm good at guessing who's done what but your books often surprise me. I can never figure out who the murderer is until you reveal them. You're a heck of a writer."

Flattery. "Thank you. I work hard on my books and I'm proud of them." Frank smiled at the young man. He was basically humble when it came to praise, most times, but it did feel good to be appreciated and for once he accepted the compliment with a smile. "Oh, my present work in progress, of course, is another murder mystery, but I don't really like talking about them until they're finished." He lightly tapped his head. "I keep it all in here until then. Not ready for prime time yet, you know?"

"Oh, being a writer myself, I understand completely." Toby nodded knowingly. He was a gawky, big boned farm boy with clear blue eyes and short blond hair who was a lot smarter than his obvious innocence portrayed. Samantha had told Frank that Toby was an excellent writer and had dreams of being a published author someday. So Frank, seeing that look he'd seen many times before on other faces now on the young reporter's, was waiting for the inevitable declaration and the inevitable request.

"You know I'm working on a novel myself," the young man's voice had fallen to a whisper.

"You don't say?" Wait for it. Wait for it.

"It's true. I've been working on it for years now and finally have the first third of it done…I hate to ask this, but would you, could you, perhaps take a look at it one day and let me know if I'm on the right track? Let me know what you think of"

Frank couldn't count the number of times he'd been asked this. Way too many. In fact, if he'd stop his own writing to read and critique other people's work as often as he'd been asked, he'd never have time to write his own books. So, as much as he hated to say this to any hopeful writer, it had become a standard reply to gently but firmly let the petitioners down and refuse the request. "Toby, I learned many years ago that if I read everyone else's stuff I'd never be able to write my own novels. So I make it a point, across the board to say no, I can't. I'm sorry. It's nothing against you.

What Lies Beneath the Graves

Samantha says you're a fine writer and I wish you all the luck in the world."

Oh, all right." The young man appeared disappointed but hid it well, standing up straighter. "I understand." Then he perked up. "Well then, as a successful murder mystery writer could you give me any advice?"

And Frank told him what he told every want-to-be-novelist. "If you're a true writer, I mean a writer in your heart, bones and soul, you will keep writing no matter what, rejections or not, and you will never give up. If you do that and keep perfecting your craft, you'll eventually succeed. I guarantee it." He didn't always say that last part but with Samantha's recommendation of Toby's writing, he could for him.

Again the young man seemed disappointed. "Really? That's your advice?"

Frank almost laughed but seeing the crestfallen expression on the reporter's face, he didn't. The young never got it. The old did, but rarely the young. "One day you'll understand, fellow writer. The truth is being a writer is not easy, believe me. It is perseverance and determination which will give you what you want in the end–and learning your craft. For now, just keep writing on your novel and only do it if it makes you happy. Oh, and write what you want to write, never what someone else wants you to."

Toby seemed to think about that and surprisingly rewarded Frank with a smile. "Thanks for the advice. I think I understand what you're saying."

After Toby had left Frank returned to the storeroom and the boxes. After another two hours of a futile search, he was ready to take a break when Myrtle entered the storeroom.

"Hi there Frank. Where's Samantha? I didn't see her out there in the office."

"Hi Myrtle. Oh, she's at the doctor's. You know, that baby is coming soon."

"I know. About a month yet to go, huh?"

"About that."

"She's okay, isn't she?" Myrtle's voice was concerned.

"As far as we know she is. It's only a check-up."

"Good." Myrtle paused and then said, "That girl reporter out there–"

"Jasmine," Frank supplied.

"Yeah, yeah, Jasmine, she said you were in here, tearing through the boxes looking for something or other. I assume you're looking for information on our sailor ghost, right?"

"Uh, you didn't tell her *what* I was looking for, did you?"

"Nah, I'm not dumb. I told her I didn't know what in the heck you were looking for. And I came in here."

"Good. No need to start a treasure hunt."

"Boy, you're not kidding. Because I now remember hearing some old lady years and years ago when I first moved here–had to be over sixty years past at least–going on about how after some rich elderly geezer who lived outside of town died the entire town, or a lot of them anyway, were going nuts vandalizing, wrecking his house, knocking down walls and everything, and digging up his yard and even a graveyard looking for some buried treasure he'd discovered on his travels years before. Caskets were dug up, desecrated, and strewn everywhere in the gold fever. It was a huge town scandal she said.

"I woke up this morning," Myrtle softly slapped her forehead, "and her words just rushed back to me. Old lady's memory, you know. It comes and goes. I bet that was the ghost sailor's treasure they were hunting for, wasn't it?"

"Yep. And I have discovered one important thing…that ghost's name was Bartholomew Masterson and he built and lived in Evelyn's house, or now Glinda's house. He died there, too. That could be some of the reasons your niece had that psychic insight. The connection is the house and the land. He wants something from her, from us."

"Ah, so you found out his name and you're sure he was the one who built Evelyn's, now Glinda's, house?"

"Remember I went to city hall yesterday and looked up the real estate records and…." Frank took Myrtle's wrist and tugged her out of the storeroom into the other room and up to Samantha's desk where he'd left the book. He picked it up and handed it to Myrtle. "I found this book at Claudia's bookstore yesterday."

Myrtle took the book and peered at the title. "Yeah, it's a book all right." Her eyes had gone wide and her face had a smirk on it. "An old book at that."

"Not just any book. Look at page forty-nine."

Myrtle did. She skimmed through the two pages and when she glanced up at him, her smirk had disappeared. "Hmm, okay, this confirms some things. So the center of this mystery is that Glinda's ghost is most likely this Masterson and there's a lost treasure that could still be out on Glinda's land somewhere?"

"Gold jewelry and old coins I think."

"And some of it could still be in the ground somewhere on Glinda's land? Oh my, my, my." Myrtle was checking to see if anyone was around to hear what she was saying. Jasmine, though, appeared to be busy in the corner and was not paying any attention to them. "Maybe we can get Glinda to ask the ghost, if she sees him again, if he is really this Masterson and where he buried the gold?"

Frank laughed. "Myrtle, only you would think of that. But, no, there is no proof whatsoever that Masterson left any of his gold lying around or buried anywhere. So far it's only an urban legend."

Myrtle was staring at the door. "You know who we should ask? Glinda. Maybe she's spoken to the ghost again and maybe he's already told her about his treasure."

"Perhaps. Wouldn't Glinda have called us if the sailor had appeared to her again?"

"Yeah, I guess she would have. Or at least she would have called me. We're so very close, you know?" Myrtle's expression was one of prideful smugness.

"I know you two are." Frank noticed beyond

the windows the day had turned unnaturally dark. A storm was moving in. "I guess I had better get back to looking through those boxes. I still have quite a few to go through. How would you like to help me, Myrtle?"

"Nah, I saw those boxes and there's way too much dust and grime on them for my liking. And I'm way too old to be digging around in old storerooms." She made a face. "Besides I have more errands to run before the skies unload on us. I saw on the weather this morning we're expecting a deluge of rain and by the looks of the sky out there it's not far off. Sorry, but I got to get going."

Frank didn't argue. Myrtle never did care much for grunt work. Now if the gold was hidden in one of those dusty boxes there'd be no way to keep her from tearing into them. Myrtle liked a more instant gratification.

"I'll see you later," the old woman said then spun around and waddled out of the building. Frank watched her go across the street and hurry away out of sight. He could hear her singing one of Perry Como's songs at the top of her lungs all the way down the street. "*Can the ocean keep from rushin' to the shore, it's just impossible. If I had you, could I ever want for more, it's just impossible!*"

What a character.

Shaking his head, he returned to his task. He was sick of the dirty boxes and the microfiche but until he found what he was looking for or reached the last box, he wasn't giving up. He kept scrutinizing the tiny pieces of film on the microfiche reader. "Well, this makes me appreciate our modern computers and laptops so much more," he muttered under his breath. "Microfiche is a pain in the butt. No wonder it's obsolete. It should be."

After a while he heard the rain thundering on the roof and windows, but he kept working determined to find out more about Bartholomew Masterson and his life if he could.

*****

Myrtle was in a hurry to get where she wanted to go, she had to beat the rain, but got side-tracked by a quick stop at The Delicious Circle. She was going to take a box of Glinda's favorite pastries to her. The girl had a real sweet tooth. Since she was always eating Glinda's goodies she thought she'd bring her own this time. One had to give once and a while, or so she believed.

She had passed the hardware store, singing one of her favorite Perry Como songs as she went, waving hello to Luke inside and he waving back, when she saw the old man down the street. It gave her a start. It'd been a while since she'd seen him wandering the sidewalks. She didn't know his name. He was dressed like a refugee with his baggy dirty clothes and his tattered fedora. She'd seen him a few times before over the years, knew of him and that he had a very ill wife; they lived outside of town somewhere and kept to themselves, but she had never actually officially met him. He constantly disappeared around a corner or a building before she could confront him and she'd tried to catch up with him many times. Oh well. Some people merely wanted to be left alone, she understood that. But it was odd he was shambling around town in the daylight, looking like a zombie. Very odd. Maybe he was a ghost…nah, his edges were too solid and he wasn't floating.

She gazed down at the sidewalk for a moment or two to avoid a gaping crack and when she looked up again, the man in the fedora was gone. Nothing new there. If she'd had an inkling of which way he'd gone, she would have chased after him. Talked to him. She was tired of his disappearing act. But she had no idea so she kept walking towards her destination. The rain was coming and she had to hurry.

"Hi there, Myrtle," Kate greeted her when she went into the donut shop. "You do know it's supposed to storm like crazy here any minute? You shouldn't be out here when it does."

"I know, I know," Myrtle brushed off her warning. "By my calculations, though, it won't start raining for another, ooh, twenty-nine minutes or so. More than enough time to get what I want here and scoot over to my niece's house."

"Oh, you're going to Glinda's?"

"Yep."

"Where's your wagon today, Myrtle?"

"Ah, I left it home. I have places to go today and things to do and the wagon isn't part of it. For today anyway. I have to make good time." Myrtle's lips barely cracked a smile.

Kate's eyes were on her when she asked, "So…what can I get you today, traveler?" Kate had given Myrtle that name years ago because Myrtle was always walking everywhere, always on the go. It was a fond nick-name so Myrtle didn't mind it.

She liked Kate. Kate was a sweet lady and often gave her samples or free pastries.

Myrtle peaked into the glass cases and picked out a variety of a dozen donuts, careful to get a few jelly for Glinda. Those were her favorites, well, along with chocolate-covered cake ones. Kate threw in three extra donuts and didn't charge her for them.

"Anything new with you, donut lady?"

"Not too much. I'm thinking about building on to the shop."

"Really? Why?"

"Well, I'd like to start serving sandwiches and sides. I'll keep it simple, mainly lunch items. I'm hoping it'd bring in more customers."

"Hmm, need more money, huh?" Myrtle was watching the day grow darker outside the windows. She'd better get moving. She didn't like the forest in the rainy dark. Too many creatures of the night roaming around. Too many ghosts.

"That's part of it. But there isn't really a sandwich shop here in town and I thought it would be nice to have one. You know, for people on the go wanting a quick meal without going to a real restaurant."

"You got a point there. If you do expand and open a sandwich counter be sure to make those little chicken salad sandwiches on those crescent roll thingies. I really like them. I'd be a customer for sure."

"Chicken salad on croissants are an excellent suggestion and I will be sure to include them on the menu."

"Be sure you do."

What Lies Beneath the Graves

"How is Glinda doing?" the donut lady inquired, closing the large white bag, taking the money from Myrtle and putting it away.

"She's doing just fine." Myrtle covered her mouth with her one hand. She'd almost blurted out about the sailor's ghost, the hidden treasure and the new adventure she and her gang were embarking on, but stopped herself just in time. She shut up. Frank wanted her to keep things quiet. She'd have a chance to blab all about it when she got to Glinda's.

"Seen any ghosts lately?" Kate suddenly inquired and Myrtle felt a moment of panic until she realized the woman wasn't asking about the sailor's ghost but about ghosts in general. The wood's ghosts.

Myrtle grabbed a hunk of glazed donut with her fingers from one in the bag and popped it into her mouth. So good. "Not today so far. But the day is young and I will be going into the forest here pretty soon." She frowned at the bag in her hand. "They'll smell the donuts, no doubt, and will probably fall all over me. I guess I better get moving. Can I have another, bigger, bag? I don't want the ghosts to smell my donuts."

"Sure." Smiling, Kate reached down and pulled out another bag.

Myrtle dumped her donut bag into the larger one and rolled up the top to keep the smell in. "Thanks."

"You're welcome. Bye for now. Be careful out there, Myrtle. Say hi to Glinda for me and tell her I'll be seeing her soon for another reading." Kate confided, "I have some important questions to ask her."

"I'll tell her," Myrtle replied as she sashayed out the door.

The sky was blacker than when she'd left the newspaper, the wind was wilder, so she made her old legs move faster. Darn, she should have worn a raincoat or brought an umbrella. Too late now.

She barely made it to Glinda's house before the storm hit. Good thing she knew all the fastest short cuts through town and through the woods. And a good thing she wasn't waylaid by any pesky apparitions because rain didn't faze them. She banged on the door and made funny faces at the weird Amadeus cat through the window glass. But it was just in fun. She and Amadeus had made peace with each other a long time ago. They only pretended sometimes they hadn't; it was their thing. The door opened as the water and wind exploded around her.

"Whoowe! Let me in, let me in, kiddo!"

"Aunt Myrtle," Glinda cried, yanking her inside, "what are you doing out in this weather? Don't you know there are tornado warnings out? What do you want…to be blown away–"

"–like Dorothy swept off into Oz?" Myrtle gave her an impish wink and chuckled. "Just let any old tornado even try it. I'd grab a hold of a fat tree trunk and I'd be safe enough. I've done it before."

Myrtle trailed the younger woman into the kitchen where she presented the white bag to her. "Donut snacks."

"Why thank you, Aunt. Donuts are just the perfect thing to eat during a rainstorm. I'll make us some tea and we'll have them."

Glinda always teased her. A funny noise erupted from Myrtle's mouth and she muttered, "Coffee, please." The psychic knew she hated tea.

"Well, tea for me and coffee for you, old woman." The psychic flashed her a playful smile.

Once settled at the table with their drinks and pastries the sound of the outside storm was a raucous backdrop with the crack of breaking tree limbs and unidentified objects bumping around beyond the windows, some slamming against the house.

"It's really storming out there. I think you should spend the night, Auntie." Glinda offered. "They say this storm, the rain, is going to last all evening. I also have a handmade pizza I was going to make later tonight and there's more than enough for you."

"My favorite with mushrooms and sausage?"

"Of course." It was convenient they liked the same toppings.

Myrtle was watching the rain hit the windows. The wind was howling like an angry monster. It had prematurely turned into darkness outside. She would spend the night. Glinda had fixed up a comfy bedroom last year just for her. The bed was so soft it was like a giant marshmallow. There was a television on the wall for her to watch and a padded rocker in the corner. She'd made the room hers by bringing some of her favorite books to read, her knitting and a bag of her favorite candy treats. A stuffed and lumpy teddy bear she liked to sleep with. It had belonged to her dead son when he'd been a child and it comforted her to have it at night to cuddle. She also had another one of her son's stuffed animals, a little dog, she kept at her house. "I guess I will stay. I don't fancy traipsing through the woods in this hurricane. Those ghosts would tear me apart. They're mad because I wouldn't give them any of our donuts."

Glinda sent her a sideways glance. "Too bad for them. That's one of the drawbacks of being dead. No donuts."

The women ate their pastries and drank their drinks and retired to the living room to watch television. It was Supernatural night and Myrtle loved that show. It was one of her favorites. Those two brothers were so cute, especially that tall and lanky Sam, and they were always able to beat the ghosts, vampires or any monsters who had the nerve to cross their path. They had witch and psychic friends. She felt a real kinship with them. They fought the good fight against the dark side and won. Tonight, according to the preview from last week, they were lost in this bizarre other dimensional world with a real monster, big as a house, waiting to have them for lunch. They were tied to trees for pity's sake waiting to be devoured. How were they going to get out of this mess? She couldn't wait to see.

Supernatural was an hour away, Amadeus was in Glinda's lap and the other felines were sleeping draped around the room in various places, when the knock came on the door. The storm was still raging outside and hadn't abated in the least. She and Glinda had had a nice evening together, eating pizza

What Lies Beneath the Graves

and chatting about fortune telling, spirits they'd known and any other interesting subject they could think of, though Myrtle hadn't touched on the subject of the sailor's ghost yet. She'd been saving it. Myrtle had discovered in the last two years Glinda was very much like her in so many ways. Blood did win out. It was like having a daughter, something Myrtle had always wanted, and she reveled in it.

"Now who would be visiting on a night like this?" Myrtle's eyes were on the door as her niece opened it.

"Frank, what are you doing out in this storm?" Glinda let him in and closed the door.

"Fighting the rain. The fog coming out here was bad, too. It's a thick soup all over the woods and roads. But I thought I'd stop by on my way home and let you know what I found at the newspaper today in the microfiche. You won't believe it–"

"Oh, hi there Myrtle," Frank said seeing her sitting on the couch. "Good, you're here. Saves me another stop."

"Hi there yourself, Frank. I'm spending the night with my niece. We're having a girl's night. What more did you find out? I haven't said much to Glinda about anything. I thought I'd leave that privilege to you. That and I knew you were still looking into the sailor's ghost and who it might be. Though I didn't expect you'd be out roaming around in this typhoon."

"Ah, it's not really that bad out there." Frank turned his gaze back to Glinda. "All right, now to why I am here. While searching through miles of microfiche I found a series of old articles from nineteen forty in the Journal published about a man named Bartholomew Masterson and his buried treasure. The articles were most likely released after he died. With what I learned, I strongly suspect he's the ghost who appeared to you. Here. I made copies of the articles."

"Thanks, Frank." Glinda took the pieces of paper and flicked through them for a minute or two. Then divulged, "Actually I think you're right about it being Bartholomew Masterson...the ghost visited me again. Last night. And someone called him Bart, which could be short for Bartholomew, and then Bart spoke back to him and called him brother and later called him Owen. In a vivid dream I saw Bartholomew on a ship and he, his crewmates and his brother were discussing a treasure they were going to look for. I overheard some of the crew speak about how years before a ship had wrecked on the outskirts of an island's reefs–they never said what island or where it was–I was after all only hearing part of the conversation, and they were going to dive and scrounge for the sunken treasure, salvage it from the shallows. And, for some reason I also didn't discover, they spoke of a deadly curse on the lost jewelry and gold."

"A curse, hmm. That's ominous. And his brother, you say his name was Owen, was also on the ship?" There was surprise in Frank's voice.

"I think so. He called him brother, affectionately. I guess it could have just been a shipmate term, but I don't think so. So...his full

What Lies Beneath the Graves

name is Bartholomew Masterson?" Glinda gestured Frank and Myrtle to follow her into the kitchen and they did.

"It is," Frank answered as he sat down at the table. "And there's quite a legend surrounding him and his treasure, before and after he died, let me tell you. The more I learn about this man the more intrigued I become. I also have a book you might want to read, Glinda. Page forty-nine." Frank pulled the book from his jacket pocket and placed it beside the article copies Glinda had laid on the table.

Myrtle snatched up the copies as Glinda perused the book. She opened it and quickly read it silently and then Myrtle read aloud from the newspaper articles. "'After Bartholomew Masterson was laid to rest a crowd of townspeople looted his house searching for his remaining gold. In their greedy zeal the structure was damaged and set on fire. The town's volunteer fire department was able to save most of the main structure but the kitchen and a front bedroom were destroyed. Days afterward the police were again summoned to the Masterson estate after reports of graves in the nearby cemetery were being dug up and the area was pitted with fresh holes.' By these accounts the hunt for the left behind gold became a circus. People fighting and brawling over where they'd dig or just eruptions of bad temper and hostile aggression.

"And this," Myrtle tapped the paper and resumed reading. "'It was also reported, after a particularly vicious conflict broke out among the illegal treasure hunters on the property, when some of them were transported to the hospital or jail and one man, Freddie Evans, died on scene from his injuries.' He was knifed; no one arrested for that crime, it says here. 'Two other men, David Hunter and Jess Compton, were later listed as missing.' They were never seen again as the last of these articles report.

"Wow," Myrtle finished up, "those treasure hungry trespassers were digging up graves, torching things and killing each other off indiscriminately. Tsk, tsk. It sounds like it was a real fiasco. Interesting."

"Yeah, I thought the same thing as I read those old newspaper pieces." Frank sent a fast look out the windows at the continuing rain. It had increased in force considerably, as had the wind. "It's peculiar that after Masterson's death enough people still believed there was gold hidden somewhere on his land that they had to descend on it and destroy everything hunting for it. And people were injured, went missing, and a man *died*. Crazy."

"Awful." Glinda had finished reading the pages in the book, closed it and gave it back to Frank. "But men do terrible things for money or gold in this case. It wouldn't be any different if it happened nowadays. Mankind hasn't changed that much. Greed and mistrust, immorality still exist and proliferate. By the way, did those articles ever say what Masterson died of?"

"According to the newspapers of the time he died of natural causes." Frank had gotten up and was making himself a cup of coffee. He knew where everything was in the kitchen so he helped himself. Glinda encouraged people to do that, even her clients who came for readings. For Myrtle and them, for any visitor, there was a coffee pot ready on the counter. He poured the cup and put milk and sugar in it. "He was ill a long time and died of heart failure."

"Or that's what they said." Myrtle was standing behind Frank, next in line for a cup of coffee.

Frank sat down with his cup as Myrtle prepared hers.

"Sometimes a heart attack can be caused by something else." Getting her drink, she resettled herself beside Glinda, picked up the article copies Frank had brought and resumed reading them.

"Myrtle," Frank said, "you're such a suspicious old woman."

"Of course I am. It's my job to be suspicious. And, you know…no one ever found the gold," Myrtle concluded, putting the papers down. "And I read every word of every one of these pages. Nope, it was never found."

"And I guess over time, when no one found it, it was forgotten." But her niece the psychic had a strange look on her face as she spoke. "Until now. After all these years, for some reason, Masterson wants us to find it."

Myrtle cackled. "Oh, the ghost has a reason, most times they do. He wants us to give it to his daughter."

"If she's still alive." Frank was being practical. His fingers tapped on the table. "Let's see, Masterson died in nineteen forty-nine so if his daughter was still alive and she'd been born a few years before that she'd have to around eighty-five years old. That's pretty old."

"Not really," Myrtle chimed in. "I'm not that far off of from that myself. And I know some of the old ladies and gents at the nursing home who are over ninety and still going strong. She could still be alive. She could have kids, too. A whole family tree of descendants."

"She could."

When Frank had finished his coffee he stood up. "That storm out there is supposed to get worse as the night goes on so I will take my leave of you two lovely ladies and head on home. Abby has supper waiting for me." He looked at Myrtle as he reclaimed the newspaper articles and the book and stuffed them in his rain jacket's pocket. "If you'd like, Myrtle, I could run you home?"

"Nah, thanks for offering me a ride, but I'm still staying here. Still spending the night. Glinda and I have a lot to talk about. And she's going to make pancakes for breakfast and you know how I love pancakes."

"I know." Frank was at the door. Outside the wind was wailing and the rain was slamming against the house.

Before Frank stepped out into the night Myrtle asked, "Now what do we do, Partner? What's our next step?"

"I'm not sure. Let me think about it and get back to you. I guess I'll try to find out more about the man who died on Masterson's property illegally hunting for the gold or more about the two missing individuals; if they ever showed up again. More about Masterson's death or anything else about the man and his life I can dig up, no pun intended. Or perhaps Masterson's ghost will appear to Glinda again and give us some direction."

"I'll let you know if he does," Glinda responded, walking him to the front door.

"I'm sure you will. Goodnight Glinda. Goodnight Myrtle," Frank said.

"Goodnight." Glinda smiled and shut the door behind him.

"Well, it's almost time for Supernatural, Niece."

"Yes, it is."

"Let's get our snacks and go turn on the T.V."

And the two women got ready for the show.

Chapter 5

Abigail was sipping her coffee and observing the people pass by Stella's Diner when she saw Myrtle and Glinda coming her way. Frank and she had just had a late breakfast and he'd gone off to the police station to check in. Chief Mearl had a case he wanted Frank's take on. Amazing how well the two now got along after years of butting heads. She'd been getting ready to leave for the Mexican restaurant for her day's work but with Myrtle and Glinda seeing her she had to stay a little longer. The mural was coming along beautifully and she was happy with it so far. She was just beginning it but that was often the hardest part.

Glinda and Myrtle flounced in and catching sight of her, waved, and made their way to her table by the window. "I made pancakes but, as Myrtle here says, that was hours ago," Glinda explained. "And she needed pie. I wasn't about to bake a pie this soon after breakfast so here we are. In Stella's at eleven-thirty."

"I wanted to come to town anyway." Myrtle shaded her eyes and stared out the window as she dropped in a chair. "That sun sure is bright out there. But it keeps the spirits in hiding; beats the rainstorm we had last night. The woods are all spongy mud. We had to wear rain boots and everything to walk here."

"So I see." Abigail took in the old woman's outfit with a subdued smile. As usual Myrtle was wearing a crazy combination and layers of clothes, a competing psychedelic colored shirt, another shirt on top of that, a sweater covering it all and ugly weather boots.

Glinda's clothes were fairly similar except her dress was elegant, color coordinated, of a soft silk, and it swayed gently around her ankles. Her rain boots were a lovely shade of pale pink, yet now covered in wet leaves and muck. Unlike her aunt, she had no floppy hat on her head.

"What are you doing here, Abby? I thought you were working on that mural every day?" Myrtle was gesturing to Stella to come over and take their order. But the waitress was busy with another customer and simply nodded. *Be there soon as I can,* it silently communicated.

"I am. But I have to eat, too. Mexican food isn't great for the first meal of the day. So Frank and I had breakfast here. You just missed him. He had to go into his consulting job at the sheriff's department and I was getting ready to go to the restaurant and work on the mural."

"Well, stay a little bit longer, Abby," Myrtle encouraged her. "Glinda had that second dream about our sailor's ghost and she'll tell you all about it in more detail. Thanks to Frank, who stopped by last night, as you well know, we now have the sailor's name, who he was, what happened to him, and we have a better idea what he may want."

"We do, do we?" She observed Glinda as she sat across from her, and there was a faraway look on the psychic's face. Perhaps she was communing with the spirits or hearing their voices or perhaps she was merely daydreaming. "Frank did catch me up on the new developments," she spoke to Glinda who now seemed to be listening but not reacting, "and he's going to check with Sheriff Mearl on any old police records there might be on Masterson and what else may have occurred after his death at the estate."

"That's a good idea." Enthusiasm lighting up Myrtle's gaze. "I stayed with Glinda last night, we had a girl's evening, you know. We had a fine time watching Supernatural and discussing our latest mystery. Glinda believes she'll hear from Bartholomew Masterson's ghost again. Wasn't last night, though. We're waiting. Could be he'll even know what happened to those two missing men who were looking for the gold after his death. Ghosts know things about the past and the future we normal alive people aren't privy to."

Speaking Glinda's name must have snapped the psychic's attention back to the real world and the present. "That would be David Hunter and Jess Compton, right?"

"Right. Them two. Frank also discovered their names yesterday in the old microfiche files."

Stella had been standing behind them, listening, and Myrtle noticed her.

"Hi Stella," she said, "come for our orders? I would like coffee and a piece of chocolate pie."

What Lies Beneath the Graves

"Same here," Glinda seconded, looking up and smiling, fully with them now.

"I couldn't help but overhear you mentioning the names Bartholomew Masterson, David Hunter and Jess Compton?" Stella had her order pad ready in her hands and was scribbling down the orders she'd been given. "I know who they are. Masterson was the man who was rumored to have buried a treasure of gold and jewels on his land somewhere on the outside of town and the other two are the men who were searching for that treasure and ended up dead, like many others. Nasty situation, that."

"That land is now my land, my home," Glinda informed the waitress.

Stella's sharp eyes went to the psychic. "Yes, it is."

"You know about Bartholomew Masterson and his treasure?" Abigail sent a glance first towards Glinda and then to the waitress. "You know what happened to Hunter and Compton?"

"I do. If my memory is accurate, I believe their decomposing bodies were eventually found dead in a cemetery, years after they'd gone missing. The cemetery out beyond Evelyn's, er, I mean Glinda's, house. Someone cut their throats or they cut each other's throats. As far as I know, their murderers were never caught. Terrible, terrible thing. Hunter had a family and three kids. He left his wife destitute."

"They were found dead?" Glinda inquired. "How do you know this? I thought they had only gone missing?"

"They were missing at first and later found

dead. And I know about this," the waitress pulled up a chair and sat down with them, clearly having something juicy to share, "because my Grampa Ernest used to tell me tales of the great gold rush here in Spookie, like the one they had in California in 1849? That's what he called it because for a while in, oh, around nineteen forty or so, give or take a couple years because my memory isn't as good as it once was and I can't exactly recall what years he told me, the town went completely bonkers hunting for that hidden gold after Masterson passed into the afterlife. Bonkers. They dug up everything they could on Masterson's land, tossed and set fire to his house, and still no one ever found it. My Grampa Ernest was a character and he used to tell me eerie tales of those days, the town's gold rush among other spooky happenings. He should have been a horror writer, he loved the macabre so much. He'd been fascinated with the Masterson debacle, he liked the grisly stories around it, and the murders which came after."

"More murders than those we are already aware of?" Abigail had to ask.

Stella laughed, her crimson lips curving up and showing white teeth. Her hair was even whiter than when Abigail had first met her. Her face more wrinkled, her back more bent. But she still worked just as hard at the restaurant. The waitress's gaze went to the door. A group of elderly people had come in and were seating themselves. She rose from the chair. "Oh, you don't know, do you?"

"Know what?" Now it was Glinda's turn to ask.

What Lies Beneath the Graves

"A lot of people died or were murdered, there's speculation on which one, over that gold. My Grampa Ernest told me at least a half a dozen gold seekers either vanished or their bodies were found on the grounds later shot or knifed to death; some mutilated. It's one of the reasons the gold rush finally came to an end. It was considered far too dangerous to even go out to that haunted property to look. Eventually the rush subsided and as time passed the whole thing became ancient history and evolved into one of our town's urban legends. Then Evelyn bought the abandoned property and she wouldn't let anyone ever trespass. She'd threaten to shoot them. That kept people away all right."

"Yep, my sister always had a loaded shot gun ready to chase any intruders off her land." Myrtle chuckled. "She was a wild one in her younger days, believe me."

"Haunted property?" Glinda had zeroed in on a different part of the conversation, her face now paler than when she'd entered the diner.

Stella's expression turned somber. "Another one of the prevalent stories of the time was it was Masterson's ghost who was committing the gruesome murders…protecting his treasure, which he wanted to go to his lost wife and child and not some treasure hunter who had no right to it. A daughter, I think. Story was the wife had grown angry Masterson was out on the seas treasure hunting for too long and she took their new born daughter and vamoosed. No one ever knew what became of them. The ghost yarns were another reason townsfolk stopped searching. You know how

Spookie's inhabitants fear ghosts.

"Anyway, I'll fetch your pie and coffee now. I have to take care of my other customers," she finished and bustled away.

After she'd left Myrtle slapped her thigh. "Darn gone it, we got ourselves a real murder mystery now again. Multiple murders. Imagine that? And I knew ghosts would come into it sooner or later. Every time I'm out near that graveyard beyond Glinda's house I can feel them skulking around, whispering and moaning." She visibly shuddered. "They're everywhere out there."

"Yes, they are," the psychic murmured.

"Well, that was interesting." Abigail peered out at the sunny day but still shivered. "More people have died over that gold than we knew. Wait until I tell Frank what we've found out. He'll probably want to talk to Stella himself. See if he can get more memories out of her."

Myrtle, reclining in her chair, inhaled deeply. "Glinda, you ever sense Masterson's ghost out there among all the other ghosts?"

Glinda hesitated a moment too long. "No. Not so far. Only in those two strange dreams."

"Have you ever seen any other ghosts out there since you moved in?" Myrtle had to press further and Abigail was surprised she hadn't asked her niece that question before, seeing they both claimed to see ghosts and they spent so much time together.

But Glinda didn't answer.

The three women lingered at Stella's for a while longer, chatting about other more normal everyday things. Myrtle and Glinda ate their pie and drank their coffee. Abigail didn't want to leave, she enjoyed their company, but after about twenty-minutes or so she got up, left them there, and made her way to her job. She had to keep toiling away on the mural. She'd promised Miguel she'd have it done by the end of the month which was now three weeks away. Since she'd begun the project she'd fretted perhaps she'd taken on a little too much. Three walls all to be covered from baseboard to ceiling with a Mexican village full of people, cars, buildings, flowers and animals was proving to be a lot more difficult to create than she'd thought it would be in the beginning. There were just so many facets of it she had to include. It was turning out to be a real challenge and all she could do was to keep moving forward.

The day was warm for April and the sun felt good on her skin. Outside the Mexican restaurant she paused, telephoned Frank and relayed what Stella had said about Masterson and the mysterious murders on his land after Masterson's passing.

"Ironically," he said, "Sheriff Mearl also remembered something about those bizarre crimes. We've been discussing them and other incidents about the case for the last hour or so. His cop grandfather, he was sheriff here during Masterson's time, Sheriff Lonnie Brewster, used to regale him with ghost stories about the sailor and afterwards his alleged specter. Seems Sheriff Lonnie actually knew Masterson or knew him as much as anyone of the day could know the man because he was so reclusive. Mearl's grandfather, like many other townspeople of the time, was basically interested in getting his hands on what was left of the treasure, Mearl believes. He tried befriending him but Masterson was so mistrustful of anyone who wanted to get close to him that that friendship never advanced further than a visit or two. But Sheriff Lonnie never found out where Masterson buried the rest of his plunder. Then Masterson died and Sheriff Lonnie was one of the ones, Mearl has no doubt, who was out there digging for that buried gold. As the others, he never found it.

"Mearl did reveal some things we didn't know, though you heard a few from Stella. People have died looking for that treasure. A lot of people. Here's the kicker. Sheriff Lonnie told his grandson he thought Masterson might, at the end of the man's life after years of illness and pain, have been criminally insane and had murdered an intruder or two, people looking for the gold, and buried the bodies under the basement floor or somewhere in the house. He couldn't prove it, but Sheriff Lonnie, who spent years trying to find the bodies to no avail, believed it. Too many people had gone missing and most of them had been searching for that gold."

"You're kidding?"

"Afraid not. Sheriff Lonnie believed Masterson was a murderer and he might have proven it but Sheriff Lonnie died before he could."

"Oh my, so if Masterson's ghost is haunting Glinda's place, he's an evil murderous ghost," she remarked cynically. She didn't believe in murderous remnants so she was being facetious. The dead couldn't harm the living or that was what she believed. Glinda saw spirits but spirits held no real power over humans. "Wait until I tell Glinda."

"If you believe in ghosts." Frank's tone was also flippant.

"Or murderous ghosts."

"Yeah. But I did think what Mearl told me was interesting. Seeing all this, undiscovered buried treasure, murders, and now possibly an evil ghost are connected to Glinda's new home."

"I guess. Did you find any actual police reports about Masterson?" she inquired. Frank went overboard when he was researching anything he wanted to put in his novels. And he was becoming obsessed with the Masterson urban legend.

"Mearl claims the police documents that old are stored somewhere else and he'll let me go through them whenever I want. He did warn me that when his grandfather was sheriff he wasn't much for thorough documentation. So maybe I'll find something or maybe I won't."

"Did you find out what Sheriff Mearl wanted to consult with you on? Your new case?"

"Uh huh. It's an unsolved embezzlement case at a local bank he'd like my take on. Early on an arrest was made but it turned out they had the wrong person. The case is still open. I have homework. I'll be bringing the files home to look over."

"Good. You and Nick can do your homework together."

Frank laughed. "Very funny."

Abigail signed off and went inside the restaurant, her mind relinquishing the Masterson mystery and all its side attractions and concentrating on her job, her art, what to make for dinner and if she and Frank should go see the new Star Wars movie the following weekend. The past's unsolved mysteries were one thing but she also had to live in the present.

But wait until Myrtle and Glinda learned of the latest news that Masterson might have murdered trespassers. Oh boy. Myrtle was going to have a field day with that information. She'll probably want to start looking for the victims' buried remains.

Chapter 6

"Come on in, Kate," Glinda welcomed the woman at the door, the night behind outlining her as she stood on the porch. "You're right on time."

"Good evening, Glinda. Thanks for letting me come over so late. I don't like to close the shop before seven. People expect me to be open if they want donuts."

"Being a lover of your pastries, I can understand. And eight o'clock isn't that late."

"As a thank you, though, I've brought you some of your favorites." Kate handed her a white box.

"You really didn't need to do that, but it was a sweet thought. Thank you."

The psychic led her guest through the living room and into the reading room, a space she'd lovingly adorned to create the spookiest ambience ebony velvet drapes and magical accoutrements could produce. It was a soothing, beautiful room, though, because she'd made sure it was comfortably plush. She seated Kate at the lace covered round table, put the bakery box on a side desk against the wall, and sat down across from her customer. The crystal ball and the stack of hand-painted tarot cards were in the center, surrounded by different sized healing rocks in glittering hues of purple and diamond white quartz, and Glinda reached for the deck, shuffled them, had the other woman cut them. She looked up at Kate.

"So is there something important you want to ask me before I lay the cards out?"

"A couple of things actually. Should I marry Norman?"

"Oh, really? He's asked you?"

"Not yet, but I have the feeling he's about to. He has that look in his eyes. He's been bringing me roses and boxed chocolates now for weeks. He can't do enough for me and lately has been helping me at the donut shop on his days off."

"Ah, he sounds like a good man," Glinda spoke as she laid the cards on the table face up one at a time. She smiled as her slender fingers touched one card after another as if she were adding up their meanings. "If you love him, say yes…and, yes, he's going to ask you. Very soon."

"How soon?"

"This week. Friday probably."

The donut maker stared at her. "Whoa, I better figure out what I'm going to say, huh?"

"Perhaps you should."

Glinda was studying the card spread, gently biting her bottom lip. Her eyes were riveted on what lay before her and she began to smile. "The cards here look good, Kate. Happiness. Continued prosperity in business and your private life. Your health now, that's another story." She selected a series of cards and made a few more pronouncements. Pretty general stuff. Then some fringe cards caught her eye. "It looks like you might be having a small medical emergency on the horizon. It will scare you, but with medical treatment and a new prescription, you should come out on the other side fine. Just thought I should mention it so you don't brush it off."

"Do those cards say what kind of medical crisis it will be?"

She hesitated, not because she didn't know the answer, but because it'd do no good to frighten Kate any more than she had to. "Not really. But I'd recommend you get a checkup sooner than later. Your doctor might be able to diagnose your problem before it strikes. Prevention is the key."

"Okay, I'll see my doctor. First thing tomorrow morning I'll call her and schedule a full physical. I'm due for my yearly this month anyway. Thanks, Glinda."

"What else would you like to know?"

Kate bent down to pet Amadeus, who'd been snaking around Kate's legs below the table. For some reason Glinda could never figure out the old cat liked the donut maker. The times Kate had visited them, Amadeus had ended up in her lap. The other cats hid somewhere and rarely came out until Kate was gone. Of course, they did that with almost every visitor, except Frank. All the cats loved Frank. He was a cat whisperer, to be truthful, an animal whisperer. There wasn't a cat or dog who didn't love Frank. People, too.

Since Glinda had moved to Spookie, claimed Myrtle as her great aunt, gained a beautiful home, and made friends with Frank and Abigail, she'd been grateful for all of them, especially Frank. He'd become the father she'd never known. There weren't many good men in the world. She knew that. They were as rare as unicorns. Looking at the cards and then at Kate's blissful face, she thought: Kate had found one of those rare good men and Glinda was happy for her.

"And," Kate started talking again, "I'm considering adding a sandwich lunch menu at the Delicious Circle and was wondering what the cards might have to say about it."

Glinda peered at the cards again and thoughtfully replied, "They say: *go for it*. It looks profitable. And I agree. Adding to your menu can only help your sales."

Then Kate asked a couple more questions about her life and Glinda, staring at the cards, gave her truthful answers. The cards really did look splendid for the donut maker. Glinda was relieved. She hated it when she had to give bad news.

The women sat and conversed for a while after the reading. They were friends after all. Glinda made tea and Kate caught her up on the most recent town gossip. Glinda was often amazed at how much drama the little town generated. The inhabitants were all eccentric in their own ways and something was always going on. She had grown to love it. All of it.

"I guess I shouldn't mention this," Kate said as she drank her second cup of tea, "but Myrtle was in my shop this morning and she bartered some interesting tidbits for a bag of her preferred Danish.

What Lies Beneath the Graves

She told me she, you, Frank, and Abigail are looking into the Masterson lost treasure? That you had a dream of Masterson's ghost and he wants the four of you to find it…for his daughter if she's still alive.

"And yes, I know all about Masterson's loot. I've heard about it since I was a child." Kate's eyes were intent as they came to rest on Glinda's face. "Is that true? Are you searching for that long lost and cursed wealth?"

Glinda knew she should lie, they didn't want the town to be aware of what they were up to, but she didn't believe in lying if she could help it. And she could trust Kate to keep what she told her to herself if she was asked; much better than Myrtle, who could never keep a secret no matter what it was or who asked her to. That old woman didn't know what a secret was.

"Since we're friends I'll tell you. We might be looking for Masterson's treasure, if it exists. Myrtle thinks we are. And it's true I've been visited by Masterson's ghost, though I didn't know who the ghost, clearly a sailor, was at first. Frank made the connections between this house, this land, and the man who built it in the late nineteen-thirties. Since then we've learned more about the man and the gold he was rumored to have found and that he'd left some of it behind somewhere buried on this land, or we believe he did. I've had a second dream. The man did find a fortune on his voyage. That's what we know so far. Maybe he spent every last penny on his homestead and everyday expenses and there was none left. Perhaps he didn't use all of it to build this house and live on and he did, somewhere on his life's journey, bury the rest. We don't know yet. But I have the feeling the ghost will eventually tell me everything…in time. We have a connection through this house, this land, and my psychic gift. I don't care if there's buried gold or not, money alone doesn't buy happiness, but Frank and Myrtle really want to solve what happened to the remainder of it. It's a mystery. If there's one thing I've learned, Myrtle, once she unearths a mystery of any kind, becomes obsessed and she just has to get to the bottom of it.

"But I'm surprised Myrtle spilled the beans to you about our little investigation. We don't want this to get out to the townsfolk. The last thing we need is another gold hunting stampede. I don't want people digging up by back yard or breaking into my house to search for buried gold."

"I wouldn't imagine you would," Kate commented. "But here's the thing and why I said anything at all about what Myrtle told me. The rest of the gold Masterson was said to have buried on this land somewhere…*it doesn't exist*. Telling certain people, a housekeeper and his servants, he knew would spread the false news was a spiteful joke he played on the town because he was a bitter, vindictive man. He spent the last years of his life isolated and lonely, by his choice. He hated everyone. He wanted the townspeople to go nuts hunting for the remainder of his loot, fighting and killing over it, when he was gone, but, truth was, he spent the whole kit and caboodle during his lifetime. Every gold coin, piece of jewelry and gem."

"How do you know this?" Glinda was confused. She'd believed the spirits who appeared in her dreams or visions told the truth. Could a ghost lie…and if they could, why would they? Why would Masterson lie about wanting his descendants to have a part of his treasure? She didn't know the answer but now she was wondering.

"I know this because when I was a child an acquaintance of my family, I think her name was Selma or Thelma, something like that, said a friend of her mother's was Masterson's extra housekeeper, sort of a personal attendant, for a short time anyway. It was at the end of his miserable life and he hired her from town because he was so ill, bedridden. But after a time the woman couldn't take the verbal and emotional abuse he piled on her–and he accused her of sneaking and snooping around looking for things to steal when she wasn't doing anything of the sort–and she walked out. Later she said to anyone who would listen that one day when Masterson was out of his mind with his illness he confessed there was no gold left. None. He'd spent it all and hadn't buried any of it. He thought it would be quite the joke on the town after he died if they thought there was hidden loot when there wasn't. Serve them right."

"Really?" Glinda wasn't sure if that were true, but then nothing in this world was impossible. Could be Ghosts could lie. Why not? But if there was no buried gold what was the reason for Masterson's ghost appearing to her twice, showing her the ship and the crew; letting her in on the buried treasure? She didn't know that either, but she had the premonition she'd learn what the ghost wanted from her sooner or later. He wanted something.

"Really. It's what I remember. I, too, was captivated with the buried gold stories so I recall what my mother's friend said because I didn't want to believe it. But I thought you and the others should know there might not be any jewels or gold buried anywhere. If you're thinking of looking and digging for it, it might save you some trouble."

"We hadn't got that far, but I am glad you told me. It is a curious development."

They spoke a little longer about non-related matters, cats and another expert baking class Kate was going to take, and then Glinda saw her to the door. As she watched Kate's car drive off into the night, Glinda thought: Could it be true? Could there be no hidden treasure at all? It was all a false folktale? Interesting.

She picked up her cell phone and dialed Abigail. She wanted to see what she thought of what Kate had said about Masterson's practical joke.

"Sorry for calling so late, Abigail, but Kate was just here for a reading and she told me something odd. Something I think you and Frank should know."

Glinda quickly summarized what she'd learned.

"Well, that throws a wrench in our new adventure for sure," Abigail responded. "Myrtle is not going to be happy. She's already scheming on how to find the buried gold. She has it all planned out, or so she says.

"I wonder if it's true."

"That the buried gold doesn't exist and never did?"

"It's what I'm wondering, as well. Here, I'm handing the phone to Frank. He wants to ask a question or two."

Frank got on the phone and they talked. When she was done, he only said, "If it is true then all that chaos and death which occurred after Masterson's demise was all for nothing, a tragedy. A malicious joke. Masterson did finally get back at the town he hated so much. Such a shame. I'll say one thing, Masterson must have been one miserable human being to perpetrate such a hoax.

"What do you think, Glinda? Do you believe the ghost or town gossip?"

"I'm not sure. But I have a hunch time will tell. This mystery isn't over yet." Glinda had trouble getting the words out because she unexpectedly had a feeling, a warning, of something not being right washing over her. She often had them when being with or speaking to another person. Something was wrong with Frank. It wasn't like the feeling she'd had about Kate, though, it was stronger. Twice in one day. Darn. Something very dangerous was coming Frank's way.

"Frank…before we get off the phone I have to ask: is there something wrong? Are you all right?"

"Of course. I'm fine. Why?" Frank's voice had become softer.

"Your health okay? You and Abby all right?

The kids? Are you on a new case, besides the Masterson investigation, that might be dangerous or lethal in any way?"

Frank laughed, but the laughter was restrained. "Sure, we're all okay. And no, I'm not chasing any serial killers or anything at the moment. The only other thing I'm looking into is a small bank embezzlement; working alongside Sheriff Mearl. No danger there."

"You sure?"

"I'm sure," Frank stated. "Now you let me know if you hear anything more from our ghost sailor. I don't care what anyone says, I'm going to continue looking into this matter and into Masterson's life. Try to find anyone still alive who might know something we haven't uncovered so far. I already am sure I'm going to use some of the specifics in my next book anyway. So none of this is wasted time."

"I'll let you know if our sailor visits me again. But Frank?"

"What?"

"I want you to be careful, real careful, you hear? I mean it."

"I'm always careful, friend. Always."

She hung up but another chill touched her skin and she shivered. Something bad was about to happen and she was afraid it was going to happen to Frank. She sat down at the table and did a tarot reading on his behalf, hoping they might give her more clarity to what the danger to Frank might be and when it was coming. But the cards were frustratingly vague. Yes, danger coming but no particulars.

When she went to bed that night, Amadeus snuggled up against her and then was joined by some of the other cats. A purring bed of fur and sleepy eyes. Glinda laid her head down on her pillow, still uneasy, but sleep finally found her.

*****

As if the spirit knew she had questions, Glinda had the third dream of Masterson that night. Once more it was on the ship, the Black Ghost, and Masterson's brother, Owen, was with Masterson. She overheard one of the other sailors say the ship had once been a whaling vessel the captain had purchased for practically nothing and that was about what it was worth: nothing. Huge sections of wood were rotted through, leaked and shuddered during storms. Many of the crew believed it wasn't seaworthy and, uneasy, feared it wouldn't get them home. Glinda could hear their thoughts and almost feel their growing dread the longer the ship was at sea. It was at the end of its long treasure hunt and the voyage was nearly over. They'd found chests, brimming with different sized canvas bags, tied with leather thongs, containing coins, precious gems and jewelry, in the shallow water among the sharp reefs around the island. They'd sent down divers to retrieve and bring the chests up to the ship and, upon discovering even more wealth than they'd thought was down there, began to celebrate. They'd retrieved a fortune and there was more than enough for everyone. The crew was jubilant. At first. The Black Ghost set sail on the long return journey to the coast of South Carolina.

The journey back. In the dream that's when the troubles began. Small mishaps, disagreements and squabbles between crew members erupted. There were mysterious acts of sabotage. The water supply was discovered to be tainted; food tampered with so some of the men fell ill. The crew began squabbling among themselves over how to divide the discovered wealth, who would get what and how much. The sleeping psychic never actually saw the treasure but she learned by the sailors conversations it was guarded by the captain in his quarters.

"Captain is hiding it from us! He won't even let us see it no more. What's he doing in that cabin with all that bootie?"

"I don't know, staying up all night counting it, but he's up to no good, I'd wager. That treasure belongs to all of us and he shouldn't be hoarding it...."

"Yeah, it's ours, too. Why's he hiding it, you know we should...."

"Rush in and make sure the crook isn't plotting something to keep it all...."

"He would not do that, would he?"

"Men do lots of bad things for treasure. All men. They kill each other off so there's more for them...."

"You mean some of our crew might be thinking that, too?"

"Sure, there's twenty of us to share the wealth. Be more for each if there were less of us...."

"You know, Henry's been acting pretty weird lately, come to think about it. Him, Basil and Derek always off in a dark space whispering and

plotting…something. They want the treasure for themselves, I'd lay a month's rations on it."

"No one's gonna take my share! No one!"

"We should make Henry confess what he's been up to–"

"What is the Captain doing with all that loot? We should go force our way into the Captain's cabin and grab those chests–"

"–split the booty right now amongst us so we are sure we each get our fair share!"

"We should!"

"Yah, let's do that–"

Then her dream turned nightmarishly dark. She watched the men, during the cover and gloom of night, rush into the Captain's cabin, viciously beat him down, and drag the treasure out onto the deck where they divided it among themselves–and then went crazy. Afterwards in rapid and terrifying vignettes the days and nights passed on board as the men fought over their treasure and begin to rise up against each other, no holds barred. Civility and trust were gone. The crew was maiming and killing each other over the spoils and Masterson's brother was one of the first casualties as he defended another shipmate from a mob who wanted to throw the man, an alleged thief who might or might not have taken more of the treasure than was his share and hid it, overboard. Masterson fought the mob with his brother but his brother was the one who ended up dead, bloody and floating in the shark filled waters until the creatures pulled him under.

Masterson's grief appeared to be overwhelming and changed him forever. No longer was he the amiable sailor on an exciting quest for riches, fame and fortune. He was a hollow-eyed remnant of the man who'd first stepped on the ship so many months before, his heart full of rage at his brother's murder and the atrocities he'd witnessed between his fellow men–all for greed.

In her dream vision the sea began to churn and the sky turned black. A terrible squall roared in and the ship, foundering and lost in the storm, found itself mysteriously back at the island and the vessel, leaking water and with two masts collapsed, crashed into the same rocks where the treasure had been found. Then her dream ended.

Glinda woke from the destruction and the tempest on the seas to a storm in the real world. The wind was screaming outside the windows and rain was pounding against the house. Another spring rainstorm. Seeing the carnage on the ship and watching it being pulled down beneath the waves had unnerved her and she was trembling in her bed. She'd *been* there. She'd smelled the salt of the sea, the brine on her face, felt the pitching of the ship under her dream feet…experienced the horror when Masterson's brother was butchered, dumped into the water and the sharks fought over his body. She'd sensed Masterson's blood-thirsty hunger for revenge and his growing hatred towards others. This had been the beginning of his isolation from society.

She threw off the covers, got out of bed and, going into the kitchen, brewed a cup of strong tea, added more honey than she needed, and sat down at the table to calm herself. The rain outside had slackened and listening to it she forced herself into the present. Her hands shook as she held the cup.

She was frustrated, troubled. What had happened to the crew? So the Black Ghost had wrecked…how many had lived and how many had died? She hadn't been shown that and it bothered her. It was like watching a riveting television program and not being able to see the end or reading an exciting novel only to discover the last chapters were missing. Horrible, horrible. The only comfort she had was the tragedy had occurred so long ago. It was in the past.

What were you trying to show me, tell me, Bartholomew? I sure wish you would have answered the question of the hidden treasure…does it exist or not? If it doesn't, what do you want of me? Why are you haunting my dreams?

She'd have to wait until Bartholomew chose to show or tell her what he wanted. There was no other way. Even the cards or the crystal ball wouldn't tell her, she'd tried many times. Nothing.

In bed once again she recaptured sleep as the now gentle falling rain outside soothed her. But after the turmoil and horror of the last dream, she hoped she'd be allowed to rest in peace at least for the rest of the night. She'd had enough. And she was allowed that…a deep sleep until the sun shone brightly into her windows and her cats forced her to rise and feed them.

Chapter 7

Silas had completed his daily stroll around town and up and down the country roads between Spookie and his house. He knew it was getting late and his wife, Violet, was most likely wondering where he'd been for so long. But walking, getting out of the house, away from their problems was the only way he could make it through the day sometimes. He was *so* angry. Angry at the world, at the universe...at God. This wasn't what his and Violet's golden years were supposed to have been like. Poverty and illness. Unpaid bills, endless doctors, tests and hospitals. It wasn't fair, it just wasn't fair.

He'd been battling bone cancer for over two years which had metastasized and spread to other organs and then his poor wife was diagnosed with breast cancer. How did something like that happen? They were in their eighties and here they were both fighting cancer at the same time...what were the odds? It seemed to him lately that everyone in the world had cancer. He, or now his wife, would go in for a radiation or a chemo treatment and there'd be rooms full of sorrowful-faced people waiting their turn with the machines or the intravenous poison which would be hung besides them, tubes snaking from their ports to the bottles. He'd feel so sorry for them and then, seeing his wife's ravished face and feeling the pain beneath his own flesh when he moved, he'd remember that, oh yeah, both of them were among those unfortunate ones. People with cancer.

For a moment frozen in his mind, he relived the shock of first being told he had stage three bone cancer, and then just a few months ago, when his beloved wife was informed she had stage four breast cancer. The whole last year had been a nightmare he couldn't seem to wake up from. No one knows how hard it will hit a person until they are the ones sitting before a surgeon who says nonchalantly, "I'm so sorry…you do have cancer. Here," as the surgical professional hands over a stack of business cards with hand-written dates on them, "I want you to see this doctor, a medical oncologist, and then the radiologist. The appointments have already been made for you and we will also keep your primary doctor in the loop as we proceed with treatments. I would recommend we operate within the next twenty to thirty days because that initial mass in your lower chest needs to be dealt with first and taken out. It'll be tricky because it's spread so far already and, we fear, it might have progressed into the bones. After you have blood tests, a chest ex-ray, an MRI, a CT scan and a biopsy–we've also arranged appointments for those within the next week or two–I'll set the surgery date."

First you don't want to believe it, then you get

infuriated and you think: "Oh, I don't have cancer. I don't feel sick. They're lying to me. They only want my insurance money." Because, oh, it is unbelievably expensive having cancer, he and his wife had swiftly discovered. Even with having Medicare and supplementary coverage, the many specialist visits' co-payments alone added up faster than ants in an ant hill. How did they expect old folks on Medicare to pay those exorbitant sums? Oh sure there was a cap on out-of-pocket expenses but there were an awful lot of exceptions that didn't count to it and the out-of-pocket reset every January 1st. He'd been diagnosed in November, the bills started accruing right off the bat, and by the end of December the out-of-pocket was restarted for the next year. Most old folks weren't wealthy; he and his wife weren't wealthy. He'd lost count a long time ago how much his cancer had cost them so far and the bills, just as unexplainable and undecipherable, for himself or his wife were waiting now most days in their mailbox and covered their kitchen table. They were Greek to him. He'd stopped opening the bills months ago. And his wife had been too ill as she went through a third round of chemo to care about anything other than staying out of the bathroom where she'd thrown up over and over. She spent most of her days now in bed, slipping in and out of sleep, weakly frail and always in pain even with the morphine the doctors were giving her. They were supposed to be helping her, instead they were killing her slowly. He hated them! All of them. He didn't care if he was in agony twenty-four seven, but not his sweet Violet. She didn't deserve to suffer so much and she was…suffering. She'd accepted extra rounds of radiation but now refused to have another round of chemotherapy after this one was done. Smart move. That chemo only made a person sicker no matter what the doctors said. He knew. He'd had a course or two and it hadn't gone well. He was so ill for so long he'd wished he was dead and that was no way to live. So he'd had enough of that. They both had.

"You know one of the worst things about having breast cancer," she'd confided to him in her soft voice after she'd had her twentieth radiation treatment, "is the indignity of it all. You're paraded around from one office to another in this skimpy hospital gown that's open in the front and all these doctors and their technicians are touching, examining and seeing your naked breasts. Not an easy thing to tolerate for an old church woman who's been modest all her life. Then you're flopped on this table for the treatments and your saggy breasts are hanging out bare for all to see; marked up in bright blue lines like a human tic-tac-toe game. It's all so undignified." And Violet was nothing if not dignified and had been all during their long fifty-year marriage and no doubt throughout her life. She had a gentle but strong heart and was a loving, good woman. A modest woman. He'd felt her embarrassment because he'd felt the same during many of his medical procedures, his old wrinkled body exposed for all to see. A person gave up all dignity once they had cancer.

He stared up at the sun, shaded his eyes with

his hand, and noticed the orb was on its way towards the trees on the horizon. It was later than he'd thought. The guilt at leaving his wife alone longer than he should have, as it sometimes did, plagued him. But he told himself she was sleeping and hadn't missed him. It was a lie he told himself often. Sometimes it worked and sometimes it didn't. Oh, he was a bad man.

Stumbling up the sidewalk lined in tall grass, he was home. Their house was in disrepair, it cried for fresh paint, some of the windows were cracked and the yard was a weed patch. It was a large frame built structure, creaky old and full of many high-ceilinged rooms. Violet and he had loved their house all the years they'd lived there and had always taken such good care of it, until now. There was a time he never would have let their home fall into such shabby condition but, as with most of his life, he'd let it slip away inch by inch…like his wife's life force was slipping away.

He hurried his steps, suddenly terrified he'd find his Violet, the woman he loved more than anything else in the world, lifeless in her bed. What would he do if he discovered her dead? Oh, no. He shouldn't have been gone so long, he berated himself. He shouldn't have been so selfish. As he shoved open the door and rushed inside, which is when the agony hit him, bringing him to his knees right inside the house on the living room rug. The pain was so fierce, so relentless for the minutes it entrapped him as he writhed on the rug, he must have passed out. When next his eyes opened the day had passed into night and the living room was dark.

What Lies Beneath the Graves

Some of his doctors wanted him to go to one of those rehabilitation places or a nursing home where he could be better cared for, but he wouldn't leave Violet. And if he left they'd put her in hospice somewhere else. They wouldn't be together and that was unacceptable. They wanted to end their lives as they'd lived them, together. There was no way they were taking her away from him.

With great difficulty, from memory, he dragged his useless body, now all bones and thinly stretched skin, to the table lamp and switched its feeble light on. Then, hushing his moans so as not to scare his wife, he crawled to her bedroom in the next room and up to her bed. The room was shadowy but he was fearful of turning on the bedside light for what he might see.

The body on the bed was so quiet, unmoving. He pulled himself up against the mattress and little by little extended a trembling hand until it touched something soft, warm and breathing. He exhaled a muffled sigh of relief. She was still alive. Still with him. He wasn't alone.

"Silas?" A tender voice spoke, a voice he knew well and his heart resumed beating. "Is that you, honey?"

He clicked the light on. He'd put a dimmer bulb in it weeks ago when she asked him to. The brighter watts hurt her eyes. He took the fragile, aged-spotted hand in his and inched himself up on the edge of the bed. "It's me, sweetheart. I'm so sorry to be so late. I lost track of time. It was so beautiful a day."

"It's all right, Silas. I've been sleeping. I didn't

even know night had come. I didn't even miss you."

Of course he didn't believe her but it was the game they played between themselves. He abandoned her at times and she pretended it was no big thing. She was like that, always had been. He'd been a runner all their marriage. Run here, run there. *I'm just going out for a pack of cigarettes, honey. Or I'm going to get gas in the car, be right back.* Of course he rarely was, right back. He'd disappear for hours, lollygagging here or there, wasting time, or talking to friends or strangers for hours while she waited patiently at home for him. She'd always been so understanding, forgiving. So loving. Then there'd been his temper. He'd spent his life being an angry, argumentative son-of-a- ----- but she had been able to calm him, keep him from exploding, hurting or killing someone who had riled him, and ruining his life. Her love had saved him so many times. What would he do without her? He truly didn't know.

"Are you hungry, sweetheart? Can I make you a snack or some supper? Some warm milk?"

She tried to sit up but couldn't make it and fell back down again. The face on the pillow gazed up at him with shadowed eyes and translucent skin. She'd lost so much weight in the last month the eyes in her sweet face seemed huge. Once she'd been a dark-haired beauty with wide blue eyes and skin as white as alabaster. She'd been smart, a book and an animal lover. She used to like solving crossword puzzles and drinking chocolate malts he'd go out and bring back for her. Her career had been a nurse, and she'd been an excellent one, so she knew what his illness was doing to him and her illness to her. She knew too much. She smiled at him. "Maybe some soup? I'd love a bowl of chicken soup."

"Then soup it is, my love. We'll both have soup and there are a couple of biscuits from last night left in the refrigerator I can warm up and butter for us as well. I won't be long." He fought to come to his feet without crying out again in pain. It was agony. *Get a hold of yourself, old man. Stop whimpering. Put that smile back on your face.* For he couldn't let her see how ill he was. When he was upright, his cries imprisoned in his throat, he hobbled from the room and, leaning against the wall in the hallway, he caught his breath and after he resumed his trip to the kitchen. One shuffling step at a time; holding onto the wall so he wouldn't fall in the hallway.

Tomorrow Violet had another radiation session and therapy at that big fancy hospital fifty miles away where her specialist was and he prayed the car would get them to the hospital and back. It was an old car, a nineteen ninety three Chevrolet. It had been acting up lately and sometimes he had trouble starting it. The paint was rusting and the tires were bald. That's why he walked everywhere he could and didn't use the car anymore except for their hospital or doctor visits, saving it for the necessary trips. They did their shopping or any other necessary errands on the way to the hospital or on the return trips.

He made the soup and the biscuits and carried the tray into his wife's room. He fed her in between feeding himself, because she was too weak to feed herself, and they talked in whispers about happier days.

"Remember that trip we took to Mackinac Island in nineteen eighty-three?" his wife asked. "We rode around the island on our bicycles and we came upon that flock of seagulls by the water? We threw stale bread at them and had them eating out of our hands? We laughed and laughed. When the bread was gone we had jump back on our bikes and ride away because they wouldn't stop flying at us, begging for more? Remember how beautiful they were as they rose into the sky?"

"I remember, sweetheart." He gently squeezed her hand then gave her another spoonful of soup. "You loved the island, the people, and the lake around it. I liked that there were no cars, just horses. And that Grand Hotel was magnificent. So huge. The flowers around it so beautiful."

"It was magnificent, wasn't it?" she murmured. "We strolled through the hotel's hallways and had that exquisite buffet in the main dining room overlooking the water. I love that island."

"I know you do."

"I wish we could go back there now and ride in one of those carriages. I wish we could walk down its main street and stop in the quaint little shops. Buy some more of that heavenly fudge they sell. You know, I can still almost taste it. Silas, oh, how I wish we could go back…go back in time and do it all over again."

Her voice sounded so painfully wistful he had to ask, "To the island?"

"No," and now her voice sounded on the verge of tears, "I wish we could go back in time. When we were young, strong and healthy. Go back to nineteen eighty-three and do it all over again. Our life."

"I do, too, honey. I do, too." For a moment Silas was overwhelmed with sadness that had become all too familiar of late. The past was gone. Their youth was gone. All that awaited them was more illness, pain and death. They'd lived their lives and now there were no more doors to go through. He felt like crying but, as always, fought it off. He had to stay strong for Violet.

Then he crept into bed with her, turned on the television, and before the ten o'clock news he fell asleep beside her. That's the way it was with them these days. They fell asleep early and slept late. That's what an old person did when they had cancer.

Chapter 8

Friday. Abigail was happy it was the Friday. Laura came home most weekends from college and this was one of them. Going into the IGA she was mentally thinking of what she had to buy to make Laura's favorite meal and when she'd have to start it so it'd be ready when her daughter arrived. For supper she was going to make a pot roast with all the sides, potatoes, corn and carrots, a meal her daughter was especially fond of. Perhaps a store bought chocolate cream pie for dessert? And on Sunday, she could send a container of the leftovers back to school with the girl. And that afternoon before Laura would drive back to college, Abigail decided she'd make a sumptuous brunch of waffles and fruit toppings. Laura loved them covered in cherries and whipped cream.

As she shopped, she thought about the Mexican mural she was nearly halfway done with and smiled. It was looking pretty good, she must say so herself, and she was proud of it. She couldn't wait to show it to Laura, who was becoming even a better artist than she was. Laura loved the art college she was attending and was blossoming into quite an independent young lady. Abigail couldn't wait to see her. Nick and Frank would be happy she was home, as well. Nick missed his sister though he'd never admit it. Teenage boys kept all that sappy stuff to themselves.

She was leaving the store, getting ready to slip into her car after putting the groceries in the trunk, when she saw Samantha hurrying over to her.

"What, you haven't had that baby yet?" Abigail exclaimed in a friendly tone, giving the other woman a hug. Pregnant women needed hugs, she thought. Hugs comforted anyone whose life was about to change so drastically and there were few things more changing than having a baby, fostering or adopting one, or two.

Samantha sighed and leaned against Abigail's car. She patted her huge stomach. "Nope, this alien creature in my humongous belly is never going to come out. Never." Then she grinned. "I'm due in a few weeks and I can't wait. I'm sick of being fat and grumpy. I want my figure and my life back. You know I wake up ten times a night just to pee and some mornings the heartburn is terrible."

"Heartburn means the baby will have a mop of hair. It'll probably be bright red like yours." Abigail ushered her friend around to the passenger side and opened the door. "Sit down, oh-so-pregnant lady, for a minute or two while we catch up. Your face is flushed and you look like you're going to faint."

Samantha slid into the seat and Abigail got in on the driver's side. The day was the hottest of the spring so far. For the first time it felt almost like summer.

"I just might faint," Samantha complained, her

head resting against the seat as she fanned herself with a piece of paper. It looked like a bill of some sort. "It's so hot today."

"That it is. Gonna get hotter, too. It's only April."

"I know, I know. And I don't look forward to this last segment of my pregnancy. I hate hot weather to begin with and to be like this," the hand with the fan languidly waved over her belly, "in hot weather is even worse. Yuck. I just pray the baby comes on time and not…late. I have places to go and things to do."

"You look tired, Samantha. You haven't been overdoing it, have you?"

Samantha sent her a sarcastic smirk and intoned flatly, "No." Then grinned.

"Really? Frank says you're at the newspaper every day working way too hard. Isn't it about time you take off and rest up? Do you have the baby's room ready for him yet?"

Samantha and her husband had known the child she was carrying was a boy for months and they were happy over that. "Boy first and then a girl and I'm done."

"What happens if you have a second boy?" Abigail couldn't help but voice.

"Well, still that will be it for me. I already told Kent that two kids are my limit. There are so many more things I need to do in life. Oh, I want it all. A family, a loving husband and a career. I think two children would be manageable, but no more than two."

"Yeah, two's a good number and, take my

word for it, highly manageable. How's your run for mayor going? Election time is coming up, isn't it?"

"November next year. Seven months. Which means I need to start campaigning. Mayor Riley's got posters and ads in the paper already going after his third term. He's giving speeches, making promises. Smiling and shaking hands everywhere."

"You're going to beat him easily, Sam, I know it. He's been mayor for way too long and it's time for a younger, more progressive candidate to take over the job. I know you'll be our next mayor."

Sighing, Samantha rubbed her eyes. "Am I biting off more than I can chew, Abigail? Am I pregnant-crazy for wanting to be a mother, a newspaper woman and a politician, even on just a town level? What am I thinking?"

"You will be amazing at all three, you'll see. You were born to be Wonder Woman."

Samantha laughed. "Yeah, that's what Kent says, but in different words. Of course he's not the one with a huge belly and hormonal night sweats. Men! They don't get it, do they?"

"Sometimes they don't, but sometimes they do," Abigail remarked. "So what else is new?"

The reporter scrunched up her lips and appeared to be thinking hard about something and then her expression became troubled. "Not much, except…." She turned and looked right at Abigail. "What's the name again of that art college Laura's going to?"

"Chicago Art Institute. Why?"

"Hmm," Samantha mumbled. "That's what I thought it was. I caught a story yesterday about her school on the Internet. Perhaps I shouldn't tell you this because I don't want you to worry but—"

"But what?" Abigail knew her friend well enough to know that whatever it was it was something important, perhaps something unsettling.

"There's been a couple of cases of missing students recently at your girl's school. The college had pretty much kept it under wraps but now with a third girl missing, it's coming out."

Instantly Abigail's inner alarm went off, though she'd just talked to Laura that morning and knew she wasn't one of the missing girls. Thank goodness. "Missing girls? Three of them? How long has that been going on?"

"By what I read in the article, maybe two weeks. The first girl, a sophomore, never returned to her dorm after a night out with an unknown man. The second girl a week ago and now the third one has been missing a few days. All have the same MO. Their roommates and friends claim they'd all met a new mysterious young man, never learned his name, and all three went out on first dates and never returned. The dean at the college has finally released the story since the third disappearance. It's awful. The police don't have any leads. I was afraid it was Laura's college and now I know, unfortunately, it is. Possibly Laura, when you see her next, will know something more about the situation."

"But Laura's college has over five thousand students. That's a large campus. She might not know anything."

"Or she might. I know she typically visits you

for the weekend. So if she comes home tonight she might know something about what is happening. If she does know anything pertinent, can you give me a call? I might be doing a story on the missing girls. It is news, especially since Laura goes to that college. Town connection, you know?"

"I'll let you know if I learn anything," Abigail promised.

It'd been years since Abigail had felt the anguish the disappearance of her first husband, Joel, had stirred in her; but now it flooded back in a dark wave. The hopelessness, the sadness and the escalating terror. It had been devastating when she'd learned years later that Joel had been dead and had been for all the time she'd been looking for him, but in a way knowing that truth had released her. She knew some of what those poor parents of those missing girls were feeling and she had great empathy for them. Suddenly all she wanted to do was hold Laura and Nick tightly in her arms and thank God they were safe. But oh how she felt sadness for those parents and the girls missing. She couldn't help herself and said a silent prayer that they were all right, even as she feared they weren't. A prayer couldn't hurt.

As soon as Samantha left her she pulled out her cell phone and texted Laura asking how long until she arrived home and was reassured when within a few minutes a reply of: *Leaving the dorm now and will be there by six or so. Have lots of dirty laundry. Okay to bring?* popped up on the tiny screen.

Sure. Bring all laundry you want, Abigail responded. *See you soon. Love, Abby.*

Abigail drove home and began supper, grateful her family was accounted for. Frank would be home in an hour and Nick, in honor of his sister coming home, was forgoing his band practice and would be home any minute. She couldn't wait to see them and have all of them safely beneath their roof again. Samantha's news about the missing college girls had frightened her and she couldn't stop thinking about it.

*****

When Laura walked in the house Abigail hugged her as if she hadn't seen her in months instead of a mere short week.

"You must have really missed me." Laura laughed and warmly returned her mother's hug.

"I have missed you, but mostly I'm just so happy you're here safe and sound. The world can be a dangerous place. At least when you're with us I know you're safe."

"Ah," Laura had dumped her overnight bag on the floor and her laptop knapsack on the table, "you've heard about the missing girls at my college, haven't you?"

Frank was at the stove checking the pot roast simmering in its pan and he pivoted around, his attention fully engaged. Abigail had told him about the missing students and he was angry, concerned and determined to protect Laura in any way he could. She'd almost had a fight on her hands to keep him from driving up and bringing Laura home as soon as he'd heard of the crimes.

"You don't need to, Frank," Abigail had said to him. "She's on her way home as we speak." Abigail didn't blame him. She felt the same way. On some level she would have gladly kept Laura at home and not let her return to a place where young women were disappearing, but anywhere in the world could be a dangerous place at any time so locking the girl in the house the balance of her life wasn't a solution. Laura had to be free to carve out her own life and free to live it. Danger might not always be avoided. One simply had to be prepared to protect themselves from it or fend it off. If she'd learned anything in her life, that was it.

"We've heard," Frank answered Laura, also stepping forward to hug the girl. "Your mother ran into Samantha today, who'd seen something in the media news about it."

Laura settled in a chair. She pushed the hair away from her face. Her expression was troubled. "It's been awful. I didn't know the first two missing girls, but I know the third one. Odette Benoist. She's in the room two doors down from me and we've become good friends this first year. Odette's a sweet, clever girl and an incredible artist. She wants to be an animator for the movies. Her dream is to work for Disney Studios and she has an uncle with connections who swears he can get her an apprenticeship there when she graduates from school. I didn't even know she was missing until her roommate, Diane, cornered me in the hallway this morning and asked me if I'd seen Odette anywhere recently. She hadn't been back to the dorm, their room, in two days. After I said I hadn't seen her, Diane was on her way to the campus police to report Odette missing like the other two girls. I'm really worried about Odette. She's so delicate. So innocent. Shy. She's close to her family, parents, a brother and a sister, and would never just take off without leaving word with any of them; not making contact for days, not even a text. That's not like her."

"I hope she's all right." Abigail met the gaze of the attractive young woman with the stylishly cut blond hair and copper-hued eyes before her. Gone was the sad looking, skinny waif of fourteen Abigail had first met in the library so long ago; the girl who'd dreamed of becoming an artist and having a better life than the poverty she'd been used to and had been living in, though she'd dearly loved her parents and her six siblings. After much sorrow, the death of her parents, the splitting up and relocation of her other siblings, which she saw often with her and Frank's help, she had grown up and come into her own. Laura knew what she wanted and she was going after it. Abigail was proud of her. She didn't like to see her anxious as she was now.

Frank had sat down at the table with Laura. "Tell me all you know about the disappearances," he requested with that intense look Abigail recognized. Detective Frank was in the house. Oh boy. She knew what that meant.

As Abigail tended to the rest of the supper, heating up the sourdough rolls and making a salad, she eavesdropped on Frank and Laura's conversation about Odette and the other missing students. Frank had brought out his notebook and was writing things in it. Abigail knew before he told her later he was interested in the disappearances and not just to put in a book. He was interested in the case. And why shouldn't he be? Chicago was his old turf, he still had friends on the police force, and finding missing people, among other heinous crimes, had been his specialty in his Chicago detective days and he'd been gifted at it. She had the suspicion Frank was going to do more about the situation than merely take notes.

Nick breezed in soon after and the four of them sat down to supper and caught each other up on what was going on in their lives. It felt good to be together.

She and Laura spoke about Laura's art classes, her teachers, and what she was learning. It was nice to have another artist to chat with about all things art. In some ways it almost made Abigail want to go back to art school herself…nah. She was happy to relive it through her daughter. Laura was quite a good storyteller, as well. She'd tell her comical or insightful anecdotes about her quirky teachers or strange fellow students and would habitually make Abigail laugh. The girl was so like her in so many ways and Abigail was content, at total peace, when she was home with them.

Nick offered his sister a chance to go with him the next day, Saturday, and listen to his band when they practiced and she accepted. Laura loved music almost as much as her brother and would sometimes even sing with him. She had a lovely voice and their harmonies were, as with most siblings, exceptional. Over the years Abigail had heard them sometimes singing together in Nick's bedroom late at night. But Laura wasn't interested in a singing career. All she cared about was being a famous artist, a painter.

The four of them discussed going to a movie Saturday night after Nick's band practice and out to dinner afterwards at their favorite BBQ place. It turned out to be an enjoyable evening and Abigail was happy to have everyone together even with the shadow of Laura's friend Odette missing. During dinner Abigail would steal a glance at her daughter and see the concern hovering in her eyes. She might not want to show it but she was distraught about what was going on at the college. She was worried about her classmates.

The weekend passed too quickly as most of them did when Laura was home. They sat around chatting, playing board games or cards, went to the movies; Abigail invited Myrtle and Glinda over for a Sunday breakfast of waffles so they could spend time with Laura, too.

Yet it didn't escape Abigail how often she caught Frank and Laura huddled over coffee or out on the porch seriously conversing about something or other. Most likely the kidnappings at the college. Odette. What they could do about it.

"I'd advise," Abigail spoke to Frank Saturday after the movie and dinner when they were in bed for the night, "you not mention the missing girls at Laura's college around Myrtle tomorrow morning. Unless you want her to claim it as another new grand mystery and she'll insist you both go down there, beat the bushes, and find them."

"I'd already figured that one out. The last thing we want is Myrtle sticking her nose into an investigation which she shouldn't be anywhere near. If those girls have been abducted, the kidnappers are serious criminals and the whole thing has to be handled by trained police. I asked Laura to keep it to herself when Myrtle and Glinda are over just for those reasons."

"I knew you were a clever man." She put her arms around him and kissed him goodnight.

*****

Sunday was a bright sunny morning and around eleven Myrtle and Glinda showed up. Glinda had brought a large bowl of fresh fruit, cubes of cantaloupe, chunks of watermelon, loose cherries, grapes and bananas, for everyone. Myrtle had baked homemade pecan caramel rolls. So they had a smorgasbord of a brunch.

Sitting at the table after their scrumptious feast, Myrtle was chatty as usual going on and on about her new adventure. "Laura, has Frank told you about our new marvelous mystery?"

"A little." Laura sent an understanding glance in Frank's direction. She'd remembered not to speak of the missing girls and hadn't said a word about any of it all morning. "Buried treasure this time, huh?"

"Maybe or maybe not," Frank tossed in. "Kate claims the legend of Masterson's buried treasure is all a hoax he perpetrated on the town as a vindictive joke because they'd ostracized him. So we aren't sure it ever existed."

Then Myrtle spent the next half hour gleefully bringing Laura up to date with everything that had been going on, Glinda's dreams and what they'd uncovered about Masterson and his life. So far anyway. Nick was listening attentively as well. "I don't believe there is no treasure," Myrtle groused. "No matter what Kate says, if that ghost told my niece there is buried treasure, then there is. Somewhere. We just have to wait for the ghost to tell us where he buried it...or we have to find it ourselves."

"Yeah, we can dig up Glinda's front and back yard and the cemetery grounds until it's a pit of holes or until we find the hidden gems and gold coins, or whatever the treasure consists of," Abigail snidely snapped. "I can think of a lot of other things more worth doing."

"Or we can wait until the ghost tells my niece where he put it." Myrtle winked at her.

"Sure, or we can wait for that." Abigail had already lost patience with the whole buried treasure enigma since she'd learned of the missing girls at the college. Now that was important, real. That could be life or death. It affected Laura so it affected Frank and her. The legend of Bartholomew Masterson's lost treasure had been a secret for decades and it could remain one for decades more as far as she was concerned. It was probably only a myth.

Hours later the breakfast gathering broke up and Laura got in her car and drove back to school, Myrtle and Glinda went into town for something or other and Nick took off for a late day band practice.

"I worry about Laura now at that college with what is going on," she confessed to her husband when they were alone.

"Don't. I gave her detailed instructions on how

to best protect herself. Park in well-lit and well populated areas. Always be aware of her surroundings. Don't travel on campus alone, have someone always go with her or stay in groups. I also gave her one of those key screamers, the kind where you push a button and a siren loud enough to wake the dead goes off–it'll scare off almost anyone meaning her harm–and a bottle of pepper spray. I think, if she's cautious and alert, she'll be safe."

"I still hated seeing her drive away. I couldn't bear it if something happened to her. Or Nick."

"I know." Frank had bestowed on her a sympathetic look. "But we can't be their shadows forever, sweetheart. We have to let them grow up and live their lives. We have to trust them to be able to take care of themselves."

She'd shaken her head. "I know, I know. It's the circle of life. All fledglings have to leave the nest and learn to take care of themselves."

"That they do. But I'm still worried about her."

"I know."

*****

She and Frank were getting ready to retire to bed but were enjoying a little time sitting on the front porch in the hanging swing, porch light off. They were bundled in jackets and hats because the April evening had turned chilly. Snowball was purring in Abigail's lap.

"The fog is already coming in from the woods," Abigail commented as she looked out over the yard. "It's going to be a real thick one." Sometimes the fog would be so heavy it was as if their cabin existed alone in the woods with a blanket of gray around it, silencing all the other sounds of nearby civilization. Abigail cherished that silence. One could imagine all sorts of strange creatures existing and happenings going on in the foggy woods deep in the night. She didn't fault Myrtle for not wanting to ever travel in the night woods.

"We might wake up tomorrow morning," Frank mused aloud, "and there will be nothing in the world but us and the thick gray fog."

"Oh, I thought that happens all the time?" she teased.

"Honey–" Frank started and then stopped. She heard his small outbreath and then he went on with, "what would you say to me taking a road trip tomorrow up to Chicago for a few days? I got a phone call from Kyle today and he has Tuesday off. I'd really like to go visit him. It's been a while. Kyle said I could stay at his apartment as usual. I asked the sheriff if I could have a few days off and he didn't mind. There's not much going on in Spookie right now. Would you mind if I went?"

Abigail was almost thankful. "No, you know I wouldn't mind you going to see Kyle. He's your son and I know how much you miss him. So go see him. And?" Abigail knew there was another reason her husband wanted to go to Chicago and she was waiting for it. She was pretty sure she knew what it was.

"You know me too well, wife. I made a call today to my old friend, Sam Cato. Remember him?"

"Of course I do. Your old partner on the Chicago police department. He helped us catch that

What Lies Beneath the Graves

Mud Person Killer–"

"Mud People Killer."

"Okay, Mud People. I remember Sam well. I liked him."

"Well, I spoke to him today about the missing girls from the art college and, low and behold, you won't believe it, he's actually one of the detectives on the case. Because Laura is involved by attending the school and we're concerned about her well-being and safety, I asked if I could drop by the station and talk to him about how the investigation is going. He said he'd love to see me and so would the other guys in my old department, or the ones still left. There's a handful, Sam says. They want to take me out to lunch so we can all catch up. I have an appointment at the station with Sam tomorrow afternoon at one."

"It's all right, Frank," she replied, stroking Snowball gently. The purring had stopped, the cat was sleeping. "I suspected you were going to take a trip to Chicago. Soon. I saw the way you and Laura were scheming on the back porch this morning. I know you're worried about her and her friend Odette. All the missing girls really. And," she reached over and squeezed her husband's hand, "if you think you can help protect our daughter in any way up there, then I'm behind you all the way. I hated seeing her leave today knowing what's going on at the campus. I pray they catch whoever is taking these girls, I know you also believe they've been kidnapped and aren't just missing, and the three girls are found unharmed…and alive."

"We all want that. Laura begged me to come

up tomorrow and look into this situation. Talk to some of her friends who might have seen or heard something and speak to the campus police. She's so scared for Odette and the others. She's frightened for herself. She thinks I can solve anything, any crime, so she said she'd feel better if I looked into it."

"That you're super cop, huh?"

"She thinks I am. I'm not, of course, but I do want to help find these missing students if I can. I feel so sorry for their families and friends. Also going up there will give Laura some piece of mind because I'll be close by and will be checking in with her a lot. She's afraid to go anywhere on campus now by herself."

Abigail shivered, remembering her missing husband Joel. Those had been dark, dark days. "Then go, honey. I can do without you for a couple of days. No problem. See if you can help Sam find those girls and…keep Laura safe."

"I knew you'd be okay with it. Thanks for being such an understanding spouse." He gave her a kiss as she lay in his arms. "You know Sam is now a lieutenant detective in his division. He's at the top of the heap."

"Good for him. He deserves it. Though, isn't he close to retirement?" she inquired.

"Three or four years away, I think. He was a lot younger than me. It'll be good to see him again. It's been too long since we saw him."

"Two years or so, huh?"

"About that."

"Say hi to him for me," she said, "and tell him

to come down for a visit sometime soon. He can bring the family if he wants. We have the room."

"I'll tell him."

"What about Myrtle's new mystery? The lost treasure?"

Frank chuckled. "It can wait. It's waited for nearly eighty years. I'm sure Myrtle and Glinda can handle it for a while. Probably have it all solved by the time I return. Treasure found and in the bank…if there is any to find, that is."

"Possibly. Myrtle is a determined woman. With Glinda's help she might just unearth that buried treasure."

"What time are you leaving tomorrow?" Was all she had left to ask.

"Early."

*****

Frank was right. When she awoke the next morning around eight o'clock he was up and dressed. Bag packed. She was sure there was a gun inside it. He never went anywhere without his old duty gun. "How about something to eat before you go?"

So they had breakfast, gazing out at the swirling fog beyond the windows which hid the driveway and roads, and she sent him off with a kiss and a hug. "Be careful, Frank."

"Driving in the fog? It's dissipating as we speak."

"Not that. Be careful," she stressed the words and was sure he knew what she meant.

"I'm always careful." And he was gone. She watched his truck disappear down the driveway into the fog.

She got Nick off to school and drove into town to work on the mural. By the time she was behind the wheel the fog was about gone. Good thing. She hated driving in it.

Chapter 9

It was strange to be in Chicago again, Frank brooded, as he drove into the heart of the city. Cars and trucks zipped by and around him at crazy speeds and he felt the encroachment; it made him nervous. He had never liked driving on the super highways. The sheer size of the city irked him. He'd been gone too long and was no longer used to the congestion, the noise. Usually when he visited Kyle he'd drive straight to his son's apartment or the hospital where he worked, avoiding the heavy traffic areas.

This time, revisiting his old police station, he had to go deeper into the city and before he knew it he was on the street where he'd once lived with his first wife, Jolene, and a child Kyle. Driving there had been automatic. The house, as he passed by it, looked the same with the landscaping, the beautiful brick front, and the attached carport he'd worked so hard to build so many years ago. There had been so many happy times he'd shared with Jolene and Kyle there, but seeing it again made him sad. It had taken a long time but he had a new life and was happy again. He didn't stop, he kept driving and soon was pulling into the police station's busy parking lot. A mess of old feelings assailed him and he found himself smiling. Oh, not so much for the job he'd left behind, and the darkness it often showed him of the world, but for the friends he'd made all those years ago and sometimes still missed.

Sam met him at the front desk. "Hi there stranger," his old friend greeted him. "I saw your truck pull in and thought I'd meet you. The guys are waiting in the back and, as always, they're ready for food. We ordered in pizzas in honor of your visit. Come on back."

"I thought we were going out to lunch?"

"We were until we got too busy. You know how it is. Pizzas in house is about all the time we can afford. There are too many open cases today. With the warmer weather the gangs are shooting up the streets again, knocking their rivals off and creating bloody havoc across the city. Domestic cases are skyrocketing. Murders are at an all time high."

"Sounds about normal."

"Do you miss it," Sam questioned. "The job?"

"No, I don't miss *this* job in the big city. The chaos, the overabundance of gruesome crimes and the homicides. So much overtime there's little left for family, friends or a social life. I do a little consulting in Spookie for the local sheriff's department and I have my books, my relaxing family life with a wife and two kids I love…and that's just fine with me."

"By the way, I like your novels, Frank. So believable. You're a fairly good writer for an ex-Chicago detective. I never knew you had such a prolific writer inside you. I'm impressed and envious."

"Thanks. High praise coming from you, Lieutenant Cato. I do my best."

"Are you rich and famous yet?"

"No, but I'm working on it." Frank walked around the counter as he'd done hundreds, maybe thousands, of times when he'd worked there and followed his friend into the office where a number of the old gang were waiting to see him. They shook hands all around and traded stories of their lives to catch up.

It was an enjoyable lunch reminiscing with his former colleagues. Then the gang broke up, some went off on calls, to man the phones, and some to do paperwork. The place emptied out quickly.

"Sam, can we talk about those girls missing at my daughter's college?" Frank pressed after they sat down in Sam's office. It was a small workspace, sparse but neat. There were framed pictures of Sam's wife and kids on the desk. Awards on the wall. It had once belonged to another lieutenant, Lieutenant Sheen, when Frank had worked the job. Sam had informed him Lieutenant Sheen had passed away the summer before. Cancer. A shame. Frank had liked and respected the man.

"We can do better than talk about it. I was going to drive over to the college and interview some of the students, their roommates and friends who knew the missing girls. I guess I'll be speaking to Laura then as well. My partner is at a doctor's appointment right now and took the rest of the day off. You want to ride along? It'll be like old times."

"I was waiting for you to ask me that. I'm in."

"Good. My car's waiting outside. Let's go."

The two of them exited the station, drove to the college and after parking the vehicle in front they headed to the registrar's office. Sam had telephoned the dean and his head of security earlier that morning so they were expected. After a short visit with the two men and learning the little they seemed to know, they left them to speak to one of the secretaries who might have helpful information about the missing girls.

Sam stood at the front desk and flipping open the small notebook he still carried to write things in he told Frank, "Since the dean was kind enough to give us the names of the missing girls–Alice Wood, Thandie Harris and Odette Benoist–and some of the students we need to interview, maybe these folks here can let us know where to find the students we need to speak to."

It didn't take long to get a list of the classes the students could be found in and the times they'd be arriving or leaving as well as their dorm addresses. Frank and Sam walked into the first room, an eighteenth century American history lecture, and introduced themselves to the teacher and asked to speak to a Freddie Marsden. The boy was a close acquaintance of Thandie Harris and had been one of the last people to see her before she disappeared. They explained to the boy what they wanted and then asked him the necessary questions. They didn't learn anything that would help, he'd seen Thandie in class a day or so before she'd vanished and had barely spoken to her at that time, and so they went on to interview the next friend.

The two detectives spent the following hours tracking down and talking to anyone who had known the missing girls or who had seen them last. They interrupted classes and lay in wait at the student's dorm rooms, catching them in between their classes or on breaks to talk to them.

Sam gathered his facts and scribbled copious notes. But when they finally called it a day and were driving to the station, Sam had to admit they hadn't learned much more than they'd already known. Nothing out of the ordinary had happened to any of the missing girls in the days before they were taken. One day each of them were just gone.

"These girls aren't going to be easy to find," Sam confided to Frank, shaking his head slowly as he drove. "It's like they have vanished off the face of the earth. No one's seen anything, knows anything."

"Now what?" Frank was staring out the window at the Chicago skyline. The city sparkled and shone in the sun, bright and beautiful, but he knew it was a misleading mirage. There was great darkness beneath the shininess. There was evil in the slums and barrios thriving in the shadows. He knew. He remembered.

"We go visit the parents."

"Oh, that's always fun," Frank stated caustically. But inside he was reliving the sadness he'd felt doing that duty. No matter how an officer tried to stay uninvolved, untouched, by the grief a parent felt over their missing child, he could never do it well. Their suffering, their distress and tears, always affected him. It would break his heart every time. He accompanied Sam into the missing girls' homes but remained silent as Sam did the talking and asked the questions. He was out of his jurisdiction and it was Sam's case. Frank had to admit, his friend didn't miss a trick, gathered the information and was thorough but compassionate towards the terrified parents. He promised them he and his fellow officers would do all they could to find their children. Frank's heart went out to the families because he knew the odds of getting the girls back safe were dwindling with every hour that went by.

Speaking to the bereft parents also made him worry more for Laura. If he could have he would have made her pack up her belongings and go home with him, but she'd already informed him she couldn't do that. She had to stay in college, attend her classes, and get her degree. "There's danger everywhere," she'd conveyed the night before, "so I have to learn to take care of myself. You or mom can't be with me forever." Of course, Laura was right. "I have to live my own life. Don't worry, I will be careful, I promise." So he and Abby would have to accept what Laura had decided. It was her life after all.

When Frank and Sam took leave of Odette's parents, their final stop, they returned to the college and met up with Laura after her last class at four o'clock. It was an early day for her.

"How did it go?" Her face reflected anxiety. She'd opened the door and led them into the room she shared with another girl, Sigourney Lassiter;

who wasn't there at the moment. "Did you find out anything helpful? Discover any leads? Has anyone heard anything from and of the girls or Odette?"

"No to all four," Frank answered. "I'm so sorry."

"So they're still missing?" Laura had pulled out a chair for Sam as she and Frank settled on the end of her bed. Frank felt terrible they didn't have better news for her.

"Hi Sam. It's been a while," Laura said. "You're looking well."

"Thanks. It's good to see you, too, kiddo, though not so much under these circumstances."

"I know." Laura lowered her chin into her hands, her body slummed against the wall at the head of her bed. "I can't believe none of the women have been found and nothing has been discovered about their disappearances. I feel so awful. And Odette? She's such a sweet person. So good. Why would anyone want to hurt any of them, hurt her? *Where are they? Where is she?*"

Sam didn't answer her questions, but instead said, "We talked to your dean earlier and he's introducing new safety measures across the campus for his female students from now on. Anyone can get a security escort to any of their classes or anywhere they need to go after dark or even during the day if they feel the need for protection."

Frank had welcomed that offer. "And Laura, listen, I want you to take full advantage of that, you hear? If you go anywhere on campus where you're not in sight of other people ask for an escort or make sure you have others around you at all times.

Promise me?"

"I promise. I'm scared, too. I will be extremely cautious. I'll be over-cautious. Tell mom not to worry about me and don't you either. I have the screamer and the pepper-spray and I'll use them if I have too. If mom had her way I'd carry a big stick of wood or a baseball bat for self-defense in my backpack like she used to do before she married you." Now she gave the two men a small smile, though Frank could see she was genuinely frightened.

"Oh, I remember that big stick." Frank softly chuckled. "If I recall, Myrtle used it to knock that Mud People Killer out of Abby's window when he tried to abduct Abby."

"She did. I've heard the story many times from Myrtle." Another smile from Laura. "That old woman sure was proud of herself for sending that killer flying out the window."

"She sure was."

At that point Sam announced, "Sorry to break this up, but I need to return to work. I have paperwork to complete and submit. And since you're riding with me, Frank. Time to go."

"I wish I could stay longer, Laura, but Kyle is expecting me and my truck is parked at the police station. I need to hitch a ride there with Sam. So where he goes I go." Frank got up from where he was perched on the bed.

"That's okay," she replied, "I have a big test tomorrow and have to study. Say hi to Kyle for me. I'll see you and mom on Friday. I pray Odette and the others will be found long before then."

"I do, too. And I'll say hi to Kyle for you."

"I'm going to do my best to find those missing girls, Laura," Sam said. "The whole department will. We're on the case and we won't give up until those girls are home. So just take care of yourself and stay alert."

"Goodbye, Sam."

Frank hugged Laura and the two men left. He didn't feel comfortable leaving Laura. Someone was taking girls and Frank felt helpless to protect her if he wasn't there to do it. But other than moving in with her and guarding her every minute, there was no way he could. She had her life there and he had to go back to his in Spookie.

Before he took Sam's leave, Frank requested, "Hey old partner, could you keep me updated, a text or a quick phone call once in a while, of anything crucial that develops in this investigation as it occurs?"

"You know I will. I can squeeze in a couple of texts or a call or two. I know you have a personal stake in this case."

And that was that. Frank climbed into his truck, drove across the city, and rendezvoused with his son at the hospital where the young man was getting off duty. They went to supper and caught each other up on things. But for the first time in a long time Frank wished he was still on the Chicago force. He wanted so badly to find the creep or creeps who took those girls. But there was nothing he could do. For him those days were over. It was Sam's world now and Sam's case. The man was an excellent cop so the problem was in good hands.

Frank would visit with his son, spend the night, and head home in the morning. Perhaps, on the way, he'd squeeze in another visit with Laura to be sure she was all right.

Chapter 10

When Glinda rose from her bed Monday morning she carried a cup of coffee out to the swing in her backyard and as she drank she admired the hazy azure sky and how the breeze riffled the tree limbs around her. She gulped in a breath of the fragrant air and sighed contentedly. It was going to be a spectacularly beautiful day. No rain. Warm. It was good to see spring again. She wasn't a winter person, though she did like snow if she was inside and it was outside.

She reflected on the vision she'd had the night before. It'd been a disturbing one. It hadn't been about Masterson and his treasure, but about something else. Something which had created a sick, horrified reaction deep inside her psyche and given her a feeling of great angst and sadness as she came out of the dream. At the end of the vignette she'd caught a glimpse of Abigail, Frank and Laura deep in conversation, looking anxious. Not unusual because she'd been with all of them the morning before for breakfast and had sensed something was wrong. They just hadn't shared it with her. Whatever it was, it was bad. Still...she had the undeniable urge to talk to one of them and tell them what she'd seen in her most recent but disturbing dream. Laura was miles away in Chicago and Frank was most likely at work at the sheriff's department. It was Monday morning after all. Abigail would be the easiest to track down, see, and she had a good idea where she could find her. So after her coffee Glinda got dressed, mounted her bicycle and rode into town.

There were whispers deep in the woods around her as she peddled down the country road, trying to get her attention or distract her, but she ignored them. She must speak to Abigail.

Maneuvering her bike along Main Street she stopped before her destination on the sidewalk, shoved down the kickstand and walked into the restaurant.

She had not been in South of the Border since they'd opened but she had a hunch Abigail would be there, because Myrtle had told her so. Which made sense because it was noon on a weekday and Abigail would be working hard on her Mexican mural for the restaurant's owner. Abigail had said she was nearly done with the commission and was eager to finish because she wanted to begin Samantha's promotional artwork for the mayoral campaign right afterwards.

Once Glinda's eyes accustomed themselves to the dimmer lights of the dining room she spotted Abigail in the rear corner intently painting on one of the walls. Glinda's gaze took in the expanse of the mural and she smiled. It appeared nearly done. It really was gorgeous and every object and person in it was so lifelike. It was as if she'd wandered into a quaint Mexican village a hundred years ago. And the delectable smells all around her made her hungry for chimichangas and margaritas. Well, lunch might not be too bad an idea.

Abigail had seen her, laid her brush down, and came rushing over. "Glinda, didn't I just see you yesterday?"

"You did, but I came into town expressly looking for you. I have something I need to discuss with you."

"Really?"

"Really."

Abigail sent her a strange look, but shrugged. "It's nice to see you no matter what. Let's sit down, what do you say? I've been on my feet or my knees painting for hours and could use a break."

"Sure." Glinda trailed behind her friend and they sat down at a table. The restaurant, at eleven in the morning, wasn't very busy. The lunch crowd was beginning to meander in so it was still quiet. The table was close against the wall and fairly private.

"So," Abigail began, "what do you need to see me about? If you came searching for me it must be important."

"It could be. I'm not sure. All I know is I had to talk to you or Frank about it. I found you first. I had another dream last night–" Glinda had been looking around them but now looked directly at Abigail.

"A vision about the hidden treasure again?" Abigail prompted.

"No. Something else."

They weren't sitting a minute before a man came up to them and asked her, "Hello, can I get you anything?" At first Glinda thought he was a waiter, then when Abigail greeted him she knew he was the owner.

"Hi Miguel. Glinda, this is Miguel Angel, he's the owner of this fine dining establishment. And Miguel, this is my friend Glinda Whitestar. Remember I've spoken of her? The psychic and Myrtle's grandniece?"

"Ah, the clairvoyant. Yes, I remember you talking, raving, about her. Hello Glinda Whitestar." Miguel smiled at her and bowed his head.

"I'm only taking a break," Abigail told Miguel.

"And a well-deserved break at that," the man replied, still smiling. "You've been working so industriously all morning. All week actually. The mural is almost completed and it is magnificent! It is more than I had ever hoped for. Because you've done such an amazing job on it, I'm going to treat you and your friend here to lunch…anything you both want."

"Oh, that won't be necessary," Glinda protested with a wave of her hand. "I'll pay."

"I insist." He handed her a menu he'd been holding in his hands. "It's the least I can do for my favorite artist and her friend. Lunch is on me. On the house. What do you want? And your money is no good here today. Some other day, not today."

"No–"

But Glinda didn't get the word out before Miguel gently interrupted, "If you don't tell me what you'd like, Glinda the psychic, I will just have to choose for you and have it prepared and brought out. I already know what Abigail likes."

Abigail was grinning at her as if to say: *I'm out of this. I can't change his mind.*

"Okay." Glinda yielded to her friend and the restaurant owner. "That's kind of you, Miguel. Let me have what she's having."

"Your wish is my command," Miguel announced with a flourish of the menu. "And I will be back shortly with your meals. Can I get you a drink, psychic? Again, anything you want you will have. Alcoholic included."

It surprised Glinda when Abigail ordered for her. "Bring the psychic and myself one of your small margaritas. It is early after all."

"Make mine a strawberry margarita," she modified the order. "As long as it is a small one. I'm not much of a drinker…and I'm driving."

Abigail laughed. "Yeah, she's driving a bicycle."

"Have you ever seen a tipsy person riding a bike?"

"Not really."

"They sometimes run into things." Glinda's lips produced a tiny grin.

Abigail laughed. "Don't worry, one margarita won't make you tipsy. I promise."

After Miguel had scurried away, Glinda reiterated, "That drink had better be small."

"It is. Half size of their normal drink. Miguel makes them special for me." Abigail was gazing at her wall painting. "I can't believe it. The mural is basically done. I was just adding final touches when you arrived. It's strange how when I first start a painting, any painting no matter how large or small, I think I can't do it. I'll never see it finished. I work and keep working, I agonize over if it's any good, then, almost like magic, one day I look and…it's done." She was shaking her head.

"Then we are celebrating. And I agree with Miguel, the mural is exquisite. I love it."

"Thank you."

"In fact, I think I'd like you to paint something on one of my walls in my reading room, something a little spooky befitting a psychic's world. I don't know what yet, but I can ponder on it and let you know. I can't pay you much, but I hope you give me a friend's rate if I throw in a couple readings."

"I can. And I'd love to paint something for you. I've never painted anything spooky. It'll be a challenge.

"All right, what was this about a vision?" Abigail returned to the reason Glinda was there.

"Oh, yes, the dream. I had a strange one last night. I know we were all together yesterday and it was a great brunch, no one said anything about anything being wrong, but I have to ask…is Laura okay? I mean, is there something wrong? With her? Or around her?"

Abigail's expression had become troubled. "What did you see in your dream?"

"I saw a girl in a dark cramped place, weeping and so afraid for her life, I think. A young woman really. At first I thought it was Laura, but after a while I realized it wasn't. Then I saw two more girls, one with blond hair, also weeping, and finally as the weeping faded away I did see Laura. She was in a room, her dorm room I would guess, at the college. She was alone."

"Laura? Oh no! Was *she* in danger?" Abigail's face exhibited alarm as her hand reached out for Glinda's hand.

"I don't believe so. It was more that there was a *connection* of some kind between her and all or at least one of the girls. Does this mean anything to you? Laura, no one, said anything was going on when I saw you all yesterday. Have I misread something?"

Abigail hesitated, a guilty expression shadowing her face. "There was something wrong yesterday, but Frank and I kept it away from you and Myrtle because it didn't have anything to do with either of you and why worry you, so we also asked Laura not to say anything about the situation. And we didn't want Myrtle budding in and trying to help fix or solve it as she always wants to do. You know how she is. We didn't want the interference. It was easier to keep the problem to ourselves."

"So what *is* the problem?" Glinda could tell her friend was relieved to be able to talk about it. "If you want I could promise you it won't go any further than me. I can keep a secret."

"I know you can. All I ask is you don't talk about this conversation with Myrtle. Not yet anyway." Abigail shut her eyes briefly as if she were gathering her courage or if what she had to impart was that disquieting. "Okay. Here's the problem and it's serious.

"In Chicago at Laura's art school there are

three female students missing. It's been over a week or so since the first one vanished and the other two soon after; the last one disappearing a few days ago. Until now the college and the authorities have kept it quiet, out of the media, but soon they won't be able to hide it. It'll be all over the local and national news. The third girl, Odette, who's gone missing happens to be a good friend of Laura's. That's the connection you felt. As the other girls Odette wasn't the type to leave without a word to anyone, or scare her parents and friends as it has. These girls are not just missing, Frank thinks, but have been abducted. Truth is, he's in Chicago right now visiting with his old partner from the Chicago police department, Sam Cato, trying to find out what's going on."

"And he is–you both are–terrified for Laura?"

"I'm afraid for the missing girls, too, but having Laura up there when someone's kidnapping young women is scaring the heck out of us. You said in your dream you saw and heard the missing girls weeping…so they're still alive?" Abigail's anticipation was palpable.

"I think so."

"Did you," Abigail leaned towards her, "see anything else, anything which might help the police find them?"

"Not really. The vision was too murky, disjointed. But I do sense they are still alive. What I saw was in the present."

"That's something. You should talk to Frank about what you've seen; perhaps even talk to the Chicago police. They have no leads, no suspects, nothing, to go on. Nothing. So anything you might tell them will help. We can vouch for your psychic gifts."

"You said Frank will be gone until Wednesday? I'll come over Wednesday evening and speak to him about it," Glinda said softly. "Maybe I'll *see* more by then."

It was at that moment their drinks and food came and with them Miguel. He pulled up a chair and watched them eat their lunches of chimichangas, rice and beans as he barraged Glinda with questions about her psychic readings and abilities, truly interested.

"My mother, Consuela," Miguel said as he touched her hand, "had the sight, too. She could see the future and often read peoples' fortunes for them. Almost everything she saw came true. She was the real thing."

Glinda jerked when his hand came into contact with hers, but she tried not to show her distress.

"As Glinda here is." Abigail bobbed her head. There remained unease in her eyes from their earlier conversation. "She's the real thing, as well."

"Then I'd like you to give me a reading something soon, Miss Whitestar. I have some questions I'd like to hear your answers to."

"I'm sure you do, especially about your childhood haunting."

Miguel flashed Glinda a shocked look. "Yes, some things about that. And other things."

"Anytime you'd like, Mr. Angel. I think I can help you." She gave him one of her business cards and an understanding look. "Just make an appointment. After this delicious meal you've been so kind to provide me with, I'll give you a fair price."

Miguel took the card. "I'll call you. Soon. Right now I'm needed in the kitchen. Lunch time is upon us," he excused himself, got up and hurried away.

"Looks like you scared him off, Glinda. I've never seen him act like that." Abigail was staring at her. "What haunting?"

"A particularly malevolent one. As he touched my hand I had a vision and it was frightening. When he was a child in Mexico Miguel lived in an old house for a short time and it had ghosts. Odious and destructive poltergeists and they were very powerful spirits. Years before Miguel's people moved into the house another family had been brutally murdered, tortured to death, by a drug lord and the spirits couldn't rest. A father, mother and two grown sons. Malicious, they haunt the place to this day. Miguel saw too much when he lived there and someone he dearly loved was taken from him. The spirits drove his mother, being what she was, insane and she took her life–and he saw it. He blames himself for it because he couldn't stop the ghosts from tormenting her. That's the secret Miguel hides and the truth that haunts him. He needs to talk about it, have a form of exorcism, which I can perform, so the memories leave him alone. He's suffered too much for too long with these memories."

"How did you know all this?"

"The vision, though brief, was extremely detailed."

What Lies Beneath the Graves

"Oh."

Glinda thought Abigail would ask more about Miguel's haunting, but she didn't. They finished their meals, their drinks, and Glinda didn't linger longer but left after promising to stop by Abigail's house around six on Wednesday.

*****

Glinda had not had another divination of the lost girls by the time she took her bicycle and rode over to see Frank and Abby on Wednesday evening. Nick wouldn't be home from band practice until later so it was a good time to discuss something they were still hiding from him.

In Abby's kitchen she sat with them and Frank caught her up on the investigation in Chicago. "I rode along with my old partner, Sam Cato, when I was there, interviewing anyone connected with the missing girls, visiting the college and searching the grounds for any left behind clues. We found absolutely nothing. Everything was a dead end. The department, at this point, will follow any lead, no matter how meager or outrageous. Even leads from a psychic. Time is ticking away and those girls need to be found. What did you see, Glinda? Give me every tiny detail. Leave out nothing."

She took her time, closed her eyes and delved deep into her memory, and tried to recall each nuance of her dream she could. Frank wrote down every word in his notebook. When she was done, she waited for his response.

"That's not much help, except for the knowledge the girls were alive two days ago. That's something. I wish we knew it for sure right now at this moment."

She looked intensely at Frank. "I...feel they're still alive." Then she thought of something else and was surprised she hadn't remembered it before. Perhaps she hadn't been meant to until that moment. "There is one last thing. I heard the word *factory* as the images slipped away."

"Factory? Any idea what kind of factory?"

"No, just the word *factory*. I had a flash of an image of what looked to be an *abandoned factory*."

"Well, that's something," Frank acknowledged. "I can call Sam and tell him they should start checking vacant factories around the college. It's a start. Thank you so much Glinda. And if you get any more *insights* or glimpses that might help the police further, call me immediately, please?"

"You know I will." She felt bad she couldn't give him more yet hoped in time she could.

Frank got up from the chair and moved into the living room, she could hear him on his cell phone talking to someone. Probably his old police partner.

"Thanks," Abigail echoed. She'd been at the sink finishing up the supper dishes, listening. Now, with a cup of coffee, she sat down next to Glinda. "Since Frank came home today he's been preoccupied with the crime he left behind in Chicago. If we had our way Laura would have come home with him until the missing girls are found and this kidnapper has been caught. We're so worried about her safety. But she has a full scholarship she worked so hard for, she's stubborn and, like all young people, thinks she can handle anything, can take care of herself and that nothing bad will happen to her. Though her heart is aching for her missing school mates, she doesn't want to change her life for something which only *might* occur. She told Frank there are awful things happening around the world all the time to all kinds of people. She can't let her fear keep her from her future."

"That's Laura all right, always believing the best will happen and not the worst. But I can understand how she'd feel that way. If everyone lived under that kind of fear of what *could* happen but might not, we'd all huddle in our houses and never go out into the world."

"I agree. I've had my traumas and deadly encounters over the years and usually you never see them coming. You have to live your life every day as if those bad incidents won't happen. Hope for the best. Otherwise, you'd drive yourself insane."

Glinda nodded. She knew exactly what Abigail was talking about. She'd also learned that lesson as a child. "I'll let you or Frank know the second I get another insight or see anything which might further help in the investigation. I wish I could force it, but my visions, my dreams, won't be forced."

"We know that. We're grateful for what you've already given us. Hopefully it will help. Talking about your visions, have you seen anything else about Masterson's hidden treasure?" Snowball was in Abigail's lap which reminded Glinda she had cats at home to feed and had wanted to get home before total dark. Myrtle had telephoned earlier and informed her she would be at her house before eight and would it be okay if she spent the night? She'd bring a movie DVD with her. What else…a ghost story. She didn't ask its title. Myrtle had begun spending more overnights with her and it was fine with Glinda. The old woman was getting older, had grown more fragile, and craved more human contact. Oh, Myrtle still had Frank, Abby and her friend, Richard Eggold, but had forged an unbreakable bond with her since she'd been living in Evelyn's house. In some ways it was as if Glinda had taken Evelyn's place. Myrtle would never admit it, but she loved her. And for Glinda Myrtle had become the grandmother Glinda had never had.

"Oh, the hidden treasure. Now that's a funny thing. I haven't been visited by Masterson's spirit since last week and that last dream. I was sure I'd see him again, but so far I haven't."

"Perhaps you won't," Abigail said the first thing that came to her mind, "see him again?"

"Perhaps I won't." Glinda waited until Frank returned to the kitchen, promised she'd contact him if she learned anything else which might help with the abducted girls, and then took her leave, reclaimed her bike and rode home as the oncoming night's shadows chased behind her. She refused to look at or listen to them as they chattered in the woods along the way. There was nothing they would whisper she wanted to hear. She had enough on her plate. Those missing girls were haunting her and they were more important than any buried treasure. People were way more important than money.

*****

Myrtle had fallen asleep before the end of the movie, Ghost Story, and Glinda covered her with a blanket and left her on the couch. Outside in the night she could hear owls calling to each other. Framed in the window was a huge white shining moon.

Glinda made sure the house was locked up tight and then she retired to her bed. Amadeus snuggled in beside her and by the time his purring had dissipated there were three more cats crowded around her and she slept.

She was again with Masterson but this time during a violent storm on the ship and the vessel was breaking into pieces on the rocks. She could hear the cries and screams of the drowning sailors as the water swept them away and the undercurrents took them under. The wind howled, the sea churned and there was Bartholomew in the waves fighting for his life. A huge portion of the ship's wreckage, a section of wood from some part of the ship, collided into him and he grabbed at it and held on, refusing to let the sea take him. Hanging from his arms were two canvas bags. Some of the treasure. He'd somehow saved it from the swirling water. Time spun by fast forward and in the morning there was no longer a ship nor any sailors alive…except Bartholomew Masterson. She saw him sprawled on a ledge of rocks along the shore and at his feet was that piece of the wreckage and the two canvas bags. There were other pieces of the destroyed ship scattered around him. There were bodies. Glinda watched as he woke and gathered the two bags to him and when he was strong enough he dragged himself up further onto the land and slept once more.

In her dream she followed the man as he searched the island. It wasn't a very big island but there were small wild animals scurrying about in the underbrush and there was fish in the water. She could feel his desperation to find any more of his shipmates alive. He didn't. He was alone. All the bodies he found were lifeless and he buried them the best he could in the sand or beneath layers of shrubbery and leaves because he had no tools, no way to dig their graves. Some he let the waves take back. There were too many to bury.

For a long time, it might have been years Glinda couldn't be sure, Masterson lived on the island with his salvaged treasure and scavenged the land for food and built his own shelter. It was a hard lonely life and the living, the surviving, of it did something to him. Warped him in some strange way. He morphed into a human animal with a straggly beard and hair and wild eyes. Every once in a while he'd bring out the canvas bags, dump out their contents, and stare at the gems, jewelry and gold coins. He'd touch and caress them and watch them sparkle in the sun. The bags hadn't held a lot and Glinda wondered what had happened to the rest. Perhaps some of the treasure had escaped the bags and slipped into the ocean before Masterson had snatched them up, but what he'd saved would still be worth a fortune in the outside world–if he ever got back to the outside world. She could see that fantasy in his eyes. At first. Over time she watched as his eyes dimmed and the hope, the dream faded. She could feel his growing despair.

Then in her dream she saw the new ship

coming over the sea's horizon and Masterson, his clothing now rags, waving his scrawny arms at it. The ship picked him and his bags up, now also stuffed with various objects he'd found on the island as camouflage to hide the treasure inside, and brought him back to civilization, a busy noisy city. He wouldn't let anyone touch the bags, guarded them day and night like a mad man, and as the dream left her, at port, he exited the ship that had rescued him and was traveling away from the city. But he wasn't the same man who'd left on the Black Ghost with his brother years before. He had changed. His face was gaunt, his eyes haunted, his body ravished by the time he'd starved and suffered, alone, on the island. Yet he seemed to know where he was going as the dream ended.

*****

"Oh my," Glinda murmured as she sat up in bed, "so Masterson was the only survivor of a ship wreck…and he *did* come back with some of the treasure." The sun was a bright light in her bedroom, the cats were gone and Myrtle, disheveled and clearly having just woke up herself, stood in the doorway, wearing one of Glinda's robes, staring at her with a mischievous grin on her wrinkled face.

"I heard that. Ah ha, I told you so, grandniece." Myrtle cackled. "Masterson's treasure really does exist. And there is some buried here somewhere. I'd stake my life on it."

With a sigh, Glinda replied, "My dream only told me he had rescued some of it but it doesn't prove he left any of it here after his death. I didn't see anything about that."

"Not yet. But you will. You will." Myrtle plopped down on the edge of the bed. "Tell me all about your dream. Don't leave anything out." Then the old lady stood up again. "Second thought, tell me about it over breakfast, I'm starved."

To that Glinda laughed and got out of bed. "Give me a couple minutes to wake up first, would you? I'll meet you in the kitchen, you can help me make bacon and eggs and I'll blab everything."

"Okay. I'll go make coffee." Myrtle hobbled out of the room, throwing the words back at her.

"You do that."

Over their morning meal Glinda described her dream in meticulous detail. Myrtle gobbled down her eggs and bacon, eyes animated with interest, and soaked in every word.

"You'll see more the next time," Myrtle repeated when Glinda had finished her recounting.

"I might. I do have the feeling Masterson isn't through with me yet but I don't know when I'll dream of him again. If ever."

"Well, you've seen enough, I've heard enough. The treasure existed, and I believe Masterson left some of it here somewhere. So until he visits your dreams again I'm going to start looking for that buried loot." Myrtle was grinning, tilting her head back and forth, and waving her fork in the air. She hadn't bothered to comb her gray hair and it stuck out all around her head like a gray Brillo pad. There was egg yolk around her lips.

"What! If you think I'm going to let you start digging holes all over my property like a rampaging mole searching for some trinkets which may or may not even exist, you are sadly mistaken. If you do that, before we know it, half the town would be here digging right along with you and the buried treasure stampede would start all over again. No way. You hear me? No way. Don't you dare do that."

"Oh, I don't plan on *digging* anything anywhere, not unless I discover something. I'm no fool. Besides I'm too old to be doing that sort of physical labor." The old woman gently tapped the side of her head. "Ha, I'm using my brain. I've ordered one of those metal detector thingies off of the Internet. The best one I could find. Whew, wasn't cheap either, let me tell you. It should be arriving any day now. I plan on using it to look for the treasure. You said you saw gems, jewelry and golden coins in those chests on the ship in your dream?"

"I did."

"And parts of jewelry, necklaces, rings and such, and golden coins are metal right?"

"Yes, gold is metal. Why Myrtle you continually surprise me. I guess I can go along with that plan. Using a metal detector to skim along the ground surface. Just do me a favor, if you find something do not dig anywhere until you confirm it with me, and, if you can help it, *do not* let any of the townsfolks see you running around my land with a metal detector. If you see anyone while you're out searching…hide the metal detector behind you or drop it to the ground. And don't tell anyone about what you're doing. Can you promise me those things?"

"If I do promise, does that mean you'll allow

me to search for the treasure?" Myrtle's voice was excited.

"Do I really have a choice, Auntie? I mean this place once belonged to your sister and you actually have more of a claim to it than I do. It was a great gift you gave it to me. I can't turn you down."

"Nah, I gave the house and the land to you and it's all yours. I'm no Indian giver. But I really want to locate that treasure. I've heard about it most of my life and I'm determined to find it if it's here to find."

"If it exists."

Another chuckle. "And I'll be sneaky all right. I'll make sure no one else is around when I use that metal detector. It won't be hard. No one hangs around your place unless they've come for a reading and then they are only in the house, not wandering around the grounds. There won't be anyone to see me."

"You got a point there, I guess."

"Hey, you going to eat that last piece of toast?" Myrtle pointed at the plate holding it.

"You can have it." She pushed the plate towards her aunt.

Outside dogs were barking somewhere and Glinda, shivers traveling along her skin, had a strange premonition. Something about the missing college girls. Unexpectedly an image flew into her head and out again.

Grabbing her cell phone, she stood up and moved into the living room, leaving Myrtle behind to eat her toast. She keyed in Frank's telephone number. "Frank, I have something else on those missing girls."

"You do? What have you seen?"

"I saw what appeared to be a vacant factory embedded in a large fenced in area near what looked like an outside animal, most likely dog, kennel. Both structures seemed abandoned. Also, I hate to tell you this but I also sensed time could be short now."

"Why?"

"I'm so sorry. I…fear one of those girls is going to die soon. I don't know how, just that she is going to die. I saw a fresh unmarked grave in the woods."

Frank said nothing to her pronouncement, but she could almost feel the frustration in his silence.

"Frank?"

"I'm still here. Is there anything else you can tell me?"

She paused, the horrendous images she'd seen replaying in her mind. "Only that the person you're seeking isn't one, it's two. I saw two men. A younger one and an older one. I also sensed they were heartless creatures and they've abducted and killed before. They might even be in the system. If you check."

"Is that all? Can you describe them?" Frank asked.

"No. Their faces were blurred, indistinct."

"Do you know how much time do we have? For the girl who is to die?"

"I don't know. But I felt it wasn't long. I'm going to ask the tarot cards later about all of this and perhaps they'll give me more. I'll let you know if they do. Goodbye Frank."

She looked up to see Myrtle loitering in the doorway. "What's going on? Who were you talking to?"

"No one. A customer."

"Uh huh." Myrtle snickered and went back into the kitchen.

Glinda followed, wondering how long they could keep the secret of the missing girls from her aunt. Myrtle always seemed to find out things eventually. It was something she was good at.

*****

That afternoon after Myrtle had gone home Glinda took her tarot cards and dealt them out, asking the questions: *Where are the missing girls? Who has them? Are they still alive?* And laying the cards out on the table face up one by one.

She did it three times but the cards would say nothing; or nothing that made any sense, that is. It was as if she'd asked totally different questions. So odd.

With a heavy heart, she tucked the cards away, telling herself she'd try again before she went to bed. But it bothered her they wouldn't or couldn't help her. That rarely happened. She didn't want to dwell on what their contrariness probably meant…that true evil was behind the abductions and the story wasn't over yet.

Much later that evening Glinda tried the cards again. And after three more strange readings she understood. One of the girls was no longer alive. One of them was dead. She didn't know how she'd tell Frank, Abby and Laura. She decided to wait until morning to call them. No sense ruining their night's sleep. There was nothing any of them could do right then.

Chapter 11

Myrtle walked away from Glinda's house in the shadows of the thick hanging clouds above her. They cloaked the sun and made the earth as gloomy as twilight. She was glad she'd worn her heaviest sweater and her long wool skirt because the morning was chilly. When was it ever going to warm up, she fretted. She dragged her wagon behind her because it was her day for dropping by the nursing home and seeing if any of them needed anything from the stores. It was little enough to do for the sick ones, but they acted as if she'd given them the greatest gift in the world. Running small errands for them.

She was on the sidewalk in front of Claudia's book store when she spied the old man in the black fedora shambling down on the other side of the street. She'd seen him before and had once even spoken to him a year or so ago. He'd said he was being treated for cancer. Remembering that she hobbled across the street and stood facing him.

Merely a town acquaintance, he'd never told her his name and she'd never asked. "Howdy, friend," she said, bringing her wagon to a stop and meeting his eyes. They were about the same age, she'd guess, give or take a decade, so in that they had something in common. Old people needed to stick together, help each other if they could. It was the Christian thing to do. She was struck by how much more weight he'd lost and how sad his eyes were.

What Lies Beneath the Graves

"How are you doing these days?"

At first she didn't think he was going to respond. He hung his head and tried to go around her, then stopped, and answered, "About as good as can be expected. The cancer has returned."

"So sorry about that." Trying to sound as sympathetic as she could. Since she didn't know what else to say, she said, "Out getting your exercise, huh?"

His smile was cynical. "I guess you could call it that."

She gently laid a hand on his sleeve. "You seem so down. What's wrong? Is there anything I can do? Listen, maybe?"

Then it was as if something broke in him and he began telling her about how ill he'd been and his wife was now unwell also and how he was exhausted caring for her; how afraid he was of losing her. His face was full of fear. In a guilty whisper he confided how much money their combined care was costing and how he didn't know how he was going to pay for all their needed medicine, doctor co-payments and other expenses since they were on fixed incomes. He wasn't complaining as much as venting. The way he spoke about his wife it was easy to see he loved her dearly. Myrtle listened and felt so much pity for him. Perhaps she should tell him about the hidden treasure buried on her niece's land? Nah, if she told one person by morning the town would all know. It was best to keep it to herself for now. When she found it she could help him with money for his problems. Help pay for his and his wife's medical bills like she'd done for old Lottie before she died? Yeah, that was what she'd do.

For the moment she did what she could do. "Is there anything I can get you or your wife? I always go to the IGA store today for the folks at the nursing home on Fifth Street and I could pick up something, groceries or whatnot, if you need anything, for you and your wife? If you give me a list and your address I can bring the stuff by later today?"

The elderly man frowned, his brows dipping beneath the brim of his hat. "I appreciate the offer but I'm," and here he paused as if unsure how to proceed, "a little short on funds at the moment."

Myrtle didn't know why she fibbed, but seeing the instant shame on the man's face, she did. "You don't need no money, friend. My church, St. Paul's on the other end of Main Street, gives me a stipend every week to buy things for the folks at the nursing home and other needy people. You qualify because both you and your wife are so sick. My pastors would want me to help you. Just give me a list of what you and your wife need, prescriptions at the Walmart even, your address, and I'll bring everything by later today."

The man's eyes were now rimmed in unshed tears, though he was shaking his head in a negative fashion. "That is so kind of you, but no thank you. We'll manage. I can't…I–" And without another word, the man spun on his worn shoes and hurried away, head down and a wrinkled hand holding his fedora tightly on his head. She thought of chasing after him, but knowing what loss of pride did to a person, she just stood there and watched him go down the street and disappear into an alleyway.

With a sigh, she continued on her journey to the nursing home. At least there were people there who needed what she had to give. She went on her rounds, stopping in the rooms and visiting with the lonely sick and old ones. After running some errands for a few of them, when she was done, she took her empty wagon, and singing at the top of her voice through the woods, she traipsed home, content she'd helped who she could help that day. The thought of supper, toasted cheese sandwiches and tomato soup, drew her on. The day had been long and she was ready to prop up her feet and, after supper, to watch television. She'd recorded some PBS murder mysteries days before and couldn't wait to see them.

She was rewarded for her good day's work when she found a large package on her front porch. "Hot dog," she cried, lifting it and dragging it into her home, "my metal detector is here!" It was all there, shiny, complicated and very expensive–it was the best. A Vision Pro XJ9 with the detector, with a LCD screen and a nifty carrying case. Unpacking it, she took out the instructions and sat at her kitchen table with the whole apparatus and read how to use it.

Glancing out the window, she muttered, "Too bad it's getting dark outside. Ghosts will soon be roaming the woods. I'll have to wait until tomorrow morning before I can try it out. Oh, well, it'll give me time to learn more about it." Which she did. By the time she went to bed she figured she was an expert on the Vision Pro XJ9. She was so eager for the morning to come so she could hunt for the treasure that sleep was elusive and it took her a long time to achieve it.

*****

At dawn, Myrtle opened her eyes and seeing the light outside, climbed out of bed and prepared for her day of looking for a hidden fortune. She giggled, she was so excited over the prospect of treasure hunting. What fun she would have. Putting on warm clothes because the early morning was still cold, she packed snacks and a bottle of water. The metal detector wasn't too heavy for her to haul around, but it wasn't lightweight, either. Good thing she was in good health for her age, probably because she walked everywhere. Walking was good exercise. It kept her young.

When she was ready, had gathered the metal detector paraphernalia together and the case was hanging from her shoulder, she made her way to Glinda's house through the forest shortcuts. By the end of her journey the metal detector had gained a lot of weight, more like an anchor. Whew, this treasure hunting wasn't going to be so easy, she thought. She knocked on her niece's front door.

"What are you doing here so early?" Standing there in the doorway in her robe, Glinda rubbed her eyes and yawned. Her hair was loose and flowing, silver white in the morning's light. Her green eyes sleepy. She was barefooted. That magic cat of hers snarled at Myrtle from behind his mistress, his fluffy tail jerking every which way.

Myrtle pushed the metal detector case at her

niece. "Look, I got it! The metal detector. They delivered it to my house yesterday. I'm ready to begin searching for that ghost sailor's hidden gold. You want to come with me?"

"Aagh, not until I have my tea and toast and wake up all the way. Come on in, old woman. I have something to tell you. I had another dream of Masterson."

"Woo-hoo! This time did he tell you where he might have buried his treasure?" Myrtle slipped past Glinda and into the house. She dropped her equipment on the sofa and followed the younger woman into the kitchen.

"I'm afraid he didn't, not this time, either," Glinda confessed. "The dream just uncovered more of his story. There was a ship wreck. All on board perishing except Masterson who somehow snagged two bags of what I think were jewels and coins. How he was washed ashore with them, clinging to a piece of floating flotsam; survived for years alone, forgotten, on an island until he nearly went mad. But, eventually, miraculously, he was rescued, and then after his voyage back across the ocean to civilization he hid and transported his small horde of wealth out of the city. There the dream ended. I don't know anything else after that. So far anyway."

"But it proves he recovered some of the treasure and brought it back with him? Right?"

"Right, but not necessarily that there was any left when he died, though." Glinda was making her tea, popping slices of bread into the toaster. The demon cat was under the table and every so often dashed out and swatted and bit at Myrtle's feet.

Myrtle wanted to stomp the creature's tail, but didn't because Glinda loved him so much. Besides, she wouldn't really hurt an animal anyway no matter how much it pestered her.

"Make me some of that toast, would you please? Three pieces with some of your homemade strawberry preserves on them. That batch you made last summer was so yummy."

"Ah, you like anything sweet. But I'll bring out the preserves. Go ahead and help yourself to some coffee, Auntie, unless you want tea?"

Myrtle grimaced. "Yeck, you and your tea. You're so funny. But I think I'll just have a glass of milk, if it's okay with you." She didn't wait for an answer, she rarely did, and fetched the carton from the refrigerator, poured a portion into a glass, and sat down with it. The tea thing was a private joke between the two of them.

"What else did you learn from your dream?" Myrtle wanted to know when Glinda set down the strawberry toast before her.

"That's about it. More or less."

"Oh." Myrtle's frown showed disappointment. "Okay then. So, do you want to come with me when I go searching for the buried treasure?"

Glinda laughed. She sat down with her cup of tea and her plate of buttered toast and sent an apologetic look towards Myrtle. "Sorry, I can't. I have readings this morning and through the afternoon. A psychic has to make a living you know. But you go and have fun."

"What you really mean is you don't believe there is any treasure buried out there, do you?"

What Lies Beneath the Graves

Glinda cocked her head, pushing her hair away from around her face so she could drink her tea. "I don't know if there is or there isn't. I just have work to do."

"Well, then, I'll do it by myself. I think I'll start with your front and back yard and then work my way to the cemetery. That could take some time, I imagine."

"No doubt. But, Auntie, don't overdo it. If you become tired, take a break."

"Ah," Myrtle protested, "I know my limits. I'll take my time. Don't worry."

The two women ate their toast, chatted, and after they were done Myrtle took her leave. "I'll come back by later if I find anything."

"Yes, please do that." Glinda's smile was warm. "I'd really like to know."

Amadeus was sitting in the doorway glaring at Myrtle. What was it with that cat? He was behaving as if he were protecting his mistress from something or someone. Her. Odd. Glinda had nothing to fear from Myrtle. On the contrary, Myrtle would do anything to keep her niece safe, protect her with her own life if need be. She loved her more than anyone else in the world, even more than she loved Abby and Frank.

Myrtle collected her treasure hunting gear and headed outside. But she couldn't shake the suspicion her niece was keeping something from her. Something important. When she returned later she'd make Glinda tell her what it was or she wouldn't leave until she did.

*****

It didn't take long before Myrtle had the knack of using the detector's wand, had almost become an expert, and learned how she should hover the thing slowly and vigilantly over the ground before her feet as she walked. Deciding to begin her search in the cemetery, she'd started at the entrance between the tombstones and was careful to remember what parts she'd already gone over. It was fun to know she might find a cache of priceless gold coins or jewelry at any moment beneath the soil. It was something she'd never done before, hunt for treasure, and she loved doing new things. This was another adventure. At first it was a bit spooky weaving between the graves and stones, stepping on the flattened mounds covered in weeds, but after a while she got used to it. Being daylight with the sun sparkling over her, she wasn't too concerned the dead would rise up and scold her for disturbing their eternal rest. If they were even there or even cared.

In her long life Myrtle had come to the uneasy conclusion that burying people in coffins beneath the earth was senseless, barbaric even, and a waste of precious land. Why? Bodies, after death, were nothing. Empty hulks. The souls were up in heaven, blithe and happy. They didn't care what happened to their mortal remains. And Myrtle truly believed there would come a time in human history, perhaps thousands of years from now, where the land would be needed for the living and then goodbye tombstones, mausoleums and angelic stone sculptures. The graveyards would be dug up, cleared out, and the land reclaimed so people could live on it again. Just one of her predictions.

What Lies Beneath the Graves

She noticed her shadow at one point as it followed her around, and grinning, she began humming Perry Como's old song, *Me And My Shadow*.

Me and my shadow, strolling down the avenue, me and my shadow, not a soul to tell our troubles to....

The hours went by swiftly. Soon she was huffing and puffing and the metal detector had become so much heavier she could barely lift it. She'd gotten tired before she'd finished a quarter of the cemetery and squatted down on a cube shaped tombstone to rest. It was going to take a lot longer than she had thought it would. The graveyard was bigger than she'd realized. No, it was just her. She was old. She got weary quicker. Her ancient bones and muscles no longer had the endurance they'd once had. Boo hoo, but she wouldn't feel sorry for herself. So her body was used up and she was old? So what. She'd just rest more often. Glaring around at the tombstones, she mused that it beat the alternative.

Thinking of her own age and frailties, the memory of the elderly man in the black fedora returned out of nowhere to haunt her. On the street the day before he'd looked so desperate, so ill. Body sick. Heart sick. Soul sick. She had an eye for that sort of thing. Sitting there on that tombstone amid the graves of people long gone, she made a promise to herself to find out who the old man was and go visit him and his ill wife; help them if she could no matter how he protested. That was what a good Christian was supposed to do. Help people.

She could ask Frank, Sheriff Mearl or one of the pastors at her church about fedora. Someone would know who he was and where he lived. Then she'd find and help him.

Fifteen minutes later she got up, and after noting where she'd left off in the cemetery with a line of small rocks, gathered her metal detector, and headed back to Glinda's house. She had time. Tomorrow she'd continue the hunt. The sailor's treasure had been lost for decades so another day, a week or a month more wouldn't hurt anything.

When she arrived at Glinda's house she knocked and knocked and no Glinda. So with that weird magical cat gawking at her through the window's glass, she retrieved the hidden key and let herself into the house. Though she looked in every room she found no Glinda. Now that was strange. The psychic had said she had customers all day, it was afternoon, but she wasn't there.

Myrtle locked the door behind her and trudged home, leaving the metal detector on Glinda's rear porch beneath a worn blanket she'd snatched from Glinda's storage closet. She'd return later or the following morning to see what was up. She'd decided she was too pooped to continue dragging the metal detector around Glinda's property any more that day. She needed a nap.

*****

Glinda had finished her second-to-last customer and when her final client of the day called and canceled she could no longer remain idle in the house. Through all her readings during the morning and afternoon the tarot cards kept sending her veiled warnings along with messages for the person being read.

As she was setting the cards aside after her last customer left, the vision came to her. It was brief, violent and left her shaking with tears in her eyes. *She had to tell Frank what she'd seen.*

She could have telephoned him but after the vision she had to see him in person. The message had been clear. Something or someone wanted her to confer with Frank immediately. She thought of leaving a note for Myrtle, who was out hunting for treasure somewhere, but didn't because then the old woman would track her down or end up at Frank's place. Abby and Frank still wanted to leave Myrtle out of the loop when it came to the missing college girls. No one wanted her to run off to Chicago and butt into that investigation and, heaven knew, she would if she could. If Frank, Abby or Laura were involved Myrtle would think she should be as well.

Glinda rode her bicycle into town. Most days Frank would be consulting for the sheriff's department and could be found at their office so she pedaled down Main Street and put her kickstand down in front of the police department.

She caught Frank literally leaving the building.

"Glinda? What are you doing here?" He was closing the station door behind him.

"Looking for you."

He sent her a strange look. "For me?"

"Yes, you. I've learned more about those missing girls. I need to talk to you."

Instead of answering her, he took her by the arm and steered her to his truck. "Get in and we'll talk."

Once inside Frank turned to her. "Good timing. I was on my way to ask you something anyway so you saved me the trouble. What did you want to tell me?"

In a solemn mood she told him and felt awful when his demeanor darkened. She hated telling him one of the girls was dead. He didn't ask which one, though she didn't know.

"So you believe the girls are being held not in the abandoned factory but in a building near the dog kennel's grounds that is close to an abandoned factory?" Frank reiterated. "And there are no dogs at the kennel. It's deserted?"

"I think so. I saw only empty pens and rusted fences as if it'd been long deserted. I also saw buildings surrounding it, dilapidated, and in the distance there was a neon sign, a restaurant perhaps…Stoney's?"

Frank appeared startled. "I know that restaurant. I know where it is!"

"That's good then, isn't it? You know where to look now." Outside the truck some of the townsfolks were bustling by her, some waved and some smiled at her or Frank.

Frank seemed elated. "We know where to look. Thank you Glinda."

"I'm glad I could help in any way. I felt for those poor missing girls, too. And now that one of them is…." She couldn't say the word but sighed. "I want them found.

"And what had you wanted to see me about?"

"It plays right into what you just revealed. I've been hired temporarily as a consultant on the kidnapping case by the Chicago Police Department. I'll be working with my old partner Sam Cato, whose usual partner is now on medical leave facing heart surgery. Sam asked for me specifically. I'm driving back up there tonight, lodging at my son's apartment, and I was asked if you would agree to accompany me and join the case as well? Unofficially, if that would be easier for you. We could really use you, especially since you seem to be receiving messages about these girls already. If what you say is correct then the other two girls don't have much time. Oh, and my son said you could also stay at his place. He has the room."

Glinda hesitated, unsure what to do, until another ephemeral image of two weeping girls crowded into her mind and she slowly nodded her head. "I'll come with you. I want to do anything I can to help. Those girls need to be rescued and as quickly as it can be done or they will die. If my psychic abilities can help you and the Chicago police department in any way find these students then it's yours to use."

"All right." Frank appeared grateful she'd accepted without much persuasion. "Can you be ready to go in an hour or so? I'll pick you up. Sam Cato and the team want to meet with us tonight at the Chicago police station. They have an all-out hunt for the girls planned for sunrise tomorrow. And now, thanks to you, we'll have a good idea where to look."

"You'll pick me up in an hour, huh?"

"I know. It's not much time. But I can load your bicycle into the bed of the truck and run you home so you can pack. I'll be back for you once I drive home and do the same."

"Thank you, but you don't have to drop me off and come back. I can pack while you wait. I'm an old hand at it. Packing and leaving on a dime. How long should I pack for?" Glinda was fighting to calm her thoughts because they were racing in so many directions. The cards had slyly insinuated the horror which would exist at the end of the investigation. There was more she could have told Frank but her mouth couldn't form the words. Her mind couldn't hold the images they were so horrific. She didn't want to go to Chicago, she didn't want to find what they would find, but she couldn't say no to Frank or the missing girls. Her gift came with its own responsibilities. Helping others, if she could, was only one of them.

"I don't know. Until we locate the missing students. But, I won't force you to stay in Chicago if you don't want to. Sam and the team merely want to meet you; talk to you. I'll bring you back home, or have someone else bring you home, whenever you ask me to."

"Sam and the team want to meet me? To decide if I'm a quack or the real thing, huh?"

"I told them you were the real thing."

"Thanks," she said softly.

Frank retrieved the bicycle and drove her home.

Myrtle welcomed them at the door. "Niece, I wondered where you'd gone. I didn't have any luck finding the treasure today, but it sure wore me out. I came back but you weren't here and you said you'd be. So I went home, took a short nap and returned because I was worried. I've been waiting for you. Where were you? Oh, hi Frank. What are you doing here?"

Oh oh. Glinda contemplated lying but she detested doing that under all but the direst circumstances. This wasn't one of them. But Frank stepped in and took care of it for her.

"Hi Myrtle. Let's sit down and while Glinda packs I'll fill you in."

"Glinda packing? Where is she going?" Myrtle demanded to know, overly protective as she always was since discovering they were related.

While Glinda went to her bedroom and packed she could hear Frank in the other room explaining what was going on to her aunt. By the tone of his voice she could hear he was being diplomatic yet firm. When she came out of the room, dressed in blue jeans, shirt, boots and a rain jacket, with a suitcase full of clothes and necessities Myrtle was prattling on about her treasure hunting and showing Frank the metal detector. So everything was okay.

Myrtle looked at her. "I know about the missing students at Laura's school and that you are going with Frank to try and find them. It's all right. I'll stay here, as Frank has asked, and take care of your animals and your house. A very important task. That way I can keep searching for the treasure. Silly Frank. He thought I'd want to go with you and help in Chicago. Not me. Not now. I don't like the big cities, too noisy and crowded. I trust all of you to save those girls. Me, I have to find the treasure. So don't worry about me, Niece. I'm fine staying here."

Now that was an unforeseen but welcome development. "That's a perfect solution, Myrtle. I was reluctant to leave my cats and house but with you here to care for them, I feel so much better about going. Thank you."

*****

In the truck as they left the house, Glinda sent a glance at Frank. "I don't know what you told her but it worked. Good job, Frank."

"It wasn't difficult. I got her yakking about the hidden treasure and how she couldn't stop looking for it now that she had the metal detector. She's on her own adventure. And we needed her to take care of your animals and this house. She was needed. It was fairly easy."

Glinda knew he wasn't telling the whole truth. "She wanted to come with us to Chicago, didn't she?"

"Of course she did," Frank admitted, grinning. "At first. But I told her it was strictly police business. Chicago wasn't a quaint little town like Spookie and the police department wouldn't allow amateurs on official investigations, wouldn't let her help no matter how good she was at solving mysteries, so she couldn't go. We'd handle the situation and when it was over we'd have quite a story to tell her. She wasn't happy about it, but she accepted it. Continuing to look for Masterson's treasure was a good consolation prize. She's really into the hunt."

"I know she is." Glinda observed the scenery going past the truck's window and tried to blank her mind from the images that kept materializing in her head. Crying, terrified young women locked in a dark prison somewhere. Fresh graves. It was easier that way. Soon enough she'd have to face what was coming. Whatever it was. All she knew was it wasn't good. Her visions never lied.

Well, while she and Frank were alone and before they got to Frank's house and Abby was there to send them off to Chicago, she thought: no time like the present. She had to tell him. "We're going to have to be really careful."

"Why?" There was an oddness in his voice.

"Something really bad is waiting for us...for you. I just want you to be ready."

"Is that the danger you warned me of before?"

"I'm...not sure."

"Any specific advice, Psychic?"

"No," she didn't tell him the entire truth, "it's only a premonition right now, no specifics. Just promise me you'll be careful when we get to Chicago?"

She thought he was going to laugh at her, but he didn't. "Okay. I promise." They pulled into his driveway and their conversation ended.

Chapter 12

The three of them, Abby, Glinda and Frank, sat at the kitchen table after Frank arrived with Glinda and deliberated their next move. He explained to Abby about being asked to join the investigation in Chicago and about Glinda's latest vision. She already knew about Glinda's first vision. He confided everything to Abby.

"So you're driving back to Chicago to be a consultant on the missing girls' case and Glinda is going with you to also consult?" Abigail asked. "Are you leaving right away?"

"Right away," Frank answered. "Sam personally asked me to help and I couldn't say no. Not with Laura also being endangered by these abductions. I hated leaving her the other day knowing what was going on."

Abigail met his gaze. "I know you hated leaving. I hated her going back up there, too. There's a lunatic or more than one, if Glinda is correct, preying on young girls and all I want to do is keep our girl safe here at home." She reached out a hand and took his. "But if there's any way you or Glinda can help find these monsters, save those girls, more power to you. I'm behind you all the way. I know I'll sleep better knowing you're up there looking into things."

He took her hand and held it gently. "Me, too. So when Sam called I couldn't say no, even though I hadn't talked to you about any of this yet. I knew you'd understand. And when I told him what Glinda has been seeing he requested she come as well. He wants to speak to her. I know he's hoping she'll see more; something, anything more, that can help us. Glinda fears those two missing girls might not have much time left to live unless we find them sooner than later. At first I didn't want to become involved, I really didn't. But now, with what Glinda's seen, I feel I don't have much choice and not just because of Laura. Glinda believes I'm supposed to be on this case; it's somehow vital that I am.

"And when Glinda presented me with clues to where the girls could be I thought she would be a help in locating them. And Sam agrees."

"So you're staying at Kyle's?" his wife affirmed. "Does he know this?"

"I should hope so. I already called him and he said it was all right we crash at his apartment as long as we needed to. I think he even liked the idea of having us there. Especially when I said Glinda was coming." He threw a sly smile at Glinda.

Kyle, on his rare visits, had met Glinda a handful of times since she'd moved to Spookie and Frank suspected a serious affection was growing between them. It had occurred to him more than once how nice it would be if the two young people became closer, a lot closer. After all, in another year or two Kyle would have to decide if he'd be moving back to Spookie to take over Doc Andy's practice because Doc Andy was retiring. Could be Glinda would be another sweet incentive. Abby, too, was aware of this possible love connection and approved. She thought Kyle and Glinda would make a perfect couple, since both of their life's goals were to help people. Abby and Myrtle believed theirs was a match fate was guiding. Besides, Myrtle said they looked so cute together.

"Oh, I suspect Kyle loves the idea of having Glinda under his roof," Abby whispered in his ear so Glinda wouldn't hear.

Then she said, "Here, Frank, go pack and I'll make you and Glinda some sandwiches to take along for the ride. You haven't had any lunch yet."

"I'll help," Glinda offered, coming to her feet.

"And I'll take that help."

From the bedroom while he packed he snooped on his wife and Glinda's conversation as they prepared the brown bag lunches. Some of their dialogue he could make out and some he couldn't. But his mind was on the case and what would be waiting for them in Chicago. He packed quickly and rejoined the women in the kitchen.

He knew the moment he reentered the kitchen something had changed, something was wrong. The expression on Abigail's face said it all.

Glinda swung around to face him and he saw the same troubled expression on her features. "We need to leave now."

"You had another vision?"

"I'll tell you about it on the way," the psychic replied. "We need to go. There's even less time than I had thought. It may already be too late."

Frank enfolded Abby in his arms. She was trembling. Apparently, Glinda had informed her of what it was that was wrong. "It'll be all right, sweetheart. Whatever it is, we'll try to take care of it." He kissed her goodbye.

"Call me as soon you know anything?" She returned the kiss.

"I will."

*****

The truck sped towards Chicago as a light rain cascaded around it, streaming down its hood and fenders. They'd left Spookie far behind them before Glinda disclosed what she'd seen.

"So one of those girls will die tonight?" Frank slowed the truck down because the rain had made the roads slick and visibility practically nonexistent. If they didn't get to Chicago in one piece they wouldn't be able to help anyone.

"I'm afraid so. If what I saw in that fleeting flash of a vison in your kitchen was accurate."

"Aren't they always?"

"Mostly. Though sometimes they're disjointed, confusing, and I can misread them. So I'm careful how I decipher each one. In the one I just had I was shown someone, a girl I've never seen and did not know, weeping hysterically in a darkened bunker-like enclosure. I had the suspicion it might be one of the remaining college girls. I saw two shadowy men digging a grave in a wooded area."

"Is there anything else you can tell me? Something that has come to you since having that vision?"

Glinda remained silent a moment and then replied, "Like I said I saw an enclosure, a prison. Now, after thinking about it, I believe it was a...shed. The last thing in my vision was a shot of the outside of it. An old shed with peeling red paint; perhaps used as a storage for supplies or machinery."

"A shed?"

"I think so. Or it appeared to be one."

Frank was thoughtful as they continued the journey. The rain was falling heavier and Frank hoped it would let up before they had to start traipsing around in a wood, field or weed patch somewhere. The city came into view and a short while later they pulled into the parking lot at Kyle's apartment complex. They made a hasty stop to unload their suitcases and check in with Kyle, who was waiting there to let them in.

His son was delighted to have Glinda there but not as delighted for the reason they'd had to come to Chicago. The evening news had reported on the missing college girls and the town was abuzz with it. Kyle knew what was going on and, besides feeling sadness for the women who'd been taken, was worried about his sister. Yet he was still happy to see them.

It wasn't lost on Frank how friendly Kyle was to Glinda from the minute they arrived. He took her suitcase and escorted her into the apartment, all smiles. He even gave her his own room for as long as they'd be there. He'd already cleared his stuff out and put clean sheets on the bed. "I'll sleep on the couch," he said. "When I'm here, that is. I'm beginning a twelve hour shift later tonight and will be on duty long shifts all week. I won't be here much anyway. So, Glinda, you are welcome to my room."

Glinda didn't argue. She allowed him to carry her suitcase into the room and set it on the bed.

What Lies Beneath the Graves

Frank looked around. His son had cleaned up the whole apartment. It was a heck of a lot neater than when he'd been there earlier in the week.

"When I knew you two were coming I stocked the fridge with real food." Kyle was smiling like a teenager at the psychic. "Since I eat most of my meals at the hospital there wasn't much real food in the apartment. Oh, and I had a few more keys made. One for each of you so you can come and go without me being here." He handed them both a key. "Just be sure to lock up whenever you leave. There have been frequent break-ins and burglaries in the neighborhood recently so, above everything, be vigilant."

They promised.

Frank and Glinda took their leave and Frank drove to the police station. When they walked in they were surrounded by a crowd of uniformed police asking questions or talking at once.

"They've been waiting for us," Glinda whispered.

Lieutenant Sam Cato worked his way through the throng, calling for quiet as he went, and stood in front of them. Frank introduced Glinda to him and then the rest of the team. Afterwards Sam ushered them into his office and spent some time speaking with him and Glinda.

Strangely enough Sam didn't appear skeptical of Glinda's clairvoyant pronouncements. He listened and after posing a question or two to her, got up from his desk.

"So you believe me?" she asked as Sam got to the door.

"Well, I can't say I was a great believer in psychic abilities before this, but Frank and Abigail vouch for you and your unique gifts so I can do nothing less than believe what you say. So enough talk. We're ready to go out and find those girls. We have all the necessary warrants to search the property in question. The property, Glinda, you helped us pinpoint. I took care of the paperwork and arrangements while you two were driving up here."

"Okay. We should get looking now," Frank said. "Glinda thinks one of the girls might die tonight so we shouldn't waste any time or daylight." He glanced at Glinda.

She nodded. "Let's go."

*****

Under a cloudy sky the rain had slacked off and Frank was thankful. It was hard enough tramping through the brush and rubbish littered across the property they'd pulled up to without a curtain of rain and a swamp of mud hampering their advancement. The land around them looked like a junkyard. The parcel of land allegedly owned by two brothers was over five acres in size. It was a lot of area to search.

"This is the place." Sam was staring over the vacant lot dotted with dilapidated structures and a rundown house. The rest of the officers, there were six of them, had parked their vehicles a ways down the gravel road so as not to alert whoever was around. They'd stealthily walked in, hands lightly resting on the butts of their holstered guns, and stood awaiting instructions.

Frank could see Stoney's restaurant in the

distance high above them on a hill, its sign blinking on and off. On the edge of the land there was a dog kennel. The cages were rusty and empty. The entire place had a sinister feel to it, Frank thought. Glancing at Glinda he wondered if she felt the same menacing vibes. Their eyes met and she nodded. She felt it, too.

"There's evil here," she murmured, her gaze sweeping the murky green spaces around them. "I can feel it. Bad things have been done here. Bad things will be done unless we can stop them."

Sam looked over his shoulder at her. "We'll stop them. Where do we look first? Any…idea?"

"This way." Glinda marched past Frank and Sam and through the weeds parallel to one of the outbuildings, her eyes on something in the distance.

The police officers trailed her silently.

They approached a thicket of trees and after zigzagging in and among them deeper into the woods Glinda stopped and pointed to a mound of fresh ground at her feet. There were tears on her cheeks. "I think this is where the first girl is. And she hasn't been there long."

Sam stared at the pile of dirt. "Start digging," he directed the two police officers at his side who'd followed them into the woods with shovels in their hands. Glinda had requested they bring the digging tools.

The dead girl had been buried in a shallow grave in a blood-soaked sheet. It didn't take the officers long to unearth her hand and then her body.

Frank wasn't sure which girl was dead below them but he knew two of the parents he'd met the other day would hear the worst news of their lives tonight and he ached for them.

Glinda stepped over to another hole in the ground; also newly dug by the looks of it. This one was unoccupied. A dirt-encrusted shovel was leaning by a nearby tree. "Thank God we're not too late for her," she whispered. Frank assumed she meant the second girl.

Sam, after calling in the medical examiner to collect the dead girl's body, had two of his officers remain at the graves.

"Where to now?" Frank was scrutinizing the hilly terrain around them.

"This way." Glinda stomped through the bushes towards the shabby house. "We'll look everywhere. I'm not real sure where the girls are being kept but I feel they're around here somewhere."

"In a shed with peeling red paint?"

"Possibly. Just because it was in my vision doesn't mean it's here."

The police officers, Sam, Frank and Glinda spent thirty minutes or so thrashing and searching the property. Evening was coming and the sun was leaving. Shadows were materializing everywhere, hiding the harsh lines of day. There was a chill in the air that only came from the woods.

They peered into the out-buildings and shacks. Spreading out they covered the grounds. They found no one, but no more dead bodies or fresh graves, either, which Frank was grateful for. They were near the house, dark windows and termite-eaten wood surrounded by piles of rusting cars, old appliances and junk, when Frank heard a car start up, coming from somewhere behind the house. Then the vehicle, an older model Chrysler, came around the house, into sight and careened past them at a breakneck speed. There were two men in it. It didn't get far. Frank shot at the wheels, shot at the windshield more than once and shattered it. He wasn't sure he'd hit either of the killers but he hoped he had. The car went out of control and smashed into a tree partway down the driveway. The engine exploded and caught fire.

The police stormed the burning vehicle.

The two men inside were dragged out of the car and they didn't want to come willingly. One was bleeding and one was shooting at them with a rifle. Darn, Frank brooded, unfortunately he hadn't killed them.

Sam was the one to bring the tall killer down with a well-paced bullet. The shorter, skinnier brute with a beard threw his hands up. "I give up. I give up! Look, you've shot me. I'm bleeding!"

Frank couldn't help himself. He strode up to the man and punched him as hard as he could, bringing him to his knees. Then he kicked him. Twice. "That's for the girl you murdered and the despicable way you buried her," he spat in an angry voice. "And the fear you've put into so many innocents. Children and parents."

He grabbed the man's shoulders in a fierce grip and shook him. "Where are the other two girls? Tell me now. *Where are they!*"

The man wouldn't answer. He stared sullenly at Frank, then hung his head; shoulders defiantly held stiff.

It was at that moment Glinda interrupted. "Look, Frank, on the far side of the house beneath the trees."

He sent his gaze in the direction she was pointing. In the descending gloom of twilight, he could barely make out the outline of a shed all but hidden by overgrown limbs and leaves.

"Call an ambulance for the one who's been shot and cuff this S.O.B.," Sam said to the officers at his side. Officer Harper, an older officer who'd been Sam's second-in-command since Frank had retired, dragged the one killer to his feet and cuffed him while Officer Brown, a younger recruit, put in the call for an ambulance for the other suspect who remained motionless on the ground.

There were muffled cries and shouts on the evening air. Someone was pounding on something.

The rest of them rushed towards the house and the shed. Up close Frank saw it had peeling paint and in the dim light the color looked to be reddish. There was a padlocked door on the other side. Frank shot the lock off and Sam, another officer, and he rushed in, switching on flashlights as they went because it was black inside. Frank prayed as they entered that the girls, if they were there, were still alive. They were.

Inside there were three cots, two unoccupied, and a pair of weeping young women in the other, clenched in each other's arms, their wrists handcuffed and, each with a lengthy chain, fastened to the floor; giving them just enough movement so they could lie down or sit together. Frank was so relieved to see them he could have shouted out in joy. The girls blinked in the light. Their faces were bruised and their eyes were like trapped animals until they realized they were being rescued instead of further abused. And their smiles came out like the sun.

One of them cried, "*It's the police. We've been saved! Thank God.*" While the other girl kept crying, her shoulders heaving, her body shuddering.

Glinda went to the girls, comforting them. Her arms gathering them to her. "It's all right. You're safe now. The police are here. You're safe."

One of the officers came in and handed Sam the keys to unlock the girls' chains. "I got them off the man we shot," he stated flatly.

"When you go out call in another ambulance for these girls, Officer Macy, they need to be transported to the hospital immediately," Sam addressed the officer. "Then go and bring back one of the squad cars so our victims can have a place to wait for it in. We're getting them out of here."

Officer Macy nodded, bowed his head to get out the low height door, and left the shed.

Sam used the key to free the girls and they were helped outside. Even in the fading light, the two victims were pitiful. Their clothes and faces were dirty. They shivered and jerked at every noise and refused to meet anyone's eyes. Which made sense because of what they'd probably been through. Glinda produced a bottle of water from a pouch hanging on her shoulder and gave it to the girls, who'd said they were thirsty and starving. Sam gave them each a candy bar and a box of raisins he'd had in his pocket. They'd be driven to the hospital and when they were ready their statements would be taken.

Frank didn't want to know what they'd been through. It was here where he and Glinda would be bowing out. Their jobs were done. He'd leave the follow up to the proper authorities. He'd only helped because of what Glinda had seen and because Laura had been endangered. The whole experience had only reminded him of how happy he was to be retired and out of the old detective and crime rat race. How happy he was in Spookie. It was much more satisfying to write about crime than to be out in the field actually fighting it.

Once the ambulances had come and gone, the perps in one and the victims in another, Frank told Sam, "Glinda and I are going now. We've done what we came here to do. We helped you find the girls. We're leaving the rest of this case up to you and the department. I'm retired, remember? We're going home."

Sam didn't argue with him. He'd known they were only temporary assistants. There wasn't anything else they could do. It was up to the justice system now. "I remember. And I want to thank both of you for all your help."

Sam was looking at Glinda. "And I want to thank you. The Chicago police department and the families of the girls you helped us save thank you. Could we call on you one day again if we ever need your, er, special abilities?"

"Call me," she answered with a tired smile, "and I'll let you know if I will or can help. If the cards and the universe agree."

"Good enough."

Frank and Glinda were chauffeured to the police station and after giving their statements they drove in the dark to Kyle's apartment. It'd been a very long day and they were both exhausted.

They were surprised to see Kyle waiting for them. "Dad, I was working last time you were here. So I traded shifts tonight with another doctor. I wanted to be here when you two returned. I see you so rarely I thought it'd be nice to spend some quality time with you."

And spend time with Glinda, Frank mused. But it was good, as always, to see and spend time with his son so he didn't question anything.

After he talked to Abby on the phone and caught her up on what had happened that day, told her they'd be home tomorrow, he called Sam and got an update.

Sam had been solemn as he'd apprised Frank on the surviving girls' conditions. "Their parents have been notified and are on their way to the hospital to be with their daughters. The girls have been through so much. The doctors say they're still in shock. But physically, aside from bruises, cuts, and one of the girls has a broken arm, they will recover. Not sure how if ever they will recover from the experience, though. The two kidnappers, brothers Arthur and Wesley Addy, hadn't fed the girls since they'd abducted them. They are shiftless, lowlifes who we now suspect have been moving from one state to another the last decade, hiding in abandoned houses, stealing whatever they could get their hands on, mugging people or robbing gas stations and abducting young girls to torture and kill.

"The brothers had been exceptionally cruel, taunting and beating the girls if they gave them any trouble. The way they treated them was inhuman. They are inhuman. Monsters. Thank God we now have them in custody so they can't kill any more young women. We've contacted other police departments in other states connecting the dots. It seems they've left a long string of murders behind them."

"Why did they kill the third girl and how did she die? Who was she?"

"She was Alice Wood. We rescued Thandie Harris and Odette Benoist. As far as I can deduce Alice was murdered for the same reason they've killed all their victims over the years. It was how they got their kicks. They were vicious, evil-minded brutes who for some demented reason hated women. Who knows why? Killing made they feel powerful. We don't have a medical report on exactly how the dead girl died. Not yet anyway. When we find out something more I'll let you know when I know. We've only begun interrogating Wesley Addy–boy, is he one messed up nut case–at the station. His wound was only superficial and a paramedic took care of it in the ambulance on the way to the jail. His brother is in the hospital right now having bullets dug out of him." Sam had chuckled. "Somehow the man got all shot up."

"Ah, too bad." Frank didn't care that Arthur Addy was having bullets dug out of him. He wished he could have put more in the creep.

"Frank, I'll let you know how things progress here with the case and what else we find out about these two animals. It looks like it'll be quite a story. They've been murdering girls for a long time. Catching them is a massive win for the good guys. Please tell Glinda we couldn't have found and stopped them without her help. We're deeply indebted to her."

"I'll tell her."

"And I want to thank you as well, old friend, for your help. I owe you."

"No, you don't." Frank had been watching his son flirting with Glinda across the room and he smiled at them. "I was protecting Laura."

"And all the other vulnerable female students at the college."

"That, too."

Frank and Sam spoke for a little longer, then said goodnight and hung up. He put in a final call to his daughter Laura. "It's over, Laura. We got the two men who have been kidnapping your classmates. They're in custody right now."

"The girls?"

He hated telling her but he did. "Odette is all right. She's been through a lot and has some injuries, mainly a broken arm. Thandie Harris is alive, too. They're both at the hospital getting treatment. I'm sorry, Alice Wood didn't make it. We didn't get there in time."

"Oh, no." Laura moaned. "I didn't know Alice very well. She wasn't in any of my classes, but I feel so bad for her and her parents. I'm happy, though, you saved the others and Odette is alive. I'll have to see her as soon as the hospital releases her. I imagine she won't be coming back to her dorm room for a while."

"Probably not right away. She'll most likely go home to her family."

"I'll wait until tomorrow and try calling her."

Frank could tell by the graveness in her voice she'd been deeply affected by the kidnappings and the one girl's death. "You can sleep peacefully now, sweetheart. Thanks to Glinda and everyone on the Chicago police force the criminals are now behind bars or will be soon and two of their victims are now safe. Their crime spree is over."

"And thanks to you," Laura added softly. "You were the connection between Glinda and the abductions. Is she going to help fight the bad guys from now on?"

"When she's asked, I believe. Goodnight, Laura."

"Goodnight, Frank. I'll see you on Friday evening." The cell phone on her end clicked off.

He'd never asked her to call him father, though he called her his daughter as did Abby. But he'd known her father before the man had been murdered five years before, he'd been a good man and father, so he didn't hold it against her not to give him that title; perhaps one day she would. He knew she loved him and Abby and that was all that mattered.

With all the phone calls done, Frank returned to his real life. He spent the evening watching Kyle fall over himself trying to impress Glinda and he tried to forget the shell-shocked and abused looks he'd seen on those two poor girls' battered faces. And he tried, in vain, to forget the blood-soaked body in the shallow grave. He couldn't. And with what Sam had divulged about the killers' cross-country across decades murdering spree he knew he'd have nightmares for a while. How many more victims and shallow graves would be uncovered as the investigation into the two men, their history, and their serial killings went forward? He felt weary just thinking about it.

Oh, yes, he was glad his police career was behind him. He liked his life the way it was, simple and good, with Abby, his books, his town, the children and consulting with the local sheriff's department when he felt like it. He'd leave the job of finding the really bad guys up to Sam and younger hungrier men. He'd served his time. Now his life was in Spookie.

He and Glinda spent the night and had breakfast with Kyle before they got in the truck and drove home. Frank was glad to see the town come into view. He was home.

Chapter 13

Abigail was at The Delicious Circle visiting with Kate, sipping coffee and eating a crème horn. She'd already consumed a chicken salad on a sesame bun sandwich. It'd been delicious as all the sandwiches were that Kate made. As far as Abigail was concerned, the new lunch menu was a hit. It was nice to be able to eat something substantial before she began gobbling down pastries.

After Kate had had the surgery for her melanoma, a small but growing spot found on her back, a medical problem she said Glinda had warned her of when she'd read her cards, she'd moved quickly to return to work and expand her menu. Abigail was just happy her friend was okay. They'd caught the melanoma early and Kate's chances of survival were high.

"I'm okay thanks to Glinda," Kate avowed. "She advised me to see my doctor. That it was important and she was right on the money. That girl is a marvel."

"Isn't she, though?" Abigail had replied with a knowing smile.

Frank had telephoned her earlier that morning and said after he and Glinda made a stop at the Chicago Police Station for a final wrap-up they'd be heading home to Spookie. She was happy the abducted college girls' case was solved and over, the culprits now behind bars, for many reasons. Her husband and friend were coming home–and Laura, and all the other young women at the art school, were now safe. She said she was proud of him and Glinda for helping to apprehend the two serial killers and get them off the streets forever. Because of her husband and Glinda now many women would not be terrorized, tortured and lose their lives. They were heroes. But there'd been danger and she'd worried, it was over, and she wanted them home. She wanted their lives back to normal. Well, as normal as living in the same town with Myrtle and Glinda could be.

Peering out through the glass windows Abigail observed the curtain of rain outside, the fog swirling around the streets and buildings. The fog had been exceptionally thick all morning, though the temperature had risen to sixty-three degrees. Safe and dry in the donut shop Abigail continued gossiping with her friend, Kate.

"I hear Norman popped the question," Abigail grilled her. "Did you say yes?"

Kate laughed. "He did pop the question…the night before my surgery."

"That was a while ago. What answer did you give him?"

"At the time I told him to ask me again next month. After the surgery."

"Has he?"

"He did yesterday."

Abigail stared at her. "And?"

"I said I would marry him in June. June twentieth. It's my late mother's birthday. A perfect day for our wedding. You and your family are of course invited. I think we'll have a small wedding at St. Paul's with a party here afterwards."

Abigail exhaled and the joy on her face was genuine. "Congratulations. What are your plans for after the wedding? I sure hope you're going to stay here in Spookie and keep this shop open. I've become addicted to your donuts. Please don't leave."

"Of course. I'd never give up this shop. It's my life and Norman knows it. Truth is, he's offered to quit his job at the flour mill and help me run and expand it. I'd have a working partner which would give me more time to bake and more free time for us to enjoy life. Last night Norman and I also discussed living arrangements. In the beginning he'll move in upstairs with me and then we'll start looking for a house in town nearby, purchase it and move in. He says his mother, who he lives with and helps, understands and is happy for him, for us. Of course, he'll continue helping her, we both will, but he'll be living somewhere else with me."

Kate had a blissful contentment about her Abigail had never seen before. "I'm so happy for both of you. Frank and I will have to give a party for you two real soon so we can meet him."

"Any time. We'll be there. Norman loves barbeque by the way and I know how Frank loves to grill steaks."

"I'll remember that and with warm weather coming it might be an option."

"So...has Samantha had her baby yet?" Kate was swiping off the counter with a wet washcloth. She couldn't tolerate crumbs on it.

"No, not until the end of May. She has about three more weeks to go. But she keeps saying the baby could come early because the women in her family, her mother and grandmother, all had early deliveries."

"She get that nursery done yet?"

"Almost. Crib's ready. They figured out how to put it together. I think they only have to complete the finishing touches like pictures on the wall and put in a supply of baby necessities, onesies, diapers and such. I know Samantha and Kent are eager for the baby to arrive."

Kate hung the washcloth on a hook behind the counter. "Is Samantha really going to run for Mayor in November?"

"Oh, she's in a hundred and ten percent. I'm getting ready to start producing her campaign brochures, posters and online ads. I never thought I'd work at a newspaper again creating and uploading ads, in this case political ads, but for Samantha I will. She'll make an excellent mayor."

"You think she's got any chance to win?"

"I know she will. She's got the smarts, the ambition and the plans. She wants to keep the small town ambience in Spookie but still make it more convenient, modern, for its people. And she's got so many excellent ideas on how to do it."

"I'd vote for her," Kate declared. "It's time we get new blood in the old town's politics. Out with the old, in with the new, I say. A woman mayor. And it's about time.

"Switching subjects, friend. How's the treasure hunt going?"

"Uh, what treasure hunt?" Abigail was more than surprised Kate knew about it.

"Oh, the secret Masterson's treasure hunt Myrtle traded me information about for a bag of free donuts last week and I told her, and later Glinda when I was having a reading done, that my family had an old friend when I was a child who was Masterson's personal housekeeper for a short while at the very end of his wretched life and she swore he confessed one day in a fever there was never any treasure left, he'd spent it all, and he only started the rumors about burying the last of it to spite the townspeople; so they'd go crazy after his demise searching for something which didn't exist. He was an unhappy human being our family friend always said. He had had a miserable life and despised everyone. Lying about a non-existent treasure was his revenge on the townspeople. It worked real well, too, I'd say. It did drive the townspeople bonkers searching for it."

Abigail couldn't help it, she laughed out loud. "And you told this to Myrtle?"

"I did. But I don't think she believed me."

"Nope." Abigail sighed. "She did not. Don't spread any of this around, besides the ones who already know, which are Frank, Glinda, Myrtle and myself, but Myrtle has been searching for that buried treasure for days now out at Glinda's with a very expensive metal detector. She swears she's going to find it."

Now it was Kate's turn to laugh. "Well, good luck to her then. She's going to need it. I believed what my old family friend told us. There is no treasure. Nada. Zippo."

As if talking about the old woman suddenly

materialized her, Myrtle came barging into the shop, closing her umbrella as she came through the door.

"Hi Kate. Hi Abigail." Myrtle found a stool beside Abigail and plopped herself down. "Give me a cup of your coffee, Kate, and one of those crème horns like Abigail here has. Please."

"Coming up," Kate told her.

And aside to Abigail Myrtle whispered, "Hunting for buried treasure all morning sure makes a person hungry, but I can't do any more searching today because of the rain. Darn it."

"Any luck?" Abigail whispered in response, playing along, trying not to show her amusement since she knew they were whispering for no reason. Kate knew all about the treasure because Myrtle had told her.

"Not yet. But I'm working hard. You should see the muscles I've grown. Woo wee. I almost have the whole cemetery sectioned off and combed."

Kate put the pastry and the coffee in front of Myrtle and Myrtle gave her a crinkled well-worn dollar bill.

Myrtle continued speaking to her in a low voice. "But that's not the reason I came looking for you, Abby. I've been in most of the shops in town and tracked you down. Claudia said she saw you come in here so here I am." Myrtle took a bite of the crème horn and made the happy face she always made when she was eating something she loved. When she was eating anything really.

"Why are you looking for me?"

"I wanted to know how Frank and Glinda are doing in Chicago. I didn't want to call and pester them if they were on the job, you know, corralling bad guys and slapping handcuffs on them, but I am anxious as to what's happened. I been having these weird feelings all day. Something *has* happened."

"Actually they should be on their way home right now. With Glinda's help they caught the kidnappers and saved two of the girls."

"Two? Ah, one of them didn't make it?"

"Alice Wood. But they saved the girl who was scheduled to die last night if they wouldn't have found them. And Odette, Laura's friend, was one of them rescued."

"That's good. Except for the one dead girl. I'm glad the whole mess is over and Frank and Glinda are coming home. A shame the third girl died, though. That's awful. Awful." Myrtle let a sad look settle on her face for a second and then rattled on. "No need to go into details, I expect Glinda will tell me everything when she gets home. She always does. It gives us something to yak about."

Myrtle was staring at the rain through the glass when she said, "The other reason I was looking for you is I want you to help me find someone who most likely lives around town somewhere. Rally our forces so to speak. Maybe we could get Samantha to help us, too, or some of the other shop owners. Maybe even Frank."

Kate had been listening to their conversation. "Who are you looking for?"

"I never found out his name. I asked enough times but he'd never tell me. Wily old fox. I've seen him around town for years, though. He's a tall, skinny old timer, married, not in the best of health and he wears this beat up black fedora–"

"Silas Smith," Kate supplied the name.

"That's his name?"

"Yep. He comes in here every so often for donuts." Kate sent a glance at Abigail. "Ask Frank about him. He knows him. It wasn't but about a week ago Silas was in here and so was Frank. Frank bought him a coffee and donuts because Silas was short of money. I think he's often short of money. Silas and his wife have fallen on real hard times from what I can piece together with bits of conversation I've overheard. I don't know their entire story but from what other people who know of him have said he's real sick. Cancer, I think. His wife has been ill, too. Really bad luck. Why are you looking for him?"

"I've talked to him on the street before and last time something in his manner touched my heart." Myrtle placed her hand on her chest. "I felt he was a lost person. He needed help but he wouldn't take any from me when I offered it. Not comfort or even a penny. Too prideful, I'd say. Lately, for some reason I don't understand, I can't get him off my mind. He's kinda haunting me. Today, while I was busy," she tossed Abigail a conspiratorial look, "doing something I couldn't get him off my mind. I think he's in deep trouble somehow. So, since I always listen to that little voice in my head, I've decided I need to find out where he and his wife live and pay them a visit. See for myself. Sooner than later. Could be I can discover why he's haunting me."

"Why that is so kind of you, Myrtle." Kate reached into the glass case and brought out another crème horn and put it in front of her. "On the house."

Myrtle smiled like a child and lifted the sweet to her mouth. "Oh boy, thanks."

"And," Kate announced, "I also know about where Silas and his wife live. After he came in last week and I overheard what Frank said to him, I was curious. I began asking people if they knew him. Another old timer, Barnaby Evans, who lives on the edge of town told me Silas lives at the very end of Cherry Street out in the woods about five miles from here in a rundown wreck of a house. I don't know the address but it shouldn't be too difficult to find."

"Hot dog!" Myrtle slapped her hand on the counter. "Now I know where they live. I think I even know the house.

"Abby?"

Abigail knew before Myrtle asked her what the request would be but played dumb. "Uh huh?"

"Could I get a ride with you out there? I have this really strong feeling these people need us. Now. They need someone to help them. And Pastor Dan always says we should help people who need help."

Kate was watching them, an eyebrow gently lifting. She grinned at Abigail. "Tell you what, if you take Myrtle to their house I'll throw in a box of donuts to take to them. I know which ones Silas likes. It'll get you in the door, I'm sure."

"Of course, Myrtle, I'll take you," Abigail

conceded. "You want to go now?" She knew Frank and Glinda wouldn't be home until later so she had the time. She'd finished Miguel's mural and was taking a short break before starting Samantha's political campaign advertising. She had time to do a good deed.

"I do. I want that old man to stop haunting me. I have important work I need to get back to. So drink your coffee, Abby, and we'll take a ride out there."

Abigail finished her drink, accepted the box of donuts from Kate and she and Myrtle left. The rain had increased into a downpour, so she was glad she'd brought her umbrella. She shared it with Myrtle, even though Myrtle had brought her own.

In the car she turned to her passenger. "Send me in the right direction."

And Myrtle did.

Chapter 14

Silas had been napping on the living room couch when someone started knocking on the front door. Now who could that be? They rarely got visitors anymore. When they'd moved to Spookie thirty years before they'd had friends, but now most of them were old and sick as they were or were dead, and thus had begun their creeping isolation. Years past Violet's church people would come by with warm meals and comforting conversation. Violet had enjoyed those visits. They'd caught her up on the world outside their home and made her feel part of the congregation where once she'd never missed a Sunday morning. But that had been years ago before Violet had become so very ill. The church and its congregation had forgotten them as had the rest of the world.

He got up and hobbled to the front door. As he opened it rainwater blew in along with a gust of wind. He hadn't taken his customary walk because the rain had drummed a heavy beat most of the day on the outside land, too heavy to stroll out in, and the day had darkened early to evening. He'd been waiting for the rain to let up, had laid down on the couch and next thing he knew he'd been sleeping. That's how it was being old. One minute you were awake and the next you were drowsing. It didn't matter where you were, you fell asleep.

"Hello?" He blinked at the two women out on his porch standing beneath a bright yellow umbrella. One of them, the younger, held a large grocery bag clutched in her arms, while the older one held on firmly to the umbrella's handle. The wind was trying to blow it away. He didn't recognize the younger female but the other one was the old woman with the wagon who kept accosting him on the street wanting to offer him help. Maybe they were the new crop of church women.

"What can I do for you, ladies?"

The old woman blurted out, "You can let us in, Silas, before the wind blows us into another state."

He didn't want them to come in but Violet would be upset with him if he were to be rude to any church people so, against his better judgement, he opened the door wider. "Then, by all means, come on in. But if you're here to see Violet, she's asleep right now and I won't wake her. She's been very ill fighting that cancer of hers, can't sleep much because of the pain, and needs her rest when she can get it."

"That's okay. We came to see you and bring you and your wife some provisions," Myrtle stated once they were inside and Silas had shut the door.

"How did you know where I lived?"

"Kate at the donut shop said Barnaby Evans mentioned you lived out on the end of Cherry Street and I kind of guessed what house. I guessed right, huh?"

"It's the only house at the end of the street. So it's not hard to miss."

"Well, show us the kitchen, Silas, and we'll put these groceries away for you. By the way, we've never officially met, I'm Myrtle Schmitt and this is my friend Abigail Lester."

"Hello Myrtle and Abigail."

The old woman who called herself Myrtle didn't wait for an invitation but sauntered towards the kitchen as if she owned the place.

Silas followed them into the kitchen. It was a mess and momentarily he felt the old embarrassment and then, as he now did with so many other emotions good and bad, he let it go. Who cared if dishes were piled up in the sink and the floor hadn't been mopped in ages? What did any of that nonsense mean anyway? The house was cleaned, the house got dirty again. It was a vicious circle. Violet used to take care of those things and try as he might he couldn't seem to keep up. He watched Myrtle dump the bag on the cluttered table, making room for it with a swipe of her hand.

"Lester…Lester," he mumbled glancing at the younger lady. "Are you related to Frank Lester, ex-detective and donut aficionado?"

"I'm married to him," she admitted. She was staring around the kitchen probably taking note of all the dirty corners and dusty counters.

He felt that stab of embarrassment again and shook it off. "Oh, I like him. He's a kind man."

"I know."

"I hear he writes murder mysteries?"

"He does," she said. "Pretty good ones, too."

Myrtle was taking the groceries out of the bag and he couldn't help but smile. "A box of Kate's donuts. Chicken Noodle soup, Fig Newtons, biscuits, milk, eggs, bread and frozen lasagna. Chocolate milk and jelly beans. Some of my wife's favorite foods and snacks. How did you know we were low on the basics and what we liked?"

The old woman lightly tapped the side of her head. "I'm intuitive, that's how. I sometimes know things."

Silas shook his head. What an odd woman. Most likely off her rocker. Pulling wagons around town like a homeless person and bursting into stranger's homes and forcing free food on them didn't make her a candidate for normalcy.

"Oh, I almost forgot, the donuts are a gift from Kate at The Delicious Circle."

"Tell her thank you for us."

"I will be sure to do that."

What happened next took him by surprise and he stood there with his mouth open. Violet, his bed ridden wife who hadn't been out of her room in weeks except to go to doctor and hospital visits, ambled into the kitchen in her nightgown with a big smile and wide eyes. Her skinny arms were open.

"Oh Silas, why didn't you tell me we had guests? If I had known we were having visitors I would have straightened up the house and put on some nicer clothes."

"Violet!" he exclaimed as he rushed to put his arms around and support her. "You shouldn't be out of bed, sweetheart. You know what the doctors said. You need rest."

His wife shoved his arms away and went towards the women. "I know you," she said to Myrtle. "You're the wanderer of Spookie town, the singer of Perry Como songs who travels the streets pulling your wagon behind you."

"That's me all right." Myrtle performed a slight

bow. "Singer of Perry Como songs. But, sorry, I don't know who you are."

"I'm Violet Smith, Silas's wife."

Silas guided her to a chair and lowered her into it. She was trembling, weak, and the blood was draining from her face, but she was still smiling. He was still trying to take in the fact his wife was out of her room, her bed. It had really surprised him.

"Oh, look, my favorite cookies." His wife reached out for the package, opened it, and stuffed a Fig Newton into her mouth. "Ooh, so good.

"Did you bring these groceries for us?" she queried Myrtle.

Myrtle nodded.

"That was so kind of you both." Violet acknowledged the younger woman, Abigail, with a nod of her own. "Silas, where are your manners? One good turn deserves another. Offer our guests some refreshments, why don't you?"

So Silas poured the chocolate milk into four glasses and they sat at the table, drank and ate Fig Newtons. He noticed Myrtle and Abigail didn't eat many cookies and poured most of their chocolate milk back into the carton before they drank what was left. As much as he wanted to ask the ladies to leave so he could put his wife back to bed again where she needed to be, he understood she'd been hungry for company as much as sustenance and she was enjoying their visit. He'd seen her smile so rarely lately. So he allowed them to stay.

They didn't intrude on their privacy for long and he was glad of it. The women chatted about trivial things, women's things, and the town; people they found out they knew in common and he sat there and listened. His wife smiled, and laughed softly once in a while and it made him feel good she did. It'd been a long time since she'd shown any joy or interest in anything other than her cancer and it made his heart lighter.

When the uninvited visitors were ready to leave Silas first ushered his wife to her bed and returned to escort them to the door. The rain had stopped.

"Thank you for the groceries and the visit," he told them in as gentle a voice as he could muster these days. "It cheered my wife up so much. She's been having a hard time of it since she started her last cancer treatment."

"What kind she got?" Myrtle asked.

"Breast cancer. Stage four." It was hard even now to say the words. He hated saying them. It seemed unreal that his beloved Violet could have this terrible disease.

"Oh, I'm so sorry." For the first time the older woman's expression reflected more pity than the earlier compassion. "And you? You have cancer as well I've heard."

"I do." He didn't want to tell her, didn't want her or anyone else's pity, but something about her kindness made him answer. "And my cancer has spread to my bones."

"Real bad luck all right, you both having cancer at the same time."

He said nothing.

Standing on the porch, the old lady squinted her eyes at him before he closed the door. Right before he did she handed him a scrap of paper with letters and numbers on it. "That's my name and telephone number, Silas. If you ever need anything, money, food, a visitor for you or your wife to cheer you or her up, or just someone to help you with her, call me, you hear? I know how hard it is to care for a sick loved one. I've done my share of it in my time. Yet a person can't always carry the burden alone."

He was afraid tears would sneak out of his eyes so he turned his head away long enough to wipe them off. "Thank you. Both of you. Your visit helped my wife more than you know."

To the younger woman he added, "Say hello to that husband of yours. Maybe next time you come over he'll tag along. He told me he was a detective in Chicago for years. My father was a cop, too. So we have something in common." He couldn't believe he'd offered the invitation, it'd simply slipped out. Perhaps he was lonelier than he'd thought. His wife as well.

"I'll tell him." Abigail smiled. He thought she had a rather pretty smile. It reminded him of his Violet's smile when she was young. Those days felt like a different life.

Then he shut the door and it was only him and his wife again. He went to check on her. For the first time in a long time, though, he felt lighter and stronger. All it had taken was someone else acting as if they cared.

*****

"That was a generous thing you did, Myrtle," Abigail professed as they were getting into the car.

What Lies Beneath the Graves

"Taking food to those two old people."

"Ah," Myrtle waved her admiration away, "you were with me, too. You helped me get the groceries and drove me over there. We both helped them."

"But it was your idea and it was a kind thing to do. You want to come home with me?" Abigail started the car and pulled it out of the driveway. "I think Frank and Glinda should be back from Chicago by now."

"Sure. Frank can catch me up on his murder case…since you two hid it from me for so long." Myrtle tried to sound petulant, but Abigail knew she hadn't cared too much because of her treasure hunt.

"I told you why we did that."

"I know, I know. I was joshing you. I have no desire to go to Chicago for any reason. I loathe big cities. Too crowded, too noisy. Yeck. I'm happy solving mysteries around here; there's usually somebody doing something to someone. Yet I sure am curious to hear all about it from Glinda and Frank when they get home. I'm so happy they rescued at least two of those young women, they're alive and…now Laura will be safe." Myrtle's body visibly shuddered in the seat beside her. "Only evil monsters steal and kill children. I hope they're put behind bars for the rest of their miserable lives. They deserve it.

"Did I tell you about some of the weird things my metal detector has been unearthing as I'm looking for the treasure? Well…."

Abigail maneuvered the car down the highway as Myrtle rattled on about every moment and detail of her search for Masterson's lost treasure when all

Abigail could think about was that Frank would be home when she got there. She'd been so scared for him, Glinda and, of course, Laura. She'd decided she didn't like her husband going up to the big city to solve crimes. She wanted him at home, safe and close by.

Frank's truck was in the driveway.

"Good, you're home." Frank embraced her when she walked in the kitchen. He was making sandwiches for him and Glinda. "Where have you two been?" His gaze included Myrtle.

After she'd said hello to Glinda, Abigail provided him with a condensed version of where they'd been and why.

"Oh, so you met Silas Smith and his wife, huh?" Frank had brought his sandwich to the table and sat down. "I'm glad you two helped that old gentleman. Rumor is he used to be a college professor. English, I think. I don't know where he taught, but all you have to do is speak with him and you realize he's very educated. It's a shame his and his wife's lives are so troubled in their golden years. I'll go visit him myself now I know where he lives and that he won't chase me off."

Abigail settled down at the table on Glinda's left side. Myrtle was rummaging through the cabinets, probably foraging for sweets. She never could get enough. "So...give Myrtle and I a rundown on how you found and arrested those kidnappers in Chicago. I want to hear everything."

Frank described the series of events he, Glinda and Sam Cato had gone through once they'd gotten to Chicago and how the authorities now suspected the brothers had been stealing and killing young girls all across the country for many years.

"So they're serial killers and they're in jail now?" she spoke when he was finished.

"They are serial killers. They're vicious, cruel and heartless. But about them both being behind bars, now there's a strange twist to their incarceration. Sam told me this morning when we were at the station, that one of the brothers, Arthur Addy, had a fatal heart attack last night. He died. So we only have the other brother, Wesley, to prosecute."

"Ha! God stepped in and punished him, that's what happened," Myrtle piped up. Now also at the table, she'd found a candy bar and was munching on it. "Good riddance. One less murderer the state has to spend our money on and has to send to the gas chamber."

Abigail couldn't help but comment. "Well, if that heart attack was God's justice, then why didn't both brothers have them and die? They're equally guilty."

"God wants the other one to confess to all the atrocities and murders him and his evil brother did," Myrtle said. "There are most likely many parents who would like to stop agonizing over what happened to their missing children. That other brother will soon be singing like a bird. He'll confess to the police who and where the bodies are and give those poor parents closure."

Abigail exchanged an incredulous glance with her husband but knew better than to contradict the woman. Over the years Abigail had learned Myrtle had countless strange notions about many things and it was best to merely nod or shake one's head and let it go. But she was right about the victims' family and friends wanting closure if their loved ones had been missing for a long time and, in reality, had been murdered. Abigail understood that need for closure completely. Not knowing what had happened to her own husband for two years had been agony and finally discovering he'd been murdered, dead for the two years, had been heartbreaking but it had also been a relief in some ways.

"Leastways," Glinda inserted into the conversation, "the killers were caught, they won't be committing any more atrocious crimes, and now Laura and her classmates no longer have to be afraid. Evil has been stopped. Justice has been and will be done."

"Yeah," Myrtle concluded, "chalk one up for the good guys. You two did well."

"So," Frank had finished his sandwich, reclining in his chair and was grinning at Myrtle, "have you found Masterson's lost treasure yet?"

Myrtle threw her wadded up candy bar wrapper at him. He ducked and it missed him.

Snowball was suddenly there attacking the wrapper on the floor, batting it with her paws across the room. Everyone laughed.

"Don't you worry, Frank my boy, I will find that treasure. Ask Glinda. She's seen it in my cards."

Frank addressed the psychic. "You've seen it in her cards? Really?"

Glinda inhaled thoughtfully. "Well, not exactly

that my aunt will find it, but I know the treasure existed from my dreams of Masterson and the last time I read the tarot cards there was a *promise* of riches all over them. Someone is going to find *something*. Myrtle just happens to think it will be her. I also believe Masterson isn't done with me. He has more to show me."

"What! It might not be me who finds the treasure? No way, Niece. I'm going to find that treasure." Myrtle tapped her chest. "Me."

The others in the room kept quiet as the cat meowed.

Chapter 15

Glinda had been home for hours and night had come. It felt good being home again with her animals and her house all around her. She felt safe in Spookie. Chicago had been a difficult experience. It was always hard to be around evil. Those two brothers and the cruelties and murders they'd perpetrated over the many years of their senseless killing spree had been of the darkest evil and their crimes made her skin crawl. She'd looked at the two siblings and had seen far too much in their narrowed eyes. *The future if they wouldn't have been caught...and thank God they had been caught and stopped.* She'd seen things in her mind, what could have been, she'd have a hard time forgetting. When the brothers had attempted to escape from their burning car, they'd been too close to her and she'd felt their malevolence. Her head had begun to hurt so much, she could barely concentrate on what her gift was telling her...that the kidnapped girls were also near. Then she spied the shed. They found and saved the young women and she was grateful for that.

She was only glad it was over. The surprising turn of events that the one brother had died of a heart attack in jail had been an unexpected bonus. She was sure he'd been the worse of the two siblings. He'd been the one to actually do the murders her inner voice whispered to her and he'd put Alice Wood into that grave. He'd deserved to die, it was only a pity he hadn't suffered more;

suffered as his victims over the years had suffered. But God had his reasons for what He did so she didn't question the man's death. It was God's will.

She went to bed and before she fell asleep Amadeus climbed in beside her. As she slipped into dreamland the other cats also surrounded her. They must have missed her. There were always cats sneaking into her bed. She didn't mind. Their purring let her know she was home.

The long night passed without her having a dream or a vision. She woke up as dawn was stealing into her bedroom. All the cats, even Amadeus, were gone. They were probably waiting in the kitchen to have their breakfast and then to be let outside. Dawn. Too early to get up, she mused, and closing her eyes, drifted away again. That's when she had the dream.

*****

Masterson was traveling by train across a beautiful countryside. He sat and stared out the window, beside him on the extra seat there was a battered chest his arm rested upon. She knew the treasure was inside that chest, or what was left of the treasure. He was no longer a young man, more middle-aged, or perhaps his experiences, his ship journeys, his brother's violent death and his long lonely island exile had prematurely aged him. His hair was gray and his wrinkled face slack. His eyes were dull. He muttered to himself as the train chugged along its tracks. *"I must find them. Is she still alive? Did she have the child she was carrying when I left her? I never meant to be gone so long. I only went to find my fortune…for them. I promised her I'd return and marry her, be a father to my child. She was sure she was having a girl. Please let me find them...my lost love and my daughter. It is all I care about. Finding them will return the happiness and peace of mind I lost so long ago. Finding them will fix everything wrong in my lonely life. Nothing must stop me."*

Glinda somehow understood Masterson was returning to the last place he'd lived with his beloved Darcy. In a small town called Spookie deep in the foggy woods. The two of them had resided in a ramshackle cabin they hadn't owned, just squatted in. Always cautious that no one knew they lived there.

In her dream she observed Masterson leave the train and drag his chest to the only traveler's lodging there was, not much more than a humble boarding house, on Main Street. He booked a room and locked the chest inside it. And after he had dinner in a tiny diner called Roadside he walked the streets of a Spookie. Glinda barely recognized the Spookie of over eighty years ago. The shops, far fewer than in the present town, were simpler and had different names above their doors. There were no sidewalks, or streetlights and the roads, even Main Street, were dirt. It was the quaint small town she had come to love but it wasn't. There were no townspeople mulling around self-absorbed, heads down, intent on texting or talking on their cell phones.

By the cars and the way the citizens were dressed she guessed it had to be around the nineteen forties or so. Masterson wandered down the streets, shoulders hunched, head down, and avoided looking at or speaking to any of the townsfolks he passed. They, in turn, ignored him. It was not a good way to try to be accepted into a community. The night ended as the fog closed in and concealed the man and the town. And she had the feeling a great amount of time passed.

The subsequent scene in her dream was Masterson building his house…Evelyn's house…now her house. Ah, the structure was beautiful as it was originally built, fresh and strong with beautiful gardens and flowers everywhere around it. Masterson was on the work site barking orders to a gang of sullen unfriendly workers. The laborers grumbled and made faces at him behind his back. What had Masterson done to make the laborers dislike him so? She caught snatches of the men's secret conversations:

"The boss says he liquidated gold coins to get the cash for all this…imagine that? But he's so tight with his money and he's an uppity fellow. Look at this fancy house he's building. He's no better than we are. My father said Masterson lived here before with his lover out on the edge of town in a shack, poor as a church mouse both of them. It is only because he came into money somehow that he can lord it over us. And he does lord it over us. They say…."

"Fancy clothes and an up turned nose does not a gentleman make…."

"Rumor is he found a great treasure while sailing the oceans…."

"And he's hid it somewhere on this land of his

so no one will ever take it....

"That's what they say...."

"We ought to find it and grab our share. It would serve him right. He never worked for that gold. Just found it somewhere and ran off with it. We could come out here at night and look...."

"That's stealing, Benedict."

"Well, didn't he steal it also? It was never his to keep so why shouldn't we claim it if we also find it?"

"You got a point there."

"We should look for that treasure...."

The house was rising before her eyes, in fast-forward time. Glinda wasn't sure how much time had passed since his arrival in town but Masterson himself had changed. There was more gray in his long hair, he'd grown an unkempt beard, and he moved with a pronounced limp, using a cane; there was pain on his face. As he supervised the construction the days and weeks also sped by in fast time and eventually the house was finished and the ex-sailor was an even older man behind an elaborately carved desk in a richly decorated and furnished room, a study perhaps, speaking to a fashionably dressed individual in city clothes. Something told Glinda the city man was a private detective. Something about his authoritarian manner. A stout man in a suit and vest, his hair was short-cropped and he had a stern clean-shaven face, sharp eyes and clipped speech. There was a hat on his head which again reminded her of the nineteen forties.

What Lies Beneath the Graves

"Find her and my daughter, Dudley, and I'll pay you three times your normal fee," Masterson was saying to the private detective. *"Do it before I die."*

"You say it's been ten years you have been searching for them?" Dudley questioned.

"It's been longer. But I know they are out there somewhere and you will not give up until you find them. Have you learned anything of importance yet?"

"Other than those two townsmen who claim the woman you are searching for, Darcy Stevens, as she was known by at the time she lived here, had left the town for an unknown destination a year after you boarded your ship and sailed, no sir. But I have many more leads to follow."

"Then go follow them." Masterson's face was gaunt, his eyes haunted. If it had been a decade since he'd come to Spookie he had unbelievably aged. Glinda felt sorry for him. It was clear to see he was a man with a broken spirit and heart.

The detective excused himself and took his leave.

That's when Glinda watched Masterson open a safe behind the desk and pull out a simple wooden box…with a pile of golden coins and a few pieces of expensive looking jewelry in it. It wasn't a big box, about a foot or so in length and less in width and depth. He took a beautiful ruby ring and a diamond necklace from the box and as they lay in his hand, he twisted them so they glittered all colors of the rainbow. He then counted out the coins into a messy stack on his desk, as if he were admiring them, and the gold gleamed in the soft lights of the room as the dream shattered and dispersed again. She could hear the winds of time soughing through the air around her. Again years, a kaleidoscope, were speeding by.

And suddenly Glinda was no longer sleeping in her bed. She was plodding through a muddy field and an old man was dragging his crippled body before her. Shabbily dressed, his clothes were so worn they could have passed for rags. He had a heavy coat on but by the trees and foliage around them Glinda estimated it was early spring and it was not all that cold. The man in front of her stopped, cocked his head a bit to the right, and in the fading light of the day she saw the old man was Masterson. In his arms he cradled a box similar to the one she'd seen him take out of his safe years before. The box with the gold coins and jewelry in it. She followed him away from his home as he thrashed through the wild overgrowth and deep into the woods. It was getting dark and she wondered where he was going. Was he going to bury what was left of his treasure? Would she now have the answer Myrtle was so anxious to have?

There was the cemetery before them, neater and less overgrown with weeds and rocks than she knew it, the tombstones whole, but Masterson was passing it by as the dream again came to an abrupt, but this time a final close.

*****

Glinda opened her eyes. She was on the ground, leaning up against a tree across from the cemetery. It was still morning, but well after dawn, and there were birds singing above her in the tree limbs. She was in her nightgown and shivered, crossing her arms around her. It might be May but the morning was too cool for her sheer nightgown. She lifted herself from the wet earth, the back of her gown damp, and looked out over the present day cemetery. Well, well, her aunt had wasted days searching for that buried treasure in the cemetery to no avail. Masterson hadn't buried it there at all. Glinda was dismayed, though, that the dream had ended before she'd seen where he *had* hidden it. Perhaps eventually he would show her.

She scurried home not wanting anyone to catch her wandering around in the morning mist in her night clothes. When she got to the house she took a shower, dressed, fed the cats, let them outside and sat down to toast with apricot preserves and a cup of hot tea.

She was getting ready to call her aunt so she could tell her about the dream when the old woman knocked on her door. Glinda knew immediately it was Myrtle by her distinctive knock. It was as if a giant was banging at her door, it was so loud.

"Good morning, Niece," her aunt said with a big crafty smile on her face. "I come bearing gifts." She held up a bundle of newspapers. "Hot off the press, so to speak. Chicago newspapers. The Chicago Sun-Times, Chicago Tribune and the Chicago Daily Herald. You and Frank are big time front page celebrities since you caught those two murderous degenerates and saved those girls. I got online yesterday, located the articles you two were in, and had those newspapers delivered right to my door. Lordy, I love the Internet. I ordered extra copies for me, you and Frank for our scrapbooks. I dropped Frank's copies off before I came here. Ah, but don't worry, they didn't print your name, just that you were a psychic who'd helped on the case. They didn't even mention Frank's name, only said a retired homicide detective also assisted in solving it. But I know who they were talking about."

Glinda and Frank had both insisted on anonymity and Sam Cato had obliged them. Good. She didn't want her name spread all over the country. The news media and a herd of people would be staked out in her yard wanting one thing or another. Frank had felt the same way.

"Getting extra copies for Frank and I was considerate of you. Just put my copies on the coffee table there. I'll look at them later." Not that Glinda cared about the articles. Frank and Sam would keep her apprised of any further developments with the Addy case and, beyond that, she didn't care. She was home and all she wanted to do was forget what she'd seen and felt on that awful land with the grave, the house which had sheltered the two human monsters, and the shed. She was pleased she'd helped save two innocent lives, and possibly many more over time, but it was behind her. She was going forward. It was the only direction she could go.

"Have you had your breakfast yet?" she asked her aunt.

"I was hoping you'd ask that and invite me to have it with you."

Glinda shook her head in mock exasperation.

What Lies Beneath the Graves

"Come on in the kitchen and you can have what I'm having. Apricot preserves on toast and…you can have coffee."

"Hot dogs! I love your homemade preserves, dearie. I'll have breakfast with you, to give me strength, and then I'll continue my treasure hunt. My metal detector is on the porch waiting for me."

Glinda considered telling Myrtle about her dream and the cemetery not ever having been the hiding place for the buried booty, but decided not to. What purpose would it serve other than to make her aunt feel bad? She'd already searched the graveyard and was moving on. Best to keep that little secret to herself.

"Auntie, I think you should search the grounds past the cemetery, not the yard around the house. I remember you saying yesterday the yard around the house was next."

"Ah, have you had a vision or an insight or something about it?"

"You might say that. But mostly it's a strong hunch the treasure isn't anywhere near the house. If I were you I'd try out around and past the cemetery. Just saying."

"You're the psychic, so that's what I will do. I'll search past the cemetery next. As I recall this land continues down to the creek. That's its boundaries."

"That far, huh?" They were in the kitchen and Glinda was staring out the window at her land.

"Yep. Old Masterson bought up a huge parcel of territory here. I'm not sure how much he paid for it all those years ago, but it's probably worth a fortune these days."

"I'll never sell," Glinda said. "This is my home forever."

"Good, that's why I wanted you to have it. I'm not going to be around forever and I feel better knowing this place will be with someone who loves it as much as my sister did. Someone of our blood."

Her aunt helped herself to toast and coffee and sat down beside her. Glinda listened as the old woman described in detail what the newspapers had printed and then how she would search for the buried treasure that day. Myrtle couldn't wait for her to read the newspaper articles so she fetched them from the living room and brought them to the kitchen table, where she spread them out and read them aloud to her.

After Myrtle had read the last word, she winked at her. "You two are heroes. Those girls are alive because of you. You should be proud of yourselves. I bet Frank will get a new murder mystery book out of this."

"He might." Glinda winked back at Myrtle.

Amadeus had appeared from somewhere and was running in circles around Myrtle's feet playfully grunting and growling. Glinda knew her cat liked Myrtle but pretended he didn't. The two had a love-hate relationship. So it was a shock when the cat jumped into Myrtle's lap, curled up and began purring loudly.

Myrtle was just as shocked but, surprisingly, instead of shoving her little furry tormentor off her lap, she sat there and petted him as if his amiable attention was as normal as could be.

"I guess after over two years he's finally accepted me," Myrtle stated, clearly touched by the animal's open affection.

"I think so." Glinda exchanged a dubious look with the cat. He purred even louder. She tried not to smile. The cat was up to something, she just didn't know what but she was sure she'd find out sooner or later.

"Time to get back to work," Myrtle proclaimed after she'd eaten meal. She gently lifted the cat from her lap to the floor and straightened up. "I'll collect my metal detector and resume looking on the far side of the cemetery. Would you want to come along? It's fun, you know. Like hunting for golden Easter eggs."

"No, Myrtle, this is your quest. I have clients coming at twelve and one woman who's coming later today I really need to see. She has a big problem and she needs the cards advice. So you go ahead. Find that treasure."

She had to ask, "What would you do with that treasure if you found it, Myrtle?"

"I'd use it for good, that's what I'd do. You know I have Samantha at the newspaper trying to track down Masterson's long lost daughter and her children, if she ever had any. She's having the nearby towns' newspapers search their archives for any clues which may lead us to any of Masterson's decedents. She's looking on the Internet, too."

"Darcy Stevens," Glinda spoke the name softly. "Have her look for a Darcy Stevens. That was Masterson's woman, the one he left behind when he went to sea; the one who might have had his daughter and the two he was trying so hard the rest of his life to find. I forgot to tell you I learned that in my last dream."

"Really? And you're just now telling me this?"

"I'm sorry. The dream was only earlier this morning."

"Earlier this morning?" Myrtle gave her a sly look.

Glinda waved her look away. "You know when you wake up too early and then just slip back into sleep? I dream then, as well."

"Humph. So do I. I dream many times a night. It's exhausting. Anything else you might want to tell me?"

"At the moment, no."

"Darcy Stevens. I'll give Samantha a call right now before I go out hunting and give her the name." Myrtle seemed excited. "Could be we'll find her and Masterson's daughter, if the daughter is still alive that is, or her children or her grandchildren. And if I do find that treasure I'll give it to them. They're the rightful owners. I only want the fun of finding the loot."

Myrtle telephoned Samantha and gave her Darcy's last name then went out the front door. Through the window above the sink Glinda watched Myrtle pick up the metal detector from the porch and make her way down the yard. She had a sudden premonition. Something bad was about to happen…she just didn't know to whom, what or when. It put her on edge and she kept waiting for further enlightenment, but it didn't come. Myrtle. Was it going to happen to Myrtle? She wasn't sure or she would have run after the old woman. No, it couldn't be Myrtle. What danger could there be for her out in Glinda's backyard?

*****

Myrtle hummed a half remembered song as she swept the metal detector over the ground before her. She was carefully meticulous in her search, making sure she examined every inch of the earth around and leading down to the creek. Being spring with all the rain they'd had the last month the creek was high, swollen and the water rushed by her with a roar over and around the huge embedded rocks. The banks were muddy so she was cautious as she ran the detector over them. She wouldn't have put it past old Masterson to bury his treasure on the creek's banks or even in the creek itself. If he had put it in the creek she'd have to wait until the height of summer when the creek bed usually dried up to a trickle, to check it. No way could she walk through the water now, it was too high and swift moving.

She'd been scanning the ground for hours, most of the day, and her arms, her legs, were getting really tired. In every way she was exhausted. Ha, being old was no fun. Her mind, her heart, wanted her to run with the wind, hike through the woods like she used to, jump fences and do all the things she used to do, but her ancient body wouldn't allow any of those things anymore. It made her so mad. Why did a person have to grow old anyway? She shook her head.

Complaining and mumbling to herself she thought she was being extra careful but before she knew it she'd gotten too near to the raging water and her feet slipped in the mud; she was thrown into the water, head over heels, the metal detector flying one way and her another, and her body was rammed into and around sharp rocks as the water propelled her down the creek, thrashing and screaming for help.

What Lies Beneath the Graves

Chapter 16

Still in her nightgown and robe Abigail sat gazing from the porch out over the yard and soaked in the warm morning. It was a beautiful day and she was happy Frank was home and the whole Chicago kidnapping thing was behind them. She'd been dismayed when she'd learned Frank had shot the kidnapper's car up to stop them from escaping. If the criminals had had guns the result could have been very different. Frank could have been hurt or killed. She could hear him inside the cabin talking again to Sam Cato on the phone. Now he was giving Sam Glinda's telephone number and her address. The psychic and the cop had become friends during the time they'd spent together on the case. Frank had told her that Sam respected the psychic and was grateful she'd been able to help them. He wanted to ask her advice in the future if he ever needed it again. Abigail was surprised Glinda had agreed to that as private as she usually was. But if it helped any new victims, she'd explained, then she'd help.

She heard her husband say goodbye, call the dogs in to feed and then release them out into the fenced in backyard. A few minutes later he came out the front porch with a cup of coffee and the newspapers Myrtle had brought by for him earlier and joined her. As she enjoyed the fresh air and the scenery, he skimmed through the papers, reading the pieces on the abduction case first and then going on to read the rest of each one. Chicago had been his home for many years so he said it was nice to read its news. Said it made him extra glad he now lived in quiet little Spookie. Well, most of the time anyway.

Abigail wasn't interested in the newspapers. "Reading about bad stuff makes me paranoid and I'm paranoid enough," she'd confided when he'd shown her the papers earlier. But she was proud of him and Glinda for what they'd done. They'd saved people's lives and that was amazing.

"It sure is a pretty day, isn't it?" she commented as she pushed the swing beneath her with her feet. The slow back and forth motion soothed her.

"It sure is. Another day in paradise." He smiled at her, leaned over and gave her a kiss, bridging the space between them.

She knew why he was in such a good mood. Laura and all her classmates at the college were safe and he was home again. He knew she hated it when he was gone and especially if she thought he was in danger. So all was well in their little world again.

"What are your plans for today, sweetheart?" Frank put the newspaper he'd been reading aside and Snowball, who'd been lurking behind their chairs listening to them, pounced on it and tried to eat it. The cat realized quickly it wasn't eatable and ran off to play in the yard.

"I'm meeting Samantha in an hour at the newspaper to kick off her mayoral campaign advertising. I don't look forward to reviving memories of all those years I sat at a computer doing mindless car and real estate ads at my old job, but I promised Samantha I'd create the ads for her. At least I'll have total control over what I produce and how. Unlike the old days. And I'll get paid a heck of a lot better on top of it."

"Uh, isn't she having that baby of hers pretty soon?"

"She is, but it's not keeping her from working on the campaign. You know her. A master multi-tasker. There's so much to do, she says. Knocking on doors, talking to her future constituents and learning as much as she can about local level politics. She really wants to be a good mayor if she gets elected. Also staying so busy she can barely think helps her keep her mind off the approaching delivery. Being a first time mother, I believe she's afraid, of it, what comes afterwards, raising another human being…everything. So in to town I'll go and placate her. Keep her busy. It's going to be so much fun, working in a newspaper office again." She grimaced. "Just like old times."

"It'll be nothing like the old days," he reminded her, "you're your own boss now. An established and celebrated free-lance artist."

She tossed her head haughtily. "Yes. I am."

"Oh, I forgot to tell you. Nick has invited us to attend his band practice today at five at his friend's and bandmate's, Leroy's, garage."

"You're kidding? Nick is letting us hear his band for the first time? He's been so secretive and possessive with his music since he began playing with Leroy and Paul. What brought this on?"

"Their first gig. He informed me this morning before he caught the school bus he and the guys were playing this Saturday afternoon at Joe's Pizza Parlor on Second Street. Since it's their first performance for the public he's decided he'd like to do a smaller, more intimate tryout for us. Sort of a practice run."

Abigail was tickled with the invitation. "How about that? I've been dying to hear him and his band so I will be sure to be there. Five you say, at Leroy's garage?" Leroy Harrison lived a mile or so away from them. Leroy had been friends with Nick since they'd been in grade school and when Nick still lived at home with his parents and siblings. The two boys had formed the band six months before and three months later had added Paul Blatner, another friend of theirs, on the drums. Nick and Leroy played guitar and sang. Abigail and Frank had been catching snatches of Nick's playing for over a year through his closed bedroom door. She thought he sounded extremely talented for his young age, his music had a kind of Tom Petty vibe, and he was already writing his own songs. His band was soft rock or that was how he described it. Abigail had been dying to hear them and here she finally would have a front row seat. She couldn't stop grinning. There was a time, once when she was very young, a teenager, when she'd wanted to sing in a band. She did for a short while in the summer of her junior year of high school. Her and a couple of her friends started a band that summer but never really played out anywhere. The lead guitarist quit and that was that. She had loved singing the songs of the day, being part of a band, but had already decided she wanted to be an artist more than she wanted to be a singer, so she didn't mind the band dissolving. So it was ironic her adopted son had formed a band. But, unlike her young self, he was already a serious musician, singer, song writer; something she'd never been. The music made him happy so that was all that mattered. She and Frank were behind him a hundred percent.

"I'll meet you there, Abby. I wouldn't miss it, either. I've wanted to hear that band of Nick's for months now. I can't wait."

"Me, neither."

"I thought," Frank said, "since you and Myrtle have broken the ice, so to speak, I'd pay a visit to Silas Smith and his wife this morning. I want to see if there is anything I can do for them. Like small needed home improvements or something a younger man can do around the yard that old Silas can no longer accomplish."

"That's sweet of you, honey."

"Well, I'm going to be elderly someday myself so I thought I'd be nice to Silas and perhaps one day some young whipper-snapper will be nice to me when I'm an old man."

"Pay it forward now to be repaid at a later date, huh?"

"You can say that. Truthfully though, I want to let him know we're here to help if they need something. Make official contact."

"I'm sure they'll appreciate it. I did notice when Myrtle and I were there the other day the house looked in need of repairs. There's missing boards on the porch. That yard is a mess. The kitchen sink leaks. Just don't overextend yourself, husband. You know you're no spring chicken yourself."

"I know. If I need to do any strenuous odd jobs for them I'll take it easy. I'm still sore from that wild romp at the kidnappers' hideout." He hesitated as if he was going to say something more, then didn't. She knew the case had affected him, what he'd done, what he'd seen. And he'd talk about it to her eventually when he got his own thoughts about it in order.

They lingered on the porch a little longer, chatting and spending time together, before Abigail got up to dress and drove into town to meet Samantha and Frank went off to see Silas.

*****

"Hi there Abigail," Samantha welcomed her when she walked through the newspaper's doors. "I'm glad you're here. I've been going crazy trying to finish this ad I want to run in the paper this week. I call it my campaign launching ad. Take a look at it for me, would you? It's missing something, I just don't know what. It's so…boring. Flat."

Abigail thought Samantha looked truly well for how far along she was in her pregnancy. But the woman was basically an optimistic individual and was contented with her life. She had a good marriage, home life and she had ambitions and dreams. Perfect ingredients for a happy life; along with good health, of course.

"Here," Abigail scooted her friend out of the seat in front of the computer and took it for herself, "let me have a look at it." Minutes later, after asking for a different digital picture of Samantha she could use, one smiling, she exclaimed, "There. What do you think?"

Samantha clapped her hands together delightedly as she examined the ad on the computer screen. "Oh my, you have the magic touch all right. How did you do that? A couple of clicks here and there and voila! It's perfect now. You even rewrote the copy and it sounds better. Bravo! Thanks, Abigail."

"Okay, boss," Abigail teased. "Now give me the political material you've written up for me to use and I'll start knocking out those ads and poster templates."

"Here it is. Everything you or my future constituents would ever want to know about me and what I plan to do for Spookie when I become mayor." Samantha slipped a manila folder across the desk at her. "I've also been thinking…how about if you paint a simple political ad on the outside wall of the newspaper here? Oh, not as detailed and realistic as your usual murals, but just a text mural with a campaign message. There's my amateur rendition, a rough sketch, of it first thing in the folder. Just the concept and basic text. Feel free to change anything or even create your own version. I figure if it was a simple painting you could knock it out without much trouble. When the campaign is over I'll just have you paint over it, same color as the wall. And if I win maybe I'll leave it up forever." Her grin was impish. "Of course, I'll pay extra for it. Just shoot me a price. But remember," she tossed in a sweet voice, "we're friends."

Abigail chuckled. "And what makes you think

I give discounts to my friends?"

"Please?"

"Okay. Big big discount, and it'll be included as part of the final bill for the complete campaign. And when you become mayor, friend, I'll expect special privileges."

"Like what?"

"Oh, I don't know right now but when you are mayor I'll let you know what favors."

"I'm sure you will. But, heads up, I believe in transparent and honest governing. No corruption."

Abigail had heard the speech a time or two and fully agreed with Samantha's creed. Moving on. "So how are you feeling these days?" She glanced at Samantha's very round stomach. "It's not long now, huh?"

"Two weeks give or take a year." Samantha smiled as she rubbed her belly. "And I'm so ready for this baby to come. I want my regular slim body back. I'm sick of being fat. I want to stop having to pee every fifteen minutes and I want to be able to eat a meal without heartburn."

"Heartburn, ey? Heartburn means the baby will have a lot of hair when he or she is born."

"That's what I've been told. Another old wives' tale."

"Possibly." Abigail opened the file and started digesting the information inside of it. All the facts, figures, history and campaign promises of one Samantha Westerly. Her mind instantly began formulating how she would use the information. It was at that moment she grasped she was going to enjoy creating the mayoral advertising for

What Lies Beneath the Graves

Samantha. It was a new adventure; something she'd never done before. Her freelance art career would be there when she returned to it. This could be a nice break. And she'd be helping a friend achieve one of her life's goals. What more could a girl ask for?

"The baby's room is ready," Samantha was rattling on as Abigail worked on the computer. "We painted it yellow. That's a bright cheerful color to keep us awake during the middle of the night feeding and diaper changes. And Kent has offered to...."

"Yellow is good." Abigail's mind drifted away from the present and the baby talk as her thoughts concentrated on her new job.

Around two thirty Abigail glanced out the newspaper's front window and spotted Kate on the sidewalk heading their way, a bakery box clutched in her hands. "Looks like we're going to have a visitor."

Kate waltzed in. "Special delivery." She set the white box on the desk between Abigail and Samantha. "All your favorites, Samantha."

"She's been bringing me donuts every afternoon for the last two weeks," Samantha explained as she grabbed the box. "She says they're for the baby, but I eat them anyway. Help yourself Abigail. She brings plenty."

"And she eats them all." Kate sat down across from them. "Fancy meeting you here Abigail. What's up? You working here now?"

"Fat chance. I'm helping Samantha get ready for the mayoral election. Doing all her campaign ads and whatnot."

"For a second I thought you'd resumed your newspaper career."

"Nope. Only working to get our first female mayor here in Spookie. She's going to win, you know?"

"I know," Kate replied amiably. "I have no doubt. I've actually offered to supply sandwiches and donuts at a huge markdown for any of her campaign rallies and free for her victory celebration."

"Hey, Kate, is the wedding still on?" Abigail pestered her friend. "Still June twentieth at St. Paul's?"

"Absolutely, and with the reception to follow at the Delicious Circle."

"Hopefully I'll be my old self by then and can fit into one of my nicer outfits," Samantha voiced as she took a donut out of the box and ate it faster than Abigail had ever seen a donut eaten. "How goes the living renovations?"

"Really good," Kate said. "Norman has been working on the upstairs renovations, clearing out the space so we have a decent place to live until we can find a house. He knocked a wall down and it's nice and roomy now. I heard about Frank and Glinda catching those kidnappers in Chicago. You must be so proud."

"I am. But how did you hear about it when their names were never mentioned in the media blitz or the newspapers?"

"Myrtle," was all Kate had to say.

"Of course, how else? Did she give you all the

gory details, too?"

"All she could remember and probably excessive embellishments as well. Now tell me what really happened in Chicago, the real version."

Abigail did and afterwards the friends exchanged other town news and gossip. And so the afternoon passed. Abigail continued to work as the three talked until Kate went back to her shop.

At four thirty Abigail pulled out the memory stick from the computer, packed up the paperwork, grabbed her purse and drove to Leroy's garage excited to be attending her son's band practice.

*****

Frank was waiting for her at Leroy's house and the band was rehearsing when she strolled up the driveway and peeked into the open garage.

There within the cluttered room was Nick looking so much more mature than his sixteen years and playing his guitar with adept fingers. He'd let his hair grow long and had taken to wearing black clothes, saying it was *his look*. A handsome boy with dreamy eyes, he was growing up faster than she wanted him to, had added bulk onto his thin frame and had shot up in height to over six foot. He was going to be a heartbreaker one day.

The songs weren't any tunes she recognized, a little rock, a little blues, but she thought the three piece band sounded really good. The instruments were in sync and Leroy and Nick's voices harmonized exceptionally well. All in all, Abigail thought they sounded wonderful. Nick's voice was exceptionally beautiful. It shouldn't have surprised her, she'd heard Nick singing around the house, but it did.

As she watched her son strum his guitar and sing his heart out she remembered him as the young boy, the one she'd met so long ago in the town library; the undernourished waif, who along with his hungry sister, yearned after the donuts she'd bring in every morning as she painted her first mural. These days the two boys had little in common, just as the hungry young girl from that time had little in common with the present day Laura. She was proud of both of them and blessed the day she had decided to take them under her wing and raise them as her own. She was also proud she and Frank had worked as hard as they had to keep Laura and Nick's siblings in their lives, too. The other orphaned Brooks' brothers and sisters spent a lot of time with each other at one relative's house or another. She and Frank often hosted weekend sleepovers whenever any of the other children wanted to visit and made sure the kids knew they were always welcomed. It had made for a full joyful life and Abigail was thankful for that every day. Coming to Spookie and opening her heart to Frank, the children, friends and the town had been the best decision she'd ever made. She had an amazingly huge family.

Following a couple more songs, Nick called a break to the music making. "What do you think?" he asked her and Frank. "How do we sound?"

"I think you sound pretty darn good." Frank slapped the boy on his back. "Who originally recorded those songs?"

"No one," Nick responded. "Leroy and I wrote

the songs you heard. Yeah we do cover songs but I wanted you to hear our songs first." Nick seemed proud of himself and his band. Leroy and Paul flanked him, all teenage grins. It was easy to see Nick was the leader.

"I loved them, especially the second one," Abigail admitted. "It was haunting."

"Something Dark is Coming. That's the one I like the best," Leroy said. "My mom likes it best also."

It didn't take long to discover Paul was the quiet one while the other two did all the talking.

The rehearsal continued after the boys ran off for a few minutes, grabbed sodas, and conferred about what songs to sing next. Abigail leaned against Frank and reveled in the music.

As absorbed as she was in listening she still noticed when Frank pulled his cell phone from his pocket, put it up to his ear and moved down the driveway so he could hear whoever was on the other end.

When he touched her on the shoulder and she pivoted around, she saw by his face's expression something was wrong. He waved his hands at the musicians and the music abruptly ceased.

"We need to go, Abby. That was Glinda on the phone. She says Myrtle has been out *hunting* all day, if you know what I mean, and hasn't returned. It's getting dark and Glinda's concerned. She wants us to come over and help her look for her."

Abigail nodded. "Let's go."

Nick must have heard their conversation because he stepped forward. "Myrtle's in trouble?

I'll help."

Frank only took a moment before he accepted the kid's offer. "We could use the help, son. Night's coming and she's a frail old woman. Heaven knows what condition we might find her in, wherever she is. We suspect she's somewhere on Glinda's property. Let's go."

"Bring your car, Abby, and we'll meet you at Glinda's," Frank told her.

Nick spoke quick goodbyes to his bandmates, promising to practice longer the next day and followed Frank to his truck, while she ran to her car.

She fretted, now what trouble had that old woman gotten herself into? But beneath her irritation there was fear. Myrtle was old but she fancied she was decades younger. She was often forgetful or reckless. Oh please, Abigail thought, don't let anything bad have happened to her. Myrtle was Spookie and Spookie was Myrtle. And Abigail couldn't image her life without the old lady.

What Lies Beneath the Graves

Chapter 17

"Do you have any idea where we should start looking for her?" Abigail grilled Glinda when they got there. The psychic was dressed for outside with a jacket and boots so she could forge through the weeds and mud.

"As I recall, she was going to search out around the cemetery and down to the creek today. But that was early this morning. She usually hikes back by midday for a snack so I can't believe something isn't wrong or she would have returned hours ago. She knows I worry about her. And, more importantly, she wouldn't be out in the woods when night falls. You know how she is about the ghosts."

They all knew how Myrtle was about the ghosts. "She wouldn't be out there this late of her own volition." Abigail was looking at the darkening windows around her.

"Here," Glinda said, "are lanterns and flashlights. Let's start looking at the graveyard's edge and fan out down to the creek."

Glinda handed a flashlight to Nick. "Thank you for helping, young man. We need the extra pair of eyes."

"Anything for Myrtle," the boy retorted. He and Laura loved Myrtle like a grandmother, an eccentric grandmother, so he would be anxious for her well-being.

The group of them hurried outside and marched briskly to the graveyard, fanning out to scan the ground as best they could. They skirted the gazebo and kept going. The shadows were merging together and scaring away the daylight. It would be full dark within the hour or less, Abigail contemplated. There'd be no moon tonight, either. By the time they had reached the creek all of them had their flashlights and lanterns on, their flashlights' beams moving out ahead of them.

They thrashed through the terrain, around trees and high spring grass. They shouted out to each other as they went so they'd know where each one was. At one point, as they were getting close to the rushing creek and Abigail crossed paths with Frank she said, "This reminds me of that day we were out searching for that missing veteran, Alfred wasn't it? And those other old people, Clementine and Beatrice, who'd been involved in that land grab. Wow, that was years ago but this brings it back way too clear."

"Except this time it's Myrtle who's lost out in the woods. Who would have thought it? As much as she wanders around everywhere. The fact she might be lost is a trip. Something really has to be wrong." Frank's sharp gaze was on the landscape around them, probing and searching.

"The light's completely gone now." Glinda had come out of a wall of bushes and joined them. "This rescue mission is going to get a heck of a lot harder. I have a truly bad feeling about this. Myrtle's life beacon is weak. I've been thinking this most of the day but now I'm certain. She's in real trouble. Life-threatening trouble. *We have to find her.*"

The group of them were now walking along the creek about five feet above the water, the fast-moving stream bubbling and spitting below them. Abigail was really beginning to worry. It wasn't like Myrtle to be out in the darkness. As Glinda, a bad feeling had been growing the longer they searched.

Myrtle, Myrtle, where are you?

Owls began to hoot to each other from the evening trees. The breeze picked up and sang a spooky melody through the rustling leaves. Abigail was grateful they'd left the cemetery behind them. It was creepy enough being out by the creek, with all its eerie night creatures beginning to chirp and click, but she particularly disliked night cemeteries. She was afraid she'd see ghosts emerging from the graves. No, no graveyards in the dark.

That's when Frank turned to Glinda, twenty feet behind him with her glowing flashlight in hand, and asked in a loud voice so she'd be sure to hear, "Did Myrtle have her cell phone on her this morning? I know she doesn't always carry it, but maybe she did today."

"She might have had it on her, though she so rarely does. You all know how she feels about cell phones. She hates them. But I hadn't thought whether she had her cell phone on her or not today." Glinda had moved up next to them.

Nick had also caught up with them, his face a pale oval in the gloom.

"I should have thought about that before. Where is my mind? Okay, let's just try calling her. It can't hurt." Frank tugged his cell phone out of his pocket and keyed in a number. Abigail assumed it was Myrtle's number.

And somewhere in the distance on the night air there was a faint ringing.

"Oh my goodness," Glinda cried out, "that's Myrtle's cell phone."

The four of them followed the siren call, half stumbling and running through the now nearly lightless landscape.

"It's this way...." Frank yelled after they'd moved down along the creek about a half mile. He kept redialing the cell phone when it would go to message and they kept following it.

"Myrtle! There she is!" Nick was at the edge of the water, flashlight zeroing in on an area of the creek, pointing at something that more resembled a bag of trash half in and half out of the water and crumpled up against a row of large rocks. Somewhere nearby the cell phone was still ringing.

Abigail sent her flashlight's beam to the pile of soggy clothes in the creek. Before she could stop them both Frank and Nick jumped into the water and together fought its force to pull the body out. Abigail was terror stricken that the rushing current would sweep her husband and son away but the two men were strong and after a few setbacks, helping each other by holding hands, they managed to pull Myrtle from the stream.

Myrtle was laid gently on the bank and Glinda and Abigail kept their lights directed on the motionless body. No one said what they were all afraid of. Was Myrtle still alive?

Frank bent down over the woman and picked up her wrist. "Pulse is weak, she's unresponsive, but she's alive."

What Lies Beneath the Graves

Abigail released the breath she hadn't known she'd been holding. "Thank God," she whispered as she knelt down in the mud by her friend and beside Glinda, whose hands were now holding and rubbing Myrtle's. Abigail wiped the wet dirt and debris from the old woman's face and brushed her tangled hair back. Myrtle was so still, not prattling on about pie or laughing at her own jokes; not like her at all. Abigail had to wipe away the tears collecting in the corner of her eyes. *Please let her be all right. Please God, don't take Myrtle away from us. We all love her.*

Frank was on his cell again calling for an ambulance and after he'd hung up he said, "I'm going up to the road to wait for the ambulance so I can bring the paramedics down here to pick Myrtle up. Stay with her. Keep talking to her. Warm her up in any way you can." He draped his jacket over her.

Abigail peered up at him. In the light's shadows he was a blurry figure. "You know we will."

As Frank took off up the hill towards civilization, Nick fell in behind him and the two disappeared into the woods. The road was about a mile away.

Abigail could hear the ambulance coming, louder, louder, closer, closer, every minute until she was sure it was up on the road above them when the silence fell.

Even with Glinda's and her attention, Myrtle hadn't woke or even moved. She was as cold and still as stone laying there on the muddy bank. In her heart Abigail was more than frightened, she was numb. Tumultuous thoughts tumbled over and over in her mind. It was like Abigail's world was frozen and everything in it was waiting to see if Myrtle would live. As she waited with her old friend her mind replayed memories of Myrtle since she'd first met her so many years ago on the streets of Spookie. The odd lady in bizarre clothes who roamed the town singing her Perry Como songs loud enough to wake the dead and tugging her battered old wagon behind her. When she'd first seen her rambling the streets of the town she'd thought Myrtle was a homeless bag lady, or, in her case, wagon lady. But Abigail had soon learned the old woman was a lot more than what she appeared to be. She was more than a quirky character with a prickly exterior, she had a good and generous heart and helped so many people without announcing she did or taking credit for any of it. Then there was the time Myrtle saved her life. She could have been dead if Myrtle wouldn't have knocked the Mud People Killer over the head that night with a stick when he'd broken into the house trying to kidnap her, right before he flung himself out her upstairs bedroom window. Dead. She owed Myrtle her very life.

Please be okay Myrtle. Please don't die.

A crowd of people appeared out of the dark with lights and a stretcher, worked over the body doing things Abigail couldn't and didn't want to understand, and then carried Myrtle away. Abigail was still fighting her tears but when the crowd was gone she let them creep down her cheeks and swiped them off with unsteady fingers.

What Lies Beneath the Graves

"Can I ride with you to the hospital?" Glinda requested of Abigail, after the ambulance had driven off, and as they trekked to the house to reclaim the truck and car. They hurried because they were meeting the ambulance at the hospital and didn't want to be late.

"Of course."

They made it to the hospital in good time, only a few minutes after the ambulance had arrived. And that's when the praying began. They sat in the hard chairs in the waiting room and waited for what would happen next. It was a long wait.

"I knew this was coming," Glinda's voice was somberly tinged with guilt. "I've been feeling for days something bad was coming. Something very bad. The cards were nefarious, as well, but I couldn't decrypt what they were trying to tell me. I never should have let Myrtle go out treasure hunting by herself. She's an old woman. I should have gone with her as she wanted me to. This is my fault. What was I thinking?"

"You were thinking Myrtle already meanders all around town and across the countryside like a person thirty years her junior. Besides, you and I both know if Myrtle wants to do something, she will find a way to do it. There's no controlling that woman."

Glinda said nothing else, only sighed and looked away.

And they waited.

Chapter 18

The days were getting warmer and warmer and Glinda was happy for it. May had come in with thunderstorms and chilly nights but had leveled off to temperatures in the seventies during the day and the fifties at night. The flowers in her yard were budding or blooming and so were the trees on her property.

Grabbing the tray with the sandwiches and chocolate milk she took it out to the swing in the backyard where Myrtle, her right arm in a cast, her face still black and blue, waited for her. The night Myrtle had almost died had changed everything. She'd broken her arm as the current had sent her tumbling down the creek as well as cutting and bruising her body up. She'd been in intensive care for over a week and slowly recovered; no one had thought she would but she did. Stubborn old woman.

Weeks later when Myrtle was released from the hospital Glinda put her foot down and demanded she come live with her indefinitely. Glinda was trying to convince her to make the move permanent and wouldn't give up until it was. Myrtle didn't need to be living alone anymore. She needed someone to watch over her and care for her.

"About time you brought me something to eat, Niece. I'm famished." Myrtle was reclining in the swing, her feet not reaching the ground. She looked frailer than Glinda had ever seen her, but better than when she'd come home three weeks before. All in all everyone said it was a miracle she was alive. And Glinda wanted to keep her that way.

"Didn't I feed you two hours ago? Bacon, eggs, toast and you ate seconds?"

Myrtle's face curved up to her. "Was that only two hours ago?"

"Give or take minutes." Glinda pulled the small round table closer to the swing and set the tray on it.

"So," Myrtle said as she picked up the sandwich and aimed it for her mouth. "I heard you on the phone before you came out. What's going on?"

"Your keen hearing, Aunt, never ceases to amaze me. Abigail was asking about last minute preparations for Kate's wedding. She also wanted to know if you were feeling well enough to attend." The wedding was in three days and Martha, their real estate friend in town, was having the reception afterwards at her grand house. Martha had insisted it be there instead of at the donut shop and Martha always got her way in the end. According to Martha the donut shop was too small. But that was Martha, she loved to entertain at her fancy mansion out in the woods, they'd had many an elegant party and gathering there, even a séance once, and, in the end, Glinda was grateful it was going to be at Martha's. The garden, Glinda knew from personal experience because she'd walked its paths and admired its lush beauty, was beautiful in June and absolutely perfect for a wedding reception. Martha, with her, Abby's and Frank's help, was doing the decorating. Myrtle wanted to help, too, but Glinda had put her foot down and told her positively no way. She was still recovering. Attending the wedding was all she'd allow Myrtle to do in her condition.

"Of course I'm going to go to the wedding and the reception," Myrtle snapped. "I'm feeling fine enough to sit for a while in a church and then eat a delicious free meal in a lovely garden–and I wouldn't miss Kate and Norman's wedding for nothing. I never pass up wedding cake and I bet Kate's will be spectacular since she's baking it. Four tiers at least. I'd go in that wheelchair you have in the kitchen if I had to. It was bad enough I missed Samantha's baby shower and the birth and had to wait to see the baby until Samantha brought her here to see me. Ha, you said she was having a girl, even though she had been told by the doctor it would be a boy. I told her the same thing. A girl. And they had a girl. At least they painted the baby's room yellow. That works for a boy or a girl. I like the name they've given her, too. Clementine. Clem for short, after Kate's late mother and my old friend. I thought that was sweet of Samantha to name her after Clementine."

Glinda had never met the woman Clementine, that had been before she'd come to Spookie. But she knew and liked Samantha and was happy she'd had a healthy baby and was, Abigail reported, already at work again and going full force towards the mayoral election. Glinda had recently read Samantha's tarot cards and they'd revealed Samantha would win in a landslide. She'd be Spookie's first woman mayor. Glinda had given that good news for free to Samantha the day she came over with her baby to visit.

What Lies Beneath the Graves

Myrtle was growing more restless every day. She hated being confined to the house and the yard so it wasn't unexpected when she announced, "I think tomorrow I'll start searching for Masterson's gold again."

"How are you going to do that?" Glinda picked her sandwich up from the plate on the tray and took a bite of it. "Uh, we never did find your metal detector after you fell in the creek."

"I know. I ordered another one off the Internet last week and your laptop says delivery date is tomorrow. So back to work I go."

"How are you going to use that metal detector with only one arm?" Glinda shook her head at the woman. "And you can barely walk straight much less ramble through the hills and gullies of this place. What's the rush? The treasure has been lost for decades so what are a few more weeks?"

"Because I'm tired of sitting around like an invalid. I have a broken arm, so what, it's healing, and I don't see any reason why I can't start looking for the treasure again. It'll give me something to do instead of sitting around all the day long. I'm not dead yet, you know.

"And I figured…maybe you could help me? You could use the metal detector for me and I could show you where to look. You haven't had any more dreams about Masterson, have you?"

"Not since before your fall into the creek. He's been quiet since then."

"Darn." Myrtle snapped her fingers together. "I keep hoping he'll visit your dreams again and tell you where he buried that treasure. It sure would save a lot of time and trouble."

"It sure would. But so far he's been absent."

"So, how about helping me look for that treasure?"

"I'll make you a deal, old woman." Glinda had lifted her face to feel the breeze and it fluttered her hair. "If you allow yourself to heal for another week I'll help you look for the treasure. I don't want you to go running around outside when you've been so ill. Not yet anyway."

Myrtle pouted but seemed to think about it. She finally nodded yes. "One more week and then we look for it. Could be by then Samantha or Frank might have found out what happened to Masterson's daughter. They said they were really working hard trying to find her or her descendants."

"You still want to give her the treasure?"

"If she's alive. And if not I'm sure we'll find good uses for it. The nursing homes are full of old folks who need things. And Silas and his wife could use a new car, supplies and cash, too."

"You're not in it for the money, are you Myrtle?"

"Heck no. I just love looking for it. It's been like an exciting game, but better. It's made my life interesting again for a while. I was getting really bored." Myrtle had finished her lunch and was getting up. "I think I'm going in for a nap right now, Niece. I'm a little tired."

Well, so much for the old woman traipsing around in the woods. She wasn't feeling well enough yet. Thank goodness.

After Myrtle went inside Glinda leaned against

the swing and closed her eyes. The warm sun felt so good on her skin. After several minutes she got up and went inside. Maybe she'd take a nap, as well, before her next client showed up.

*****

The morning of Kate's wedding Myrtle climbed out of bed and with Glinda's help put on her best, brightest outfit. A dress of yellow flowers on a blue background. It was a flowing silky creation topped off with a shimmering pink shawl. Glinda had ordered it for her off the Internet at some la-di-da store as a late birthday present. It was so soft. Wearing it made her feel like a queen or something. She was excited about the wedding and had been looking forward to it for weeks. She was happy she was well enough to go. Abigail, Nick, Laura and Frank were picking them up in an hour and she had to be ready. She was in her bedroom gathering her purse.

She stared around the room and smiled. Glinda had finally talked her into, more like begged her, to moving in with her permanently and Myrtle was secretly glad of it. Glinda had fixed up her room to be so comfortably pretty. It was a large room with a smaller one, once a spacious walk-in closet, attached. The year before Glinda had found someone to transform the closet into a compact bathroom which housed a tiny sink, toilet and bathtub. It wasn't a big bathroom but it was perfect for her. It was strange now living in her dead sister's house but she could feel the love all around her of both her sisters. They were here with her and Glinda. Sometimes their ghosts talked to her in the middle of the night when the house was silent. She whispered secrets to them and they whispered their secrets to her. They kept her company. Yes, it was good she was living here.

She hadn't listed her own house with Martha yet. The real estate lady would bug her again today at the wedding to sell, no doubt, but it was hard for Myrtle. That place of hers had been her home for a very long time, contained so many memories, and she wasn't sure she could ever sell it. For now, she thought, she'd just think on it and let it be. The house wasn't hurting anyone sitting out there in the woods. Good thing she had no pets. She heard a plaintive meow and went to the window to let Amadeus in. He often came to visit her. The cat jumped on her bed and promptly fell asleep.

"Go ahead, Niece," she said to Glinda when the young woman reentered the room to see if Myrtle was ready to go, "get ready yourself. Our ride will be here soon. I'll wait for you out on the swing. I'll let you know when Frank and the gang show up."

So Glinda went to get dressed and Myrtle waited outside in the sunshine. It was a gorgeous day, perfect for a garden wedding, she thought as she looked out over the yard. She'd been doing some hard thinking, too, since her last chat with her niece, about Masterson's buried treasure. She was no longer sure if she should keep hunting for it. Had her little accident been because Masterson's ghost had decided, in the end, he didn't want his buried booty to be found? Had the ghost pushed her into the water? All interesting notions. All she knew was since her close brush with death everything had changed. Kate believed there was no hidden treasure; there had never been. What if Kate were right? That would mean she nearly died for nothing, not to mention all the days of dragging that heavy metal detector around until she was exhausted.

She heard Frank's truck horn before Nick came running around the corner of the house looking for her. "Hi there young man!"

"Hi there yourself, Aunt Myrtle." He'd started affectionately calling her that since she'd moved in with Glinda. She'd let him, though she really wasn't his aunt at all. But she liked having more family. "We're all out in the driveway waiting for you and Glinda. They said to hurry it up or we'll miss the wedding." Then the boy sprinted around the house and disappeared.

Myrtle got up from the swing and hobbled to the rear door. She'd make a short cut through the house to the driveway. It was faster and less steps. She cradled her wounded arm. It still hurt and she'd be happy when it healed and the cast would come off. The doctor had told her because of her age the healing would take longer. So she was sort of stuck with the pain and the cast for now and for heaven knew how much longer.

The truck conveyed them to St. Paul's in time for the wedding. It was a simple, yet poignant, ceremony in the church beneath the stained glass windows. Kate was lovely in her baby blue chiffon dress, her face glowing as she walked down to meet her husband to be, Norman.

Myrtle hadn't met Norman before but she sensed he was a nice enough looking middle-aged man. Looked like he'd eaten a few too many of Kate's donuts, though. He wasn't exactly chubby but he wasn't thin, either. He had short hair an odd white color even though he wasn't very old, or Myrtle didn't think he was. But when he smiled, gently took Kate's hand at the altar when the vows were over, the look of pure love in his eyes was obvious. Their kiss was sweet. She liked him.

Then everyone, with big smiles, trailed the newlyweds from the church, got in their own vehicles and drove to Martha's house.

Pouring into the garden along with the other guests, Myrtle went straight for the group of decorated tables covered in food. Martha and friends had outdone themselves. The tabletops were festooned with colorful crepe paper and balloons and beneath the food plates were expensive lace tablecloths. Under the tables there were crates of red and white wine. Martha liked wine. A lot. The variety of dishes was impressive.

The four tier wedding cake sat in all its splendor in the center of the refreshments. Myrtle had been right. Kate had fashioned a delicious looking confection with snow white icing dotted with pink, blue and yellow icing roses. Myrtle wanted to just dive in and eat the whole cake, but since she couldn't, she grabbed a few pieces of the already cut up chocolate cake on a plate beside it. The wedding cake was surrounded by stacks of glittering presents for the bride and groom. Myrtle's fingers just itched wanting to tear open the wrapping paper and see what everyone had gotten them. Since she couldn't she had to make do with touching, lifting and shaking the individual packages and trying to guess what was maybe inside. She and Glinda had gotten them something really useful. A card with money. Everyone could use that.

"Myrtle," Glinda, in her long pale green dress, had come up behind her, "not waiting for the wedding party to start sampling the fare, huh?"

"Ah, they won't mind if I nibble on a thing or two. There's so much out here they'll never miss it. That wedding made me hungry. Weddings always make me hungry." She snatched up one of Martha's teeny-weenie sandwiches and ate it, too. There were many kinds of finger foods and goodies. That Martha could really spread out an impressive feast. Of course, she had had help from Abigail and Glinda. Myrtle herself had helped a little. She'd made an apple cake. Oh, there it was at the end of the table.

The garden itself had been spruced up with benches and chairs topped with soft cushions and adorned in more balloons and crepe paper so people could sit and chat, though it normally had more than enough of them scattered around anyway. There was also a stair-stepped waterfall embedded in sparkly rocks. It was splendid. Martha's waterfall gurgled and flowed down the rocks and into a pond full of golden fish the size of teaspoons.

The day was perfect. It was sunny, not too hot, and with sapphire hued skies. For the first time since her near death drowning experience Myrtle was perfectly content. Now if she could just get rid of her uncomfortable cast. But, not to fret, that was coming.

The newlyweds had arrived amid cheers, hoots and gleeful comradery and made the rounds of the guests. Myrtle hugged both of them and wished them a long happy marriage and life. Music began to diffuse through the garden. Thank goodness Martha wasn't playing that heavy metal stuff or much of the newer songs. She said Kate preferred the softer classics from the nineteen sixties and seventies because they weren't hard on the ears. But Myrtle liked the big band sounds from her youth better. Yet it was Kate's wedding so it was her choice. There was a part of the patio cleared off and people had begun to dance.

It was a great party, Myrtle mused, as she viewed the guests eating, drinking, talking and dancing. Everyone seemed to be having a good time.

Samantha was there with her handsome husband, Kent, showing off baby Clementine. Myrtle thought the baby was fairly cute for an infant. It had a whole mop of reddish hair. Samantha cradled the child lovingly in her arms as she conversed with her friends, flitting from person to person. She had a dreamy look on her face. That's what happiness looked like.

"So how do you like being a new mama?" Myrtle spread out her arms, cast and all, gesturing for Samantha to give her the baby.

"Sit down first, Myrtle," Samantha advised. "She's heavier than she looks."

"Yeah, you just don't want me to drop her. I won't." But Myrtle settled down on the nearest cushioned bench anyway. The baby was carefully laid in her arms and the old woman cooed at her and laughed when the baby cooed back. "Smart child. She'll probably grow up to be president one day."

"She could. But I hope there's a woman in the Oval Office before that."

Myrtle glanced up at the baby's mother. "Talking about politics…how's the campaign coming, Samantha?"

Abigail had wandered close to them, a plate of food in her hands, and must have overheard the question. She joined them.

"It's going great," Samantha said. "Isn't it Abigail?"

"It is. With a tad over four months to go, we're getting the word out. I begin painting the promotional ad on the newspaper's outside wall on Monday. It won't take long. Two days at most."

"Oh goodie," Myrtle commented as she gently rocked the baby. "I'll have to mosey on out there and follow your progress. I love to watch you create your on-a-grand-scale artwork. It's fascinating how you can paint something so big and still get the proportions right."

"Practice and experience, that's how. Sure, come on by and watch me paint. It's a public area. And I don't mind an audience, you know that. I like company." Abigail took the baby from Myrtle's arms and had her time with the newcomer. The infant was the hit of the party almost as much as the newlyweds. That was what was important in life really, the good stuff like births and weddings. Wedding cake. Parties. From her great age Myrtle could vouch for those truths.

Of course, Myrtle didn't talk to anyone about Masterson's buried treasure. That was still a secret. The main topics were Frank and Glinda's stunning success at bringing the Chicago kidnappers to justice, Clementine and the coming mayoral election and, of course, how Kate and Norman's renovation of The Delicious Circle was going. Kate said she enjoyed working with her now husband. They were a good team. For the first time Myrtle believed Kate was the happiest she'd ever been. Good for her.

At one point of the day Myrtle was eavesdropping on a conversation Glinda was having with Frank:

"Glinda," Frank was saying aside in a subdued voice, "I wanted to thank you for the heads up about the danger in Chicago. Because of it I didn't let my guard down for a moment. I was looking for the danger and when it came I was ready for it."

"I think you would have been all right whether I'd warned you or not. You still know how to handle yourself even though you've been retired for years. I was afraid at your age the physical exertion would be too much for you. I shouldn't have worried. You still have it. I just don't want you going anywhere yet. Good friends are really hard to find. I didn't want you hurt or worse. It was close." Glinda had put a hand on Frank's shoulder and smiled at him. "I want my friend to hang around for a long time. I want all my friends to hang around a long time. You've all become family to me."

"Don't worry," Frank assured her. "I don't plan

on going anywhere. Abigail and the kids need me."

"Your friends need you. The town needs you. You and your mystery solving gang have saved a lot of people's lives."

"And you're now one of that gang and you helped save lives in Chicago."

Glinda, as always, was humble. "I just sent you and the police in the right direction. You and your officer friends did the rest."

That was all Myrtle could overhear because Glinda and Frank mingled away. She would have tailed them to hear the rest of what they were saying but she knew she could grill Glinda later at home about it. Glinda usually told her everything if she asked. For the moment, the dessert table beckoned and she obeyed. She'd already eaten a handful of those baby sandwiches and a plate of those tiny barbequed chicken drumsticks. All delicious.

The remains of the day were full of joy, gossip, laughter and town community. As it came to an end and the guests started going home, Myrtle had to admit it'd been a very good day. She sat on a garden bench as the evening shadows began to collect and ate her third piece of wedding cake and drank her second glass of wine. Two glasses were more than enough for her because anything more would have her on the ground.

"Are you ready to go home now?" Glinda was poised above her. "Frank is driving us home and then returning with Abigail and me to help Martha clean up."

"I'm ready all right. I wonder if Kate would mind us taking home some of this yummy cake, there's a lot of it left, and possibly some of that meat pasta Abigail made. Both would sure make a nice lunch tomorrow."

"I imagine she wouldn't mind. You go ahead and ask Martha to make us up two plates, put everything in a bag so you can carry it because of your wounded wing there, and then join us at the truck."

"Okey-dokey." And off she went in search of Martha.

Myrtle was sleepy on the drive home her mind full of all the day had held. It'd been an excellent day indeed. When Frank pulled into the driveway Glinda helped her into the house. "I'll be back as soon as the remains of the wedding feast are cleaned up, Auntie. I might even bring home some more leftovers. You get some sleep. You look ready to collapse, old woman."

"You're right. I am a little weary."

And after the truck drove away Myrtle hobbled to her room and was soon sleeping in her bed; that crazy magic cat tucked in beside her, his motor running. Since her accident the silly cat wouldn't leave her alone. He was always wanting in her lap or her bed. It was fine with her as his purring helped her fall asleep. Boy, if her late sister Evelyn, the animal hoarder, could see her now she'd be laughing. Well, maybe Evelyn did see her and the cat. It wouldn't surprise Myrtle one bit. The house was full of ghosts. Masterson's. Evelyn's. And every cat, dog, rabbit or bird that had ever lived and died in the house. And that was a whole lot of critters.

What Lies Beneath the Graves

Chapter 19

The evening after the wedding Glinda was outside getting fresh air and welcoming in the twilight. She was drowsy and had to keep shaking her head, and stretching, to stay awake. Myrtle had spent most of the day in her room watching television and napping. The wedding had taken a lot out of her, though she seemed to have had a good time. She was still recovering from the trauma and injuries of her accident so Glinda let her rest as much as she wanted. It also gave her some private time of her own, which she was used to, and she needed after all the years she'd lived alone.

Lounging on the backyard swing with a cup of steaming hot tea, she sleepily took in the scenery around her. She adored her home. She felt safe within its walls and boundaries. Her flowers were blooming and the grass had come in lush and thick. It was another warm June day and she lifted her face to the fading sun. The day before had been fun and she'd made contact with many new potential clients who would be visiting her for readings in the near future. She never failed to hand out her business cards wherever she went. The personal touch and word of mouth, to promote her business, were better than any ads on the Internet.

She was hungry and thought of going inside to rustle up a snack and check on Myrtle but as her eyes examined the edge of her yard, where the darkness was gathering, she saw something glowing in the distance. It was a figure resembling a man but it was one of light. It beckoned her and she walked towards it. The figure of light shimmered and moved and she followed it across her yard and into the surrounding woods. After trampling through the forest for a time she realized the illuminated creature was leading her towards the graveyard.

Was the figure Masterson's ghost? Was he at last going to show her where he'd buried the remainder of his treasure? If it existed?

She didn't mind zigzagging among the cemetery tombstones while there was yet a little daylight, but it was dissipating swiftly. The plot was spooky in the dusk but it'd be worse at full nighttime so she hurried along. Unlike Myrtle, spirits didn't bother her unless they were malicious entities. In the half-light she could see there were wildflowers growing everywhere, even on the graves. Last time she'd been here there'd been no wildflowers at all. Now that was odd.

A great shadow blanketed the area around her and she looked upwards. There were no clouds anywhere. So where was the shadow coming from? So strange. She paused on the fringe of the cemetery and stared at the surrounding land. In the unnatural twilight it all appeared so eerie. The figure of light had disappeared.

She was ready to pivot around and return home when she heard a voice, as if someone were muttering to themselves, and gazed up to see the man of light coming her way, though as she watched the light dissolved and a real man was revealed. It was Masterson. The elderly Masterson whom she'd followed in her last dream, though now

What Lies Beneath the Graves

he seemed even older. He was huffing and puffing as he wound his way to the cemetery and lurched between the graves. He halted a few times and seemed to be looking for something. After all these weeks he had appeared to her again. But she wasn't sleeping, was she? This wasn't a dream, was it? She pinched her arm. Ouch. What was going on? She'd had visions during the day before yet this one wasn't like any of them. The world didn't look real.

The ghost's speech was a little clearer now and she strained to understand his words as she trailed him through the graveyard. What was he saying?

Here. Here. No. maybe there. There. No. I have to hide it well where no one will ever find it. Oh, oh! Go away you demons! Leave me be! I am sick of your deceits and evil doings. Get away from me! You can't have my treasure! I won't allow it. It is mine! Mine! He put the small chest he was carrying down on a grave and waved his hands around wildly as if there were creatures attacking him. He screamed over and over and Glinda covered her ears. It was easy to see Masterson wasn't in his right mind as he ranted and raved at invisible entities. At the end of his life the poor man had conceivably been insane.

If she hadn't had seen him in her dreams as his years had gone by she never would have recognized him. He was a walking skeleton in a threadbare robe and one scuffed slipper. There was no slipper on his left foot and the foot was bleeding, leaving a trail of blood wherever he stumbled. He didn't seem to notice. What had happened to him since the last time she'd seen him? He'd looked ill then but nothing like he did now. His eyes were crimson streaked with fever and his face reflected pure terror as he fought his imaginary foes. He'd been dead a very long time but she still felt pity for the remnant. What he must have suffered at the end of his life to have such anguish pursue him into death the way it had.

The spirit, crying and moaning now, kept moving and she kept following behind. But he didn't stop in the graveyard but lurched on down a path through the woods and came out by the gazebo. He shuffled up the steps and collapsed on the bench.

She's poisoning me, he whispered. *I know it. I caught her putting something into my cup yesterday and as soon as she left the room I dumped it out. I fired her immediately. But too late. Too late. I am dying. How long has this been going on? Why do they want me dead? Do they despise me that much? What have I ever done to any of them?* He lowered his head into his hands and his body rocked in despair.

Glinda felt so sorry for the ghost she wanted to comfort him in some way, any way. But he was a spirit and couldn't see or hear her. She couldn't physically touch him.

Then the strangest thing yet occurred. She'd moved to the lowest step leading into the gazebo and was leaning over so she could hear his words better when his face lifted and he spoke directly to her as if he *knew* she was there.

My housekeeper has poisoned me. She's killed me. Who has paid her to do such a deed? His eyes were crazed and his face was wracked with pain. *I have to hide the last of my treasure…for my child. For my child! And I will leave a letter for her so if she ever comes looking for me she will find it. A letter, a letter. I will draft it as soon as I go back home. Please help me find her.*

It was so shocking the way he addressed her, as if he was really seeing her, was really speaking directly to her, she jumped back and nearly fell onto the ground.

Then the ghost staggered to his feet again and, the chest nestled in its emaciated arms, he left the gazebo and started around the base of it. Somewhere he had picked up a shovel and as she watched he found a spot on the side of the structure near a formidable sized rock and he began to dig. It was slow going because he was so weak and kept stopping to catch his breath, to rest. But finally the hole was deep enough, extremely deep by her measure, and tucked beneath the gazebo. He shoved the chest into it and began to cover it with dirt, handfuls of grass and nearby rocks. His body swayed, his breath was coming in short raspy gasps.

Seemingly with great effort he walked away using the shovel as a makeshift cane. She followed him as he dragged his feet along the edge of the cemetery and tortuously made his way to his house, losing the shovel at the end of the yard. He didn't make it inside, but crumpled on the porch into a heap. He made a series of guttural groans and lay still. She saw his spirit leave his body and float into the air.

The spirit looked right at her and said, *the*

housekeeper poisoned me. Find the treasure and give it to my daughter. Darcy, my beloved, said she'd name the child Isabel, Izzy for short. It was her mother's name. Please give it to her. And tell her, as hard as I tried, I'm sorry I never found her mother and her. So sorry.

Then Masterson's ghost vanished.

My, my, Glinda thought, Masterson didn't bury the remainder of the treasure in his yard or the graveyard as so many people had believed for so long; he was murdered by his housekeeper and…he never had the chance to write that letter to his wife and child. It explained so much.

And now, she smiled, *I know where the rest of Masterson's treasure is buried.*

She opened her eyes in surprise to find herself slumped on one of the gazebo's benches in her nightgown. Darn, she had to stop doing this. It was morning and the birds were singing in the branches around her. She'd been sleeping all the time, even when she'd been out on the swing drinking her tea and had somehow dreamed everything she'd seen. Somehow, as she'd been dreaming, she'd wandered all the way out to the gazebo. My, my, my.

She got up and made her way to the house.

Myrtle was at the kitchen table waiting for her. "Where have you been?"

Glinda gave her a big grin. "Discovering where Masterson buried his treasure."

"Hot dog!" Myrtle exclaimed. "I knew he'd tell you sooner or later. I was counting on it. Hey, now I don't need that new metal detector. Hmm, maybe I can send it back and get my money refunded. I never even took it out of the box."

"Well, you were right. He showed me. He also told me some other interesting things as well. He was murdered. Imagine that? We've been involved in a murder case all along. Besides everything else that poor man went through, in the end, someone killed him. No wonder his spirit was so tortured."

"Good, tell me the rest of it later. I'll get the shovels."

"Let's have breakfast first. There's no rush. And I'll do the digging. You can't dig with a bad arm."

"That is true, I guess. Hard to hold a shovel with one hand. I have another better idea. Let's call Frank and Abigail to go out with us and uncover the treasure. Four more hands couldn't hurt. Get what we want done quicker and then I won't have to dig at all.

"So, where is it buried? Under what grave?"

Glinda lifted her chin and grinned once more. "Masterson didn't bury his loot under a grave, nor anywhere in the graveyard, his yard, in or on the edge of the creek, as you had thought. He buried a small chest with something in it, I don't know what yet though I suspect it's gold or jewels of some kind, *under* the gazebo."

"What, under the gazebo! Really?"

"Really."

"Ooh." Myrtle was rubbing her hands together in anticipation. "I want to run out there right this minute and dig it up! See the gold and jewels shine in the sun in my hands."

"Soon. It appears that I slept the whole night

out in the woods. I need a shower, need to get dressed and we need to eat something before we go traipsing out into the forest and start digging." She patted Myrtle's wrinkled hand. "But soon."

"Okay. I'm going to call Frank and Abigail right now and tell them to come right over–"

Myrtle must have caught her mindful glance.

"–tell them to come in an hour."

Glinda nodded. "Okay. In an hour."

So as Myrtle telephoned Frank and asked them to come over, Glinda cleaned up, dressed in the appropriate clothing for digging in the dirt, and then the women had their morning meal as they waited for Frank and Abigail to arrive.

*****

Frank was as excited as a kid on Christmas morning as Glinda, with Myrtle tagging behind and being helped along by Abby, led him to where in her dream she'd seen the ghost bury the chest. The day had grown warmer and by the time they had trekked to the gazebo they were all hot and a little sweaty. And there was still digging to do.

"Here?" Frank questioned, slamming the blade of his shovel down so it would dig under the base of the gazebo. It wasn't easy to get to for all around the structure bushes and undergrowth had taken over. They had to whack through a jungle to even start digging.

"I think so," Glinda replied, inspecting the ground around the blade tip. "There was this huge rock–that one there," she pointed. "He used it as a marker. Except for being more covered in earth, it looks like the one in my dream."

What Lies Beneath the Graves

"Then here is where we'll begin shoveling earth," Frank concluded and the shovel began its work. Abigail and Glinda also picked a nearby spot and began digging as well, as Myrtle, sitting on the gazebo's steps cradling her wounded arm, observed them.

They dug for hours in the dirt where Glinda thought the chest might be. The holes got bigger and deeper, then merged together into one gigantic pit. Still no chest.

As the three continued to excavate Frank talked about his visit much earlier that morning with Silas and his wife. "I finally made it out there. Silas and I had a nice long heart-to-heart. Old guy seems to be really lonely. 6*-Once he got used to me being there he talked my arm off."

"How was his wife doing?" Myrtle inquired. "When we were there she actually came out to see us and have a snack with us."

"Not this morning," Frank answered as he lifted another shovel full of dirt and tossed it behind him. "Silas said she'd been very ill after another round of chemo. She was in bed and I didn't see her. I took them groceries and offered to help him clean up his yard and do any odd repair jobs in and around the house any time he needed me to and was surprised when he accepted without much convincing."

"That," Glinda spoke up, "was kind of you, Frank."

"I actually enjoyed the visit. We discussed many things over cups of coffee and a cheesecake I'd brought along. You know, he was a college

English professor before he retired and he's an intriguing character in his own right, full of curious stories and life experiences I can appreciate. I asked him why and when he and his wife decided to move to Spookie, of all places. He said it was because his mother had told him his father had lived in Spookie when they were both very young and in love, though they were never married. So thirty years ago when he and his wife were looking for a final home, leaving the big city of New York, he said he remembered Spookie and what his mother had said about it. That it was a quiet little town with colorful people. He said it sounded like the sort of place they wanted to grow old and die in. So they moved here."

"His father?" Glinda, taking a break from her digging, perched next to Myrtle on the steps, was suddenly intently interested, her eyes on Frank. "Who was his father?"

The hole had grown into a yawning chasm now. The pungent smell of freshly upturned earth hung on the air around them. Frank had commented earlier on how he wondered how Masterson, as ill as Glinda had said he'd appeared to be in her last dream, had had the strength to dig so deep a hole.

"Silas said he'd never known who his father was because his mother refused to speak much about him. All he ever knew was his father had been a sailor who'd abandoned his mother before him and his twin sister, Isabel, who passed away years ago, were even born. A father who'd promised to return but never did. He'd sailed off somewhere searching for sunken ships full of treasure or something and then fell off the face of the earth. Sound familiar?"

"Oh my," Glinda murmured. "This is way too much of a coincidence if you ask me. Something else is at work here. Fate, maybe, or a higher power." She sent a glance at the sky. "Did he ever mention his mother's name?"

"Let me think. I believe he said it was...oh, yeah, Darcy."

"And," Glinda repeated, "he had a *twin* sister named Isabel?"

"That's what he said."

"Was she called Izzy for short?"

"Now that I don't know." Frank had halted his digging to wipe the sweat off his face. "But I could ask him when I see him tomorrow. I'm going over there to fix a small leak he has in his bathroom. Why do you want to know?"

"Because one of the other things Masterson's ghost told me in my dream last night was his lover's name had been Darcy, she'd been pregnant when he sailed away on the ship, and she'd confided in him she was sure she was going to have a girl and if she did she'd name her...Isabel or Izzy for short, her mother's name."

Frank, Abigail and Myrtle stared at her, but it was Myrtle who spoke first. "Oh, my. Silas Smith could possibly be *Masterson's son*. Darcy must have had twins. Masterson never knew that because he was already sailing the ocean or stranded on that island of his. The girl, his daughter Isabel, is now long dead. But Silas is still alive and he's Masterson's only living descendent. Wow. What a coincidence."

Glinda looked at Frank. "If that is true, if we find the remains of Masterson's treasure it would legally belong to Silas."

"Not if," Frank stated, his voice rising a notch, "*when*. And that appears to be *now*." He plunked the tip of his shovel's blade against something hard he'd uncovered in the deep hole.

Myrtle left the steps and all of them gathered around as Frank finished unearthing and lifting out a small chest covered in moldy dirt and age.

"This chest looks like the one in my dream Masterson buried." Glinda's fingers touched the box.

"Open it," Myrtle said excitedly.

They watched as Frank used the shovel to knock the rusted lock off the chest. Inside they found a jumble of sparkling jewelry and three golden coins. Glinda had no idea what type of coins they were, Spanish perhaps, but they looked to be very, perhaps centuries, old.

"Woo-hoo, we found the rest of Masterson's treasure!" Myrtle danced around in a circle in a celebratory way, careful not to jostle her wounded arm too much. "All those people hunting, digging up everything everywhere, killing each other off, all those years for it, didn't find it, and *we found it!* What do you think it's worth Frank?"

"I have absolutely no idea, but I'm sure our historian friend and your boyfriend, Myrtle, Richard Eggold might."

"Not my boyfriend," snapped Myrtle. "Just a friend."

What Lies Beneath the Graves

Frank ignored her pronouncement. "The gold coins alone, though, as old as they are and in the mint condition they're in I'd say they're worth possibly a small fortune. Now what?" Frank was holding the open chest in his arms; staring at it as all the others were doing.

"We do what Masterson asked us to do," Glinda decided. "We give it to his child. We give it to Silas."

"All of it?" Myrtle's mouth had fallen open, but her shining eyes were still on the contents of the chest.

"All of it," Frank concurred with Glinda. "If Silas is Masterson's child the treasure belongs to him. Would you really want to keep something which doesn't belong to you, Myrtle, if you knew who it rightfully belonged to?"

"Nah, I guess not." Myrtle had plopped back down on the gazebo's middle step and waved her good hand in the air. "It's not as if I need the money. I don't. But Silas and his wife, though, they do need it bad. Their house is falling down around them, they're starving and their car is barely running. All right, we give the treasure to them. I can live with that."

And no one disagreed.

*****

As the day began to wane, Frank carried the chest to Glinda's house and put it on the table where she usually performed her psychic readings.

"I'll tell you what," Glinda proposed, "let's telephone Silas and ask him if we can come over. We have something to tell him. We can ask more about his mother and father and if we think he is who we believe he is, we present him with the treasure."

"That sounds like a plan." Abigail leaned forward in her chair. Glinda had given her a wet cloth to wipe off her sweaty face. Abigail's eyes, as everyone else's, were fixated on the pieces of jewelry and coins laid out on the table before them next to the open chest. They glittered under the room's soft lights. A real honest to goodness treasure. The people around the table kept picking up and touching the different items, oohing and aahing over them. There was an exquisitely fashioned ruby ring, an elaborate diamond necklace and a few other pieces. Each piece was stunning.

"If those coins could only talk." Frank had his cell phone in his hand and was keying in Silas's number. "Imagine the story they could tell. Who they had belonged to, how they had come to be hidden for centuries at the bottom of the ocean among the silt and fishes, being found by Masterson's shipmates, the ship wreck and how Masterson survived and salvaged a part of the treasure. I'd love to hear those tales."

"Me, too," Myrtle seconded.

Minutes later after getting off the phone, Frank announced, "I spoke to Silas. He was reluctant at first to let all of us come over. He's a private person. But I told him it was important and after he thought about it he said okay. I also believe as I said before he's desperately lonely and is hoping to alleviate that situation by opening his life to other people. He did ask, though, that we wait until tomorrow morning to visit. His wife is sleeping now and he was ready to retire himself. They go to bed early. I said we'd see him in the morning."

"That's fine with me." Myrtle covered her mouth as she yawned. "I'm beat myself. It's been quite a day."

"That it has," Glinda agreed.

"We'll leave the chest with its contents here with you, Glinda. We'll return tomorrow at ten in the morning or so, if that's all right with you two ladies?" Frank had come to his feet, his face weary from the digging and the discovery.

"Ten it is." Glinda was glad they weren't going over until the next morning. She was tired from the day as well. She glanced over and saw Myrtle dozing in her chair.

Frank took his wife's hand. "Let's go home, honey. I need a shower, a couple of strong aspirins and a soft bed. Every muscle in my body is aching. All that digging reminded me that I need more exercise or something. Maybe I should be a little younger." He laughed, his eyes straying to the treasure on the table one last time.

When they'd left Glinda helped tuck in her aunt and then, after locking the chest with its precious cargo in her cabinet, she retired for the night herself.

She couldn't wait to see Silas's reaction tomorrow when he learned his father had never really abandoned him, his mother and his sister but had been lost on an island, had always loved them, had looked for them all his life…and that now he was filthy rich.

Chapter 20

Frank drove his truck over to Silas's and had Abigail follow in her car with Myrtle and Glinda.

They'd been welcomed into Silas's house, around his table, and as the sun shone in the dirty windows, they told him they had something important to ask him and to tell him. "Something about your past."

Silas blinked his eyes and seemed, at first, not to understand what they were there for. "My wife had a hard night but she wants to come out and see Glinda and Myrtle again so she'll be out in bit. She's getting her robe and slippers on."

"Before we go any further with this conversation, say anything else, we need to know a few things. Ask you some questions." Frank leveled a serious gaze at the old man. "You told me your mother's name was Darcy? What was her last name?"

Mystified, Silas answered him, "Stevens."

"You said you never knew your father's name, though, right?"

"No. I never did." Silas's eyes were bloodshot, his face slack with illness and age. "My mother only said he'd deserted us to go searching for some long lost treasure on the high seas. He promised to return for us, but he never did. She hated him for leaving her alone. After years of waiting in Spookie, she moved us first to Boston and later, when we were older, New York. Then Violet and I moved here about thirty years ago."

What Lies Beneath the Graves

"And you had a sister who's passed away?" Glinda interrupted.

"Yes. Isabel. She died of cancer about a decade ago. Huh, unfortunately cancer runs in our family. She was a wonderful woman, a loving sister. I miss her so much even now."

"Was she called Izzy for short?" Glinda again.

"How did you know that?" the old man asked.

Violet came into the kitchen then, smiling and looking extremely frail, muttered hello to everyone and sat down beside her husband. He took her hand and smiled encouragingly at her.

"It's a long story and since you're out here now, as well, Violet, to hear it, I'll start telling it." Frank then proceeded to explain about Glinda's psychic powers, that she was Myrtle's niece, where she lived and about Masterson's ghost showing her where his long lost treasure had been buried; who they believed Masterson was to him and Isabel. He told them about the legend of the buried treasure and how people had been searching for it for a long time, to no avail. No one had ever found it. Until now. When Frank was done he lifted the chest from the floor, where he'd put it when they'd arrived, to the table and lifted the lid.

Silas stared at the jewelry and coins in the chest before him as if he were seeing a mirage. His crippled fingers picked up a coin. "You mean to say this is something my father's spirit wants me to have? The rest of his treasure?" Silas looked at them, Glinda included, as if he couldn't believe what they were saying, as if they were playing a joke on him. "This is mine? Ours?" He glanced at his wife.

Violet was also staring at the contents of the chest, her fingers covering her mouth, her eyes wide with shock. "Oh, my, these items must be worth a lot of money."

"We think they might be." Frank was smiling at their reaction. Everyone around the table was smiling.

"And it's yours," Glinda assured Silas. "All yours."

"But you three found it and it was on your land." He looked at Glinda. "Yet you're giving it to us?"

"It's yours," Glinda reiterated. "I promised your father's spirit if we found it and we found his lost daughter, or in your case his other child, we'd give it to you along with the message that he never forgot your mother or the baby–he never knew your mother was carrying twins–she was going to have. It wasn't his fault the ship wrecked and he was marooned for years alone on an island and by the time he returned to civilization your mother, your sister and you were long gone. He wanted you to know he searched all his life, hired private detectives and everything, yearned for you and missed you, but could never find any of you. He wants you to know he loved your mother and more than anything wanted to be your father. He just never had the chance. He's sorry. Now his spirit can finally rest and leave me in peace as well."

Frank thought Silas was going to cry, and tears were actually trickling down Violet's face. Then old man lowered his head into his hands and shook his head. "After all these years of carrying that burden of being unwanted by my father I finally know the truth." He peered up at Glinda. "He did love us. He'd didn't desert us on purpose. Thank you."

The six of them talked a while, Violet asked questions of her own, and Silas mused out loud about how he was going to spend the money the treasure would provide. Better care for his ailing wife, in-home nurses. Better medicine for both of them. A better car. Their house spruced up and needed repairs made. Cabinets crammed full of all the food they could ever eat. Frank offered to help Silas liquidate the treasure and convert it into cash. "Don't worry, Silas. We'll help you get the most you can get for all of it. I'll take you into town tomorrow to contact a lawyer and put the treasure into a bank vault for safe keeping until you're ready to cash it in. I also want to contact a friend of ours who might know more about what this treasure could be worth. I'll call him tonight. Later, Myrtle can even give you financial advice if you need it. She's good at that. If you have a safe place to hide it until tomorrow, Silas, I'd strongly suggest you do."

"No," Silas seemed to think for a minute, then replied, "I'd like you to keep it for me until we're ready to deposit it into the bank. I wouldn't feel safe with that many priceless valuables in the house."

"No one knows we found it; no one knows you have it."

"Well, then I guess it'll be safe here for a night or so."

Frank, Abby, Myrtle and Glinda were getting ready to leave when Silas opened the chest and picked out one of the coins. He gave it to Glinda. "This is for the four of you with my deepest gratitude. Fair is fair. It's your share for finding the treasure and uncovering the truth about my father. You have no idea what that means to me or what this unexpected wealth will mean to me and my wife. Don't you dare turn my gift down. I insist."

Glinda graciously accepted the coin and thanked him. She handed it to Myrtle, who grinned like a child. "Wow, treasure. Look how it glitters in the light. I bet it's worth a whole bundle of money."

"I'm sure it is." Frank winked at Myrtle. "We'll be finding out just how much real soon here." He turned to Silas. "Now where is that bathroom leak of yours? I came prepared, Abigail is taking the girls home, and I'm staying to fix it."

"Then see you later at home, Frank." Abigail gave him a kiss and went towards the door.

Smiling widely for the first time since they'd met him, leaving the chest with his wife who was still handling and gawking at its contents with tears in her eyes, Silas led Frank down the hall as Abigail left the house with Glinda and Myrtle.

*****

"Do you two want to come over and have some lunch with me?" Abigail asked her two passengers once they were on the road.

"Sure!" Myrtle accepted without a second asking. "I'm so excited over us finding the treasure, I sure don't want to go home yet. Do you, Niece?"

"We can spend some time with Abigail and bask in our accomplishment, Auntie. I don't have any clients today. I'm free."

What Lies Beneath the Graves

"Good," Myrtle declared. "We can have lunch out on your fabulous porch," she told Abigail. "What are we having?"

Abigail made a face. "Oh, I'll scrape up something. Leftovers. I think I have left over stew in the fridge. Would that be all right with you two ladies?"

"Sure. I'll eat anything," Myrtle said.

And Abigail knew all too well that was true.

*****

That night when the day was over, their company gone, Nick in bed, and they were alone, Abigail and Frank sat outside on the front porch for a long time. They revisited the events of the recent weeks and relaxed with their normal nightly porch therapy.

"Laura will be home tomorrow morning. She told me, with exams, she was too beat to come home tonight." Abigail informed him. "I talked to her and she's been so relieved since the kidnappers were apprehended. The whole college has been. She misses her friend, Odette though. The girl's parents took her out of school so she could have therapy and time to heal. Whatever she went through, Laura says, it's left terrible scars. The physical ones will heal but the emotional ones will take time. The girl's a mess."

"Poor child."

"But you saved them. The two girls. I'm so proud of you all. You, Glinda and Sam saved them."

"That we did. We had a lot of help, though, from Chicago's finest."

"Do you ever miss your old cop life?"

"How can I miss it when Myrtle, and now Glinda, keep pulling me back into it? Then there's the consulting with the sheriff's department."

"And your murder mysteries."

"Yeah, I guess my old cop life is alive and well but in different reincarnations. Sometimes I feel as if I'd never left police work. There's always someone needing something."

"Isn't that the truth?" She smiled at him in the light sneaking out from the house windows and blanketing the porch in a faint radiance.

They were silent until a night bird broke the stillness with its shrill call accompanied by the katydids chirping along with their own song.

"Finding that treasure sure was something, wasn't it?" Frank's voice was soft on the warm summer night. Abigail could now hear the June bugs clicking out in the woods as well, bumping into things as they always did. If she switched on any light in the house the little beetles would swarm the screens and somehow squeeze in to fly all over the rooms, dive bombing anything that moved.

"It was. I've never see coins and real jewels like that before, except in a museum. So unique. So gorgeous. I imagine the Smiths are happy tonight or as happy as they can be with their medical problems."

"They are. I spoke to Silas earlier tonight on the phone and he's already called the hospital and requested private in-home nursing care for his wife; a housekeeper, too, to help with cleaning and cooking. He's so relieved knowing he can help his wife more now. When I was done fixing their bathroom leak, I picked up groceries, prescriptions, and other essentials for them. It made me feel good to help."

"Have you thought about what we'd do with our share of the coin we were given?" She took his hand as her eyes followed Snowball bouncing around in the dark yard chasing the fireflies. She would try to jump up and swat the insects out of the air, but rarely caught them. They were too fast for her.

"A little. Nothing specific, though. You have anything you really want, wife?"

"I haven't really thought about it. How much, a wild ballpark figure, do you think the coin, or the coins, will each fetch? I'm sure you've already done research on them. Talked to Eggold."

Frank chuckled. "You know me too well. I did look the coins up on the Internet when I got home today. I took photos of them with my phone camera before I gave the chest to Silas. The coins were all different and some are worth far more than the others. Silas probably didn't realize he was giving us the most precious of all the coins. According to what I read and saw on the Internet today, and what Eggold said after I sent him a picture of it, the coin Glinda and Myrtle have in their possession right now, our coin, could be worth as much as a hundred thousand dollars or more if put up on auction."

"That's a great deal of money."

"It is. It could do a lot of good in the right places and in the right hands."

"Not our hands, huh?" Abigail pressed.

Frank was looking out over the yard. "We have everything we want or need, Abby. You know that."

"Of course I do. I don't care about the coin or the money it could bring. Don't worry, we can find something good to do with it. I'm sure you'll think of something. If not you, then Glinda and Myrtle will." Abby squeezed his hand tighter. "I overheard Myrtle planning to give her portion to the old folks in the nursing home she visits all the time. She says they need so many things and her share of the coin could provide a lot of them."

"It could.

"And speaking of our friend Myrtle, she called me tonight right before we came out here."

"She did? And?" Abigail waited for it. She knew it was coming.

"The treasure hunt is behind her. Gone and done with and she's on to something else, something new. She said she already had our next great adventure...out next great mystery. She'll be over tomorrow to tell us about it."

"Oh, no." Abigail sighed.

"Oh yes."

"I thought she was going to go on that world cruise she keeps talking about? Is the new adventure murder on a cruise ship, by chance? Please no. Being on the ocean makes me seasick."

Frank chuckled. "No, not on a cruise ship. She's not going on the cruise at all, she said. For apparently the new mystery takes precedence. She claims she can go on the cruise afterwards or anytime really. And by the way, she still wants all of us to go with her. She'll pay."

What Lies Beneath the Graves

Abigail sighed. "Oh, no, another adventure. I wonder what it is this time."

"Heavens knows. Her previous *great adventures* have involved an insane serial killer out to kidnap and murder you and me, old people missing and ghosts, possible witches everywhere in town and this last time finding a long buried legendary treasure–with Glinda's help, of course."

"I just hope it's not *werewolves loose in town* this time." Now Abigail laughed. "Or aliens."

"Either wouldn't surprise me at all. But we'll find out tomorrow what this next *great adventure* will consist of, no doubt."

"Yeah, when she shows up for a free breakfast." Abigail laughed again. "What are you planning on having for breakfast anyway?"

"I thought…perhaps French toast with blueberries."

"Myrtle will like that. So will I. Laura should be here in time for breakfast, too. She loves your French toast."

"I know she does." Frank stood up and still hand in hand the husband and wife went inside as Spookie's night fog began to creep in. By morning it would cover the yards, the woods around their house and all the nooks and crannies of the town. As always it would hide the town's mysteries and secrets until the morning sun chased them all away.

About **Kathryn Meyer Griffith**...

Since childhood I've been an artist and worked as a graphic designer in the corporate world and for newspapers for twenty-three years before I quit to write full time. But I'd already begun writing novels at 21, over forty-six years ago now, and have had twenty-eight (romantic horror, horror, romantic SF horror, romantic suspense, romantic time travel, historical romance, thrillers, and murder mysteries) previous novels and twelve short stories published. But I've gone into self-publishing in a big way since 2012; and upon getting all my older books' full rights back for the first time in 33 years, and along with my newer novels, have self-published all of them. My five Dinosaur Lake novels and Spookie Town Mysteries (Scraps of Paper, All Things Slip Away, Ghosts Beneath Us, Witches Among Us and What Lies Beneath the Graves) are my best-sellers.

I've been married to Russell for over forty years; have a son, James, two grandchildren, Joshua and Caitlyn, and a great-grandchild, Chelsie Lynn, and I live in a small quaint town in Illinois. We have a quirky cat, Sasha, and the three of us live happily in an old house in the heart of town. Though I've been an artist, and a folk/classic rock singer in my youth with my brother Jim, writing has always been my greatest passion, my butterfly stage, and I'll probably write stories until the day I die...or until my memory goes.

2012 EPIC EBOOK AWARDS *Finalist* for her horror novel **The Last Vampire** ~ 2014 EPIC EBOOK AWARDS * Finalist * for her thriller novel **Dinosaur Lake**.

*All Kathryn Meyer Griffith's books are here:
http://tinyurl.com/ld4jlow
*All her Audible.com audio books here:
http://tinyurl.com/oz7c4or

What Lies Beneath the Graves

Novels & short stories from Kathryn Meyer Griffith:
Evil Stalks the Night, The Heart of the Rose, Blood Forged, Vampire Blood, The Last Vampire (2012 EPIC EBOOK AWARDS*Finalist* in their Horror category), Witches, Witches II: Apocalypse, Witches plus bonus Witches II: Apocalypse, The Nameless One erotic horror short story, The Calling, Scraps of Paper (1st Spookie Town Murder Mystery), All Things Slip Away (2nd Spookie Town Murder Mystery), Ghosts Beneath Us (3rd Spookie Town Murder Mystery), Witches Among Us (4th Spookie Town Murder Mystery), What Lies Beneath the Graves (5th Spookie Town Murder Mystery), Egyptian Heart, Winter's Journey, The Ice Bridge, Don't Look Back, Agnes, A Time of Demons and Angels, The Woman in Crimson, Human No Longer, Four Spooky Short Stories Collection, Forever and Always, Night Carnival Short Story, Dinosaur Lake (2014 EPIC EBOOK AWARDS*Finalist*), Dinosaur Lake II: Dinosaurs Arising, Dinosaur Lake III: Infestation, Dinosaur Lake IV: Dinosaur Wars, Dinosaur Lake V: Survivors, Memories of My Childhood and Christmas Magic 1959 short story.

Her Websites:
Twitter: https://twitter.com/KathrynG64
My Blog: https://kathrynmeyergriffith.wordpress.com/
My Facebook author page:
https://www.facebook.com/KathrynMeyerGriffith67/
Facebook Author Page:
https://www.facebook.com/pg/Kathryn-Meyer-Griffith-Author-Page
208661823059299/about/?ref=page_internal
https://www.facebook.com/kathrynmeyergriffith68/
https://www.facebook.com/pages/Kathryn-Meyer-Griffith/579206748758534
http://www.authorsden.com/kathrynmeyergriffith

Kathryn Meyer Griffith

https://www.goodreads.com/author/show/889499.Kathryn_Meyer_Griffith
http://en.gravatar.com/kathrynmeyergriffith
https://www.linkedin.com/in/kathryn-meyer-griffith-99a83216/
https://www.pinterest.com/kathryn5139/
https://tinyurl.com/ycp5gqb2

CPSIA information can be obtained
at www.ICGtesting.com
Printed in the USA
LVHW052149110722
723237LV00001B/12